BETWEEN CASES

The City Between: Book Seven

W.R. GINGELL

Cover by Seedlings Design Studio

Welp. This one nearly killed me.
You lot better enjoy it.

CHAPTER ONE

IT'S FUNNY HOW PERCEPTION CHANGES STUFF. I'VE BEEN A PET to two fae and a vampire for more than a year now, and although my perception of their feelings toward me has run the gamut from an idea that they barely tolerate me to a feeling that they might actually care about me just enough to make a few changes about the place, it would never have occurred to me to think it would go any further than that.

Behindkind don't tend to care about humans that much—and when they do, it's single humans. *This human is better than the rest. That human is worthy of my notice.* That sort of thing. I didn't like that, but I could appreciate the fact that my psychos cared about me at all, even if I'd rather see them caring about everyone else, too. Or at least, caring enough to help people who needed help without it being just to appease me.

Take Zero, for example: he's fae. Not as obviously unsteady as Jin Yeong, the vampire; nor as obviously bloody. Not as tortuously clever and quietly bloodthirsty as Athelas, his fae steward. But there's a kind of ruthlessness to him that's nearly as frightening to the people he's looking after as it is to the people he's protecting them from.

You know, the kind of feeling that he's going to look after you no matter what happens; no matter what you want. Like a really over-protective big brother. At least, that's what it looked like to me, and I hadn't thought anything more of hugging him or leaning up against him on the couch than I had with Athelas. When your housemates are emotionally constipated, it takes a lot of aggressive cuddling to make them stop being stiff.

All it took to give me a different perspective was a former friend's certainty that Zero was sweet on me—just one tiny, weird idea planted in my mind—to make me start second-guessing everything.

I hadn't realised how often he touched my head as he passed me around the house these days. Even when he was reading a book and walked past the back of the couch as he paced with it, there was a light touch on the top of my head.

Not significant. Not a lingering touch. Just the sorta thing you'd do if you were making sure something was still where you'd put it down. And it wasn't as though it was something you'd do to someone you thought of as equal enough to actually like. Or did fae even think of relationships in terms of equality?

That was a scary thought, and I didn't want to think about it. I'm really good at not thinking about stuff when I don't want to think about it, especially when it takes my life from weird to *weird* weird. The problem is, when your perception changes, you suddenly see everything from that new set of lenses.

That's the bit where it alters stuff. Or maybe stuff was already like that and now you see it properly. Beggared if I know which one it is. I told you: I'm good at not thinking about stuff I don't want to think about.

Anyway, it was the situation presently in front of me that seemed most pressing in terms of perspective and change.

I'd walked out of the house that morning with a light step and a very nearly light heart, and when I'd started through a concrete tunnel that connected one side of the footpath to the other beneath a concrete bridge, the only person in front of me was a kid in a dark blue school uniform with a light blue collar, who looked to be about seven or eight.

He was a cautious little nipper, too; stared around before entering the tunnel and gave me a suspicious look for good measure. He must have been satisfied with what he saw, because he started into the tunnel after he'd given me the once-over, and I followed him with my hands in my pockets, wondering what he was up to.

It wasn't a long tunnel: just long enough to span a double-carriageway with a bit of overhang at the ends. The other end was a circle of light that darkened suddenly with the entrance of another school-kid, walking toward us. This kid was a lot bigger than the first, and I was pretty sure the little one recognised him, because the skinny shoulders in front of me stiffened, and the steady, grim footsteps faltered for a second.

It wasn't until the bigger kid was well and truly into the tunnel that it occurred to me to wonder how he'd taken up *so much light* when the tunnel was a good three meters in diameter—or, for that matter, why it seemed as though he'd risen from the ground instead of turning into the tunnel from the footpath.

Once I wondered that, I could see that the shadow didn't look quite right. If you looked at it from the perspective that trolls didn't exist and that it *had* to be a very large schoolboy, you could still fool yourself that the lumps on the sides of its head were just very prominent cauliflower ears. You could tell yourself that the squarish lump clutched in its right hand was just a lunch box and not a lump of wood for a club. You might even be able to persuade yourself that the incredible stench preceding the supposed schoolboy was the result of very bad hygiene.

But as soon as I realised how much of the tunnel it was taking up, my perspective—which *did* include trolls, by the way— switched to allow me to see the real outline of the thing: big, ugly, and radiating threat.

Ah great. It was a troll, segueing from the world between our world and the world Behind. I stepped up my speed a bit, and the kid in front of me stumbled to a stop. Whatever his perspective was, there was no doubt that he was terrified.

"Hand it over, runt," said the troll. Funnily enough, its voice still sounded like a high-schooler's.

The little kid tried. He said, "C-can't eat lunch if I give it to you."

"Don't care. Hand it over."

"Mum didn't give it to me this morning," said the kid. It was a stupid lie, but he was young and scared.

I broke into a jog, worried about the way the distance had telescoped. Between shouldn't be spreading things out this far; the troll must be doing that to make sure its prey couldn't get away if it tried to run.

Judging by the fact that it was shaking down a kid for his lunch money, I was pretty sure I knew what kind of a troll it was. I'd been studying, if only for a bit of rest between bouts of training with Zero and Jin Yeong, and cooking meals.

This troll was a bridge troll. Unlike ninety percent of trolls, who were inclined to be people-pleasers, bridge trolls were vicious, territorial, and inclined to take toll in body parts if they couldn't take it in coin.

Heck. Now what was I supposed to do? The troll had the kid by the leg now, and the poor little thing wasn't even screaming, just choking on terrified sobs with his arms wrapped around his head as he was shaken down for coins.

I hadn't come out to fight a bridge troll today. Didn't even know if I could fight one, despite all my extra training lately—this thing was flamin' big. Still, what else could I do when there was a kid choking on his own snot and about to lose his head?

I skidded to a halt in front of the troll just as a couple of two-dollar coins tinkled to the concrete, and panted, "Put the kid down."

The troll froze, a bit like a dog with something in its mouth it knows shouldn't be there. "You can't see me," it said, in a voice as cold and grating as rocks in a crusher.

"I'm not talking to myself, mate," I pointed out, catching my breath. "Look, if you just want a toll, what about we have a talk and sort out some kind of—"

It tossed the kid aside, crushing leaf-litter and aluminium cans beneath its feet as it started toward me. "You can't see me," it said again, and this time it was a threat, not a statement of disbelief.

I had no weapon. I hadn't come out to fight a troll today: I'd come out today to see a merman about a USB.

Lucky for me, the same perspective that allowed me to realise a high-schooler was actually a bridge troll made it possible for me to find weapons in this environment—in any environment in which I could access the weird world between worlds. *Between*, we call it. Catchy, right?

I'd already been looking around for a weapon; it's instinct, these days. Without hesitation, I stooped for the tattered and holey umbrella half-buried beneath leaf-litter, feeling the organic slime of something hopefully moss-based on the handle. That handle firmed beneath my grip until I held a long blade with a braided leather grip that ought to have been too big and heavy for me.

Only one, and I was used to two blades these days, but there was something special about this sword. I didn't know exactly what that was, but I had pulled it from random umbrellas on two different occasions now and I was pretty sure it wasn't supposed to work that way. The Heirling Sword had once more made an appearance for me.

I didn't have time to wonder what the implications of having the Heirling Sword in my hands were—I didn't even fully understand what the Heirling Sword *was*—because the bridge troll, already too close and ugly to boot, swung at me with its knobkerry.

I blocked the hit without even thinking about my reaction, a two-handed slice upward to the left in a block that rattled the bones in my left arm. I followed the block and ducked under its arm in one movement, finishing with another slice across the leg closest to me as the troll stumbled forward, too committed to its strike to stop. It was a glancing hit that barely drew blood, but it gave me a good idea of the speed and strength I could expect from the troll.

If I could move quicky enough, I'd be fine. If it managed to get in a hit, I was probably going to be very dead or very much in pain and then very dead.

I put up my guard again, feeling the dragging weight of the sword on my shaken arms, and the troll turned.

"Stay *still*, little flea," it said.

"Yeah, nah," I said as it lumbered forward again.

This time the troll tried to swat me back-hand and I ducked under the swing without guarding, circling to the right to confuse it. It didn't hurt that this manoeuvre took me further away from the troll's knobkerry, either. I hadn't counted on its other arm being quite as close as it was, though, or quite as fast: the troll sent me flying across the tunnel with a flat palm.

Somehow I managed to keep a grip on the sword, battering my knuckles as the weight of it slammed them into the concrete. Unfortunately, with the wind knocked out of me it was very hard to do anything but stare at the dark, curved ceiling of the tunnel, and I had to force myself up, slowly and painfully.

The troll was slow, but so was I. By the time I dragged myself up, it was very nearly on top of me. I tried to move back to bring up a guard again, but the pommel of the sword hit the concrete wall at my back. I didn't have time to pull away and try again, or even to adjust the angle of the sword, but that didn't matter because the troll tripped on the broken concrete and lurched drunkenly at me.

Luckily for me, that put the point of the sword at roughly

stomach level for the bridge troll, its knobkerry hitting far too high on the wall as it tried to catch itself. It shish-kabobbed itself without any help from me, narrowly avoiding crushing me as its head hit the wall, and I stepped to the left as the body inevitably fell away to the right, drawing out the sword as I went.

Blood, thick and jelly-like, gathered into globs and slowly slipped down the flat of the blade. The soft *pat pat* of them hitting the concrete punctuated the last gasping breath of the bridge troll, and I cleared my throat in the silence that followed.

I said, "Sorry," to the body and looked around for the kid as the troll began to moulder away into the appearance of a lumpy old mattress as the world Between sank back into itself and took on the appearance of the human world again. He was long gone, by the looks. Definitely not in the tunnel, anyway.

That didn't mean I was alone, though. I smelt him before I saw him: an almost blue waft of scent-laden breeze that hit nearly as hard as the bridge troll had done. A moment later he sauntered into the tunnel, picking his way fastidiously between the worst piles of garbage to save his pointy shoes.

Jin Yeong: vampire, lover of strong perfume and garlic, once a part of the Korean army and now a permanent pain in my neck—sometimes literally—who refused to speak English and addressed the world, understanding or not, only in Korean.

I huffed an irritated sigh as I cleaned troll blood off the sword. That was all I needed: a pointy-shoed little mosquito here to see me doing stuff I definitely shouldn't be doing and report back to Zero. I'd already had enough of that from Jin Yeong. There had been a time, not so many weeks ago, when he had pretended to be my friend and had fought for me. And okay, he'd actually been hurt: nearly died, in fact. But he'd still been with me on Zero's orders, had still been telling Zero stuff behind my back. That was hard to forget—or forgive—even though we'd fought together since.

Jin Yeong sniffed fastidiously as he approached, and in Korean, the words shaping through Between to be understandable, said, "You made a smell."

"No, the troll made a smell," I corrected him. "It's probably dandruff season for it. Don't reckon it's snow at this time of year, anyway."

"If you had not killed it, it would be stinking elsewhere," he said.

"Only until we'd gone through. Then it would have come back again to rob the next school kid. Oi," I added, scooping up the four dollars from the ground, "reckon you can find that kid again and slip this in his pockets?"

Jin Yeong considered me for a few moments as if deliberating with himself about whether or not to request payment for his services, then said, "*Kurol su isseo.*"

He disappeared while I was still cleaning myself up to make sure I was presentable to humans as opposed to vampires, and I let out a breath. No use trying to ask him not to tell Zero about this; I'd tell Zero myself. Better to get it over with and be scolded.

Besides, the sword I'd pulled out of Between still leaned against the wall where I'd propped it after cleaning, glowing with a faint edge of yellow, and that was more of a worry than the troll. I was pretty sure I wasn't supposed to be able to pull this particular sword out in the particular way I'd done it, because this sword was the Heirling Sword. Note the capital. It was a sword designed for a certain set of people—heirlings—and Zero and Athelas had been stubbornly sure for quite some time now that I was not an heirling. Right now, that wasn't looking too certain, and maybe it's just me, but the idea of having to fight to the death to claim a throne in fairyland has never really appealed to me. I was half convinced already that they were only so firm about me *not* being an heirling because they didn't want me to be one and thought they could stop it happening by the sheer force of their disapproval.

I actually expected the sword to flicker back into being an

umbrella again, but it stayed there in its sword form for the entire time that I cleaned myself up, so I picked it up again and stared at it as if I could make it talk by the staring.

"Yes, I'm curious about that, too," said a cool, familiar voice. "What exactly are you doing with Lord Sero's sword?"

Ah heck.

I turned in a swift scattering of old juice-boxes and bottle caps, the sword lifting to guard position without me thinking about it, and there was another, more worrisome pain in the neck: the golden git. The fae commander from the enforcers who brought us jobs occasionally and was technically one of the king's men but in practise—we suspected—reported directly to Zero's dad.

"Just trying not to die," I said. "What about you? Why are you sneaking around random tunnels in North Hobart?"

"I saw a stray pet," he said, with a cold smile that matched the embossing of leaves and flowers on his golden armour: beautiful and soulless. "I decided to follow it to see what it was up to."

"Thanks for the help, then," I told him, with a hefty amount of sarcasm.

He ignored it, and I knew why. His eyes were still on the sword that I should not have been holding. That I should not have been *able* to hold.

"We wondered," he said, with a small, disbelieving shake of his head. "We *wondered* why he kept you around when you were only a liability. It seemed incredible that he should make the same mistake twice, but—"

A small breath escaped me as I understood. "You're the one who messed with the café the other day, aren't you? You wanted to see what Zero would do if you trapped me in there."

"We were interested in knowing how far Lord Sero would go to protect you," he said, shrugging. "We were also curious to know why he is doing so, but I believe I'm beginning to understand."

Maybe it was the idea that I couldn't do anything about it that made me so bitter as I asked, "So who are you going to tell? Zero's dad, or the king? 'Cos if we're going to discuss stuff that makes us all wonder, that's something we're pretty curious about at home."

"Obviously Lord Sero's father will be informed of your connection with the sword," said the golden git disdainfully. "It's not necessary for the king to know right now. And I have no intention of discussing anything with you, human."

"Funny," I said, the coldness of fear stealing over one cheek and then rapidly down my neck. "Didn't think you'd actually answer that."

He shrugged. "Why would it matter? You won't be alive to tell anyone, little human."

Great, death threats at ten in the morning. Life was a real merry-go-round right now.

"Shouldn't you be asking permission to do stuff like that?" I asked, settling my weight back on my left foot and shifting a smidge to the left as I did so. I was close to the end of the tunnel, but even if I did make it out before he caught me, what then? Would Jin Yeong be back soon? Could I hold out long enough against an actual fae warrior to make it until whenever that was?

"Lord Sero's father will certainly order you put to death when he finds out," he said. "I am merely anticipating that order."

He came at me so quickly that I barely had time to settle into my guard, and sliced so strongly into that guard that the sword very nearly flew right out of my hands. I stumbled to the right, my fingers aching with the force of the blow, and didn't have time to bring up my guard again before I saw the tip of the golden fae's sword plunging toward my chest.

I don't know what I expected it to feel like, but I didn't expect it to feel like a solid shove in the sternum that sent me stumbling two steps backward while a bloody sword followed me but stopped just short of my chest.

I stared at that bloody sword tip, then at the back from which it protruded, stupidly. There was a suitcoat there, and the scent of cologne suddenly *everywhere*, but that couldn't be right because JinYeong shouldn't be between me and the golden fae; JinYeong shouldn't have a sword sticking out of his back.

The golden fae looked just as disoriented as I felt, his face a study in utter shock over JinYeong's left shoulder and one of JinYeong's hands gripping his left shoulder.

I actually thought JinYeong was dead for a frozen, sick moment. Then he laughed with blood in his lungs, and jerked the golden fae closer with the hand that was on the fae's shoulder. The sword jolted further through him as he did, sending me scrambling out of the way, and the golden fae only had a moment to make a strangled sound of realisation before JinYeong tore out his throat with his teeth.

If I'd had time to think about it, I would have thought that JinYeong would bite him. Vampire spit is deadly to anyone with full fae blood, and I would have bet my last clean hoodie that the golden fae was as fully fae as possible.

I didn't expect the savagery of throat tearing that reminded me JinYeong was very much not human—or the terrifying self-abandonment with which he had thrust himself through in order to kill the fae.

The golden fae stumbled back a step and crumpled where he stood, but I saw his eyes and I knew he was already dead before he hit the ground, his neck and chest a welter of spurting and rippling blue blood.

The Heirling Sword fell from my cold, numb fingers, hitting the concrete with a light *thwack* of whippy tines and remaining material as it turned umbrella again, and JinYeong staggered, the golden sword hilt-deep between his ribs and darkly dripping with blood where it protruded from his back.

"Ah heck," I whispered, because he had done it *again* and there was no reason for him to have done it this time. Because I was going to have to pull that sword out of his chest so he could start to heal. Because I was going to have to—

"Blood," he said as he swayed, his mouth and chin glistening blue.

I took in a breath that was very nearly a sob and seized the sword hilt, drawing it out as quickly and steadily as I could. He groaned anyway, sinking to his knees, and I caught him before he could fall too much further.

"Hang on," I said. "You want blue blood or red?"

"Blue," he gasped.

I let him settle on his haunches before I grabbed the golden fae by the plate armour and hauled him closer.

"Better be quick," I said, reefing an arm closer to Jin Yeong's nose. "You've already done for most of it."

He sank his teeth into the fae's wrist, curled over himself in pain and weakness, and the golden fae grew utterly bloodless as he drank, blue blood standing out in bright contrast against the utter white of his dead face.

I waited until Jin Yeong stopped swaying where he crouched and straightened a little, then helped him out of his suitcoat. It was pretty much toast by then, and his shirt wasn't much better. I would have helped him to wipe his face and clean up a bit, too, but he did it himself with his suitcoat and a surprisingly steady hand, then let me help him up so that we could make use of the council tap at the end of the tunnel.

The blood came out of his shirt as we washed it—or maybe it just became unnoticeable against the powder blue cotton—and Jin Yeong slowly struggled back into it, allowing me to help him. Luckily for him it was turning into a warm, sunny day that would see him dry in no time, but his cream suit-coat was a loss, and he knew it. I saw his incisors bared in a silent, annoyed snarl as he threw it back into the tunnel, behind a pile of already mouldering miscellany.

"Go home," I said to him. "Athelas will help you heal a bit quicker and you can get some more blood."

I meant to turn my back on him and go about my business, refusing to acknowledge that he'd just almost died *again*, but he caught me by a pinch of sleeve as I turned, nice and light, and that stung me to the heart because he was being gentle with me when he was the one who had just been hurt.

"*Odi ka?*"

"None of your business where I'm going," I told him angrily, without looking back at him. He had no business taking dreadful risks for me again when I didn't know why he was making them. "Go home! Get Athelas to look at you and make sure you're all right!"

I saw the shrug in my peripheral. "This little thing? It will heal."

"You're still dribbling blood," I said shortly, shooting a quick look at him. I was perfectly well aware that it wasn't just a little thing: if I hadn't been there to pull out the sword, he would have died with it in him. Fae swords and daggers often tend to have anti-vampire enchantments, I'd found. And yeah, if I hadn't been there he wouldn't have been in danger, either, but that thought did nothing to improve my mood.

JinYeong wiped the blood away with the back of his hand, then fished out a handkerchief from goodness knows where to do the job properly. "I drank a lot of blood," he said. "This is that person's blood, not mine."

It was blue, too; I don't know why that didn't register with me. The realisation made the small, shaky, angry part of me a little less shaky and angry, so I only mumbled, "Why are you following me this morning, anyway?"

JinYeong shrugged with one shoulder, and said something in Korean that made a meaning of *there is a suspicious thing about you this morning* in my head.

"Yeah?" I cleared my throat, and this time I turned back to face him. "What's that, then?"

He shrugged again.

I levelled a challenging look at him. "Zero tell you to follow me?"

Jin Yeong gazed at me for a few moments before asking, unexpectedly, "*Wae*? Will it make a difference?"

"Yeah," I said, and there was that pinch of anger again. "Zero tell you to follow me?"

"No," he said. "I came for my own reasons."

"All right," I said. "You can come with me, then."

"You could not stop me anyway," he said below his breath, but I was pretty sure he was grinning, just a little bit. Again, he asked, "Where are we going?"

"Going to see a merman about a USB," I told him. "Look, if you're coming with me, try and make sure people don't notice all *that* down your front, all right?"

"They will not see," he said. He seemed quite jaunty again, despite the fact that I could see through the gash in his shirt to the still-healing wound there. "They will be distracted by my face. You—they will notice you."

I looked down and saw the darkness of blood soaking into my hoodie. "Flamin' heck!" I said crankily, and stripped it off. Luckily I was wearing a black Monkees band t-shirt beneath the hoodie: the blood didn't show up except for a little spot on Davy's face, and that could have been interpreted as a psychedelic splash of colour.

"You know you've gotta stop doing that," I said, as I tossed the hoodie in the nearest public garbage can. "Coming out of nowhere and chucking yourself between me and swords. It's not flamin' healthy."

Jin Yeong just shrugged, and kept walking. Usually he exudes a kind of self-satisfaction that's very hard to bear, but today he just looked content, like he'd done a good day's work.

He wasn't exactly wrong, so I said grumpily, "There's not always gunna be someone there to pull out the sword and lug a dead fae closer for you to feed on so you don't die, you know."

"Then I shall pull it out myself and crawl," he said. He shot me a glance beneath his lashes and added, "I do as I please. You can't stop me doing that, either."

Then he sauntered on ahead of me as I briefly halted in a combination of frustration and sudden, completely unexpected fondness. Now, he definitely exuded self-satisfaction.

CHAPTER TWO

IT'S *VERY HARD* TO FEEL GRATEFUL TO A VAMPIRE WHO SAVES your life out of what seems like pure contrariness, let me tell you. On the other hand, that morning the sheer contrariness of it seemed to make it easier not to make a fuss about him following me. It wasn't that I trusted him more, exactly. Maybe I distrusted him less, though. Heck, maybe I was grateful, who knows? You should be grateful when someone saves your life.

Ordinarily, I wouldn't have wanted Jin Yeong to come with me to visit Marazul, even if I did fully trust him, but I was feeling fairly nervous about the whole thing. Not nervous in the *am I gunna die today* kind of way, but in a more subtly dangerous way: the kind of nervous that made me wonder if I would still be able to speak when it came to this particular merman smiling at me.

This merman and I, we'd fought together in the café the golden fae had imprisoned us in—me physically, him electronically—and by the time the whole ordeal was over, I'd felt comfortable and warm with him instead of warm and nervous. But that was a few days ago, and I was rapidly finding that I had to break through this kind of nervousness again every time I saw him.

Jin Yeong was dangerous and maybe not to be entirely trusted, but he was a familiar quantity in many ways. I'd *had* a crush before, but I didn't remember it being so alien and all-encompassing that I found it hard to breathe when my crush was nearby. I didn't like it. Didn't like not being able to do something about it. Didn't like the way it was hard to focus properly on other things when he was nearby. I wanted it to go away, wanted to be able to stop myself from going to see 'Zul, but he was the only one who could help me with the USB unless I tried to get into contact with Blackpoint.

Maybe, I thought, maybe I should just try to get over it. Ignore the feelings until they went away—stop going to see 'Zul as soon as the USB was sorted out.

And maybe I'd have to stop telling off Zero about not being able to handle his emotions when I couldn't even handle a crush.

"Where are we going?" asked Jin Yeong, and I came out of my thoughts to find that he was watching me unblinkingly.

"I told you—oh, you mean where are we meeting him? His place, this time. It's not far—and you can sit down while we're there."

I hadn't been inside 'Zul's place before, though I'd seen it from the outside. I'd met him a few times in the last two days, running errands for Zero, but I'd always met him at a café or out in the botanical gardens in areas where he could manoeuvre his wheelchair along the wide, smooth paths.

Today, we were meeting at his house. I had a feeling that if he'd been expecting me he would have tried to meet me outside again, but I didn't want to chance anyone else getting a look at what I was going to show him.

His house was easy to find: he lived on the main drag, up in the top floor of a building above a couple of shops. The whole building sat across the road from a café that used to sell the best coffee and was also, incidentally, holding humans captive to feed off their souls.

The café was gone now: Marazul and I had dealt with it just before Zero showed up to stare coldly at everyone. But 'Zul's building was still there, dark and tall and scalloped at the top like a gothic Lolita dress in cream and black.

We had to go up by the fire escape at the back because there was no entrance that I could find along the bottom level. Maybe you were supposed to enter through the shops, but I didn't think so. I wouldn't be surprised if 'Zul had tried to hide the entrance: I was pretty sure he was worried about who was going to be paying him a call these days. I was hoping that that reluctance wouldn't extend to me.

JinYeong took the stairs at first stoically and then energetically, so the dead fae's blood must be doing him some good. I tried not to sigh, and, now that the worry that he would suddenly stop and collapse was gone, I started to worry exactly what Zero was going to say when he heard about all of this.

At the final platform of the fire escape, we walked alongside windows that were opaque with the darkness of moving shadow. There was a little bit of green to that shadow, too. I didn't like the way it moved, but that could have been because I was used to stuff that shouldn't be moving, moving—and then attacking.

Metal vibrated under our feet as we crossed the corrugated platform that ended just past a single, simple door. There was no doorknob on the door, and there was no feel of what I'd come to think of as magic to it, either. There was definitely a decent layering of Between to it that meant I could have tried to push through it, but that didn't seem polite.

Besides, JinYeong has a harder time getting into places without an invitation. He can still get in, it just seems harder for him, and he'd had a bad enough day as it was. If I could make life easier for him, I probably ought to.

JinYeong tilted his chin at the camera outside the door and gave it a sharp-edged grin. I smacked him lightly in the arm and said up at the camera, "Can we come in?"

I was pretty sure Marazul could hear through it, too. He uses human technology, but he gives it a bit of an edge—a Between edge—which means that stuff that should only be able to do one thing becomes able to do three or four extra things that you wouldn't expect. I was also pretty sure that he didn't have to be on his computer to check it.

There was a pause of about thirty seconds where I wasn't sure if he would just pretend not to be home, before the door made a heavy *clunk* sort of sound and cracked open a few millimetres as if it had been released from a magnetic hold.

"C'mmon," I said to JinYeong, drawing in a deep breath. It didn't seem like enough. "Better get on with it."

I hesitated over the lintel, but that wasn't just because I was nervous. It was because as I stepped through the door, it seemed as though I was falling softly into a vast body of water.

Shadow met and engulfed me as I stumbled in, folding softly around me in ripples of green and blue shadow, cool and quiet. I looked around at the glassy corridor I had entered, and grabbed JinYeong's wrist, dizzy with wonder and amazement.

It was water. The shadows in the windows were the movement of water moving against the glass, lit from within and edged in Between of a kind that I hadn't often seen. That wasn't too surprising—'Zul also used Between in a way that I wasn't used to seeing.

JinYeong, likewise impressed, looked around the whole place, his brows rising as shadows rippled across his face. We stood in a corridor formed from glass walls that formed a smooth arch above our heads, leading further into the space that branched out into a small living room and kitchen further on, but left the rest of the place for water that continued so far into the distance that it was too dark to see the walls that must contain it.

Basically, it was the biggest fish tank I'd ever seen.

We moved into the living room, and here the light became blueish-white with an influx of natural light from the window and the warm white of the fluorescent tubes above. In that light, my skin seemed to glow white, and even Jin Yeong seemed pale.

"Ah," muttered Jin Yeong, tilting his chin to the far left of the room, where the wall met glass in a smudge of blue shadows, "here is the fish man."

"Merman," I said, without looking at Jin Yeong, but my heart wasn't in it. Without meaning to, I took a step forward, and then another until I was close enough to touch the glass. I felt it under my fingers the next moment. I hadn't meant to do that, either, but I was too fascinated watching 'Zul appear to think of anything else.

First as a movement of the water, then as a shadow; then a figure that swayed, danced, *coiled* through the shifting shadows, drawing closer in a series of spirals that grew tighter until he slipped up against the glass in front of me, suspended in shadow and light.

The scales of his tail caught the light and almost glowed from within, gold in the water that could perhaps just be reached to test the coolness of it, but it was his face that really drew attention.

In the light of my world, 'Zul's skin was a gentle, sun-kissed bronze, his eyes honey and warmth, his hair rough and curly and carefree. Here, he was bright, glittering gold in the water, sunlight cooled by the waves that seemed to move around him even though he was in a fish tank instead of the sea. Everything slimmed, smoothed, and embellished; a more beautiful and not-quite-real version of himself.

I felt a horrible insecurity, a moment where it seemed that I was looking at a changeling instead of the real 'Zul. Then he smiled at me, wide and glad and warm, and my own smile came out to answer it, easing the terrible tightness of my chest.

A pale set of knuckles knocked imperiously on the glass beside my face, and Jin Yeong said, "*Hajima.*"

At first I thought he was telling me to knock it off, but his dark eyes were fixed on Marazul, and the moment of surprise made me realise what I hadn't before: 'Zul was either using or perhaps merely exuding a kind of Between that must be similar to what Jin Yeong exerts upon most other humans. I was, oddly enough, entirely immune to Jin Yeong's particular brand of mojo; it looked like I wasn't immune to the merman brand of the same thing. I hadn't noticed it before, but then I hadn't seen 'Zul in his natural habitat before, either.

I narrowed my eyes at 'Zul and he had the grace to look away, his eyes faintly guilty. Then he caught sight of the tear in Jin Yeong's shirt, and he began to look wary as well as guilty.

With a vibration that made my teeth buzz, I somehow heard him say, through water and glass alike, "Sorry. I can't help it when I'm in here."

"Just when you're in there?" I asked. It made me uncomfortable to think that he might have been influencing me to like him from the start. It made me *more* uncomfortable to think that I hadn't noticed it before.

"Only in here," he said. "I can't do it in the human world, but in here it's the merperson equivalent of B.O."

"*Tch!*" said Jin Yeong. "*Cogitmal.*"

I threw him a look. "You're one to talk: you always have women trailing after you because you're flamin' irresistible."

"He can help it a *little bit*," Jin Yeong said coldly, and turned his shoulder in irritation.

"I'd come out," said 'Zul, after a very slight hesitation, "but the enchantment on the walls can get a bit messy and it takes me a while to get to my wheelchair."

It took a few seconds to realise that what he meant was he didn't want to struggle into his wheelchair while we watched—and that he probably didn't want our help to get in it, either.

"Sorry if it's uncomfortable for you," I said. "Us coming here, I mean. I didn't want to hand this over out in the street."

"No," he said. "I wouldn't have opened the door for you if it wasn't all right for you to come in. I haven't finished with the last thing Lord Sero asked me to do, though: Blackpoint is pretty hard to track down, and I'm fairly certain he can—"

"—sneak inside computers and hide in the internet. Yeah. Didn't Zero tell you?"

He stared at me with his mouth open. "Yes. How did you know?"

"He sneaked away from an execution team by ducking into a game and having someone smuggle him out of his mansion. Then he blew up our computer, getting out."

"Yes," muttered Jin Yeong. "My heart was recharged and I did not *require* it."

"It gave him a lot of static," I added, grinning properly for the first time since I'd entered the tunnel this morning. Jin Yeong had been attracting a lot of static electricity for these last two weeks after the shock to his heart, but so far it had only meant he gave himself a series of little shocks as it discharged, which was fun for me and not so much fun for him when he tried to take over too much of our couch.

'Zul said with some respect, "I've never seen anything like it."

"You sent a café full of people to safety via email," I pointed out.

"Yes, but I didn't know it was possible before I did it."

"Now you do," I said. "S'gunna be very useful, too."

"Yes," he said, but he sounded a bit doubtful. "Very...useful."

"Anyway, that's not what we've come about. We've come about this USB."

"What is it?"

"We don't know," I said, still brandishing the glass USB at him. I'd picked it up from the North Wind, and I was rather sure it held information about Zero's mother or my family's murder—or perhaps both. "That's what I need you for—I don't know the password and I don't know how to get to the files without a password."

He nodded. "I've got a little spell program for that sort of thing; they work better than anything else I've used. Is it a job for Lord Sero?"

"Nope," I said. "In fact, I'd rather you didn't mention it to him at all."

'Zul looked faintly ill. "Pet—"

"Don't worry," I said, smiling encouragingly. "I won't tell him if you don't."

I saw Jin Yeong's mouth open in the reflection of the glass and sent him a narrowed, sideways look that he met with a pouty, challenging one, a glint to his eye. Was he going to tell Zero after all? I could have left him behind. I could have gone alone another day but I'd brought him with me today, despite everything. There was a part of me that wanted to see if I really could trust him not to tell Zero stuff that was important to me. A part of me that wanted to believe that the Jin Yeong who had twice stood between me and the sword of a powerful fae was as trustworthy as I'd once thought him.

"Jin Yeong won't tell, either," I said. "*If* he knows what's good for him."

"I shall do as I please," said Jin Yeong, but he said it in Korean without the usual translation supplied by Between magic. In other words, for my ears only. He added, "You are not my pet; I am not yours."

"You been taking lessons from Athelas in Riddle Speak?" I said, by way of retort, and turned back to Marazul. "It won't come back to bite you. I'll make sure."

"You can't promise that," he said, and there was a half-smile on his face that looked distinctly rueful.

Jin Yeong gave vent to a derisive sort of sniff that counted for a laugh when he was trying to be insulting. I narrowed my eyes at him.

"I won't promise," I said to 'Zul. "But I'll do my best. Trust me, I don't want Zero to know about this any more than you do."

"It's frightening how you think that's comforting," he said, but now his eyes were smiling too, even if that smile was as rueful as the one on his lips. "I'll let you know when I get something."

WE DIDN'T STAY LONG, DESPITE MY PROMISE TO JINYEONG that he could sit and rest, and it was a quiet walk back home. I was thoughtful and silent, and so, surprisingly, was JinYeong. In general, his cologne was strong enough to count as an extra personality, but even it seemed diluted and mellow now that we were in the fresh air again.

It wasn't until we passed back through the tunnel that I saw the floppy, bent remains of the umbrella I'd used earlier, and spoke almost without thinking.

"Oi," I said. "There it is again. The umbrella."

It had still been at home when I got back from using it in my drop-bear adventure a while back, though; sitting in the umbrella stand in the hall where it ought to have been and still in its umbrella form. Zero hadn't mentioned that it'd gone missing, either, and I was pretty sure he would have noticed.

I nearly picked it up again, but I didn't know exactly what to do with it when it looked like a busted umbrella. I mean, I might *look* like I know what I'm doing and what's going on, but most of the time I haven't got a clue what's happening and why stuff works the way it works. I'm just mostly trying not to die, and figuring things out as I go along.

My problem is that my owners are convinced there's only one way that Between works—and Between doesn't always work that way for me. Don't know if you've ever tried to convince three Behindkind that they're wrong, but it's not easy. Part of that's understandable: I'm a human, not Behindkind, and I don't have anything like their experience when it comes to Behind and Between. My only experience is my own, and although I can understand why they're always so quick to dismiss me, it never gets any less annoying to be told that something you've just done, or seen, or caused, is impossible and can't have happened.

It's not that easy to learn when your teachers need to learn a few things themselves.

They had told me that Between worked in a certain way, and the way that the sword was behaving here today was at odds with how they had told me it worked. Of course, that was if they were telling me everything, and they had a very bad track record of not telling me everything. They also had a bad habit of protesting that something *couldn't* be right until it proved that it was, and that was the habit that worried me the most right now.

"It is dirty," said Jin Yeong. "Don't touch it. You already made enough mischief today."

"Don't pretend you don't make mischief when it comes to Zero," I retorted. "Anyway, I wasn't going to pick it up."

Jin Yeong turned on his toes and planted himself in front of me, ducking his head to put himself nose-to-nose with me. "There is mischief I *could* make—"

"If you're leading up to trying to blackmail me," I said, my hand snaking out to grab his tie, "you'd probably better remember that your tie is in reach and I can make another little playmate for the tie frog that's hanging around Hobart somewhere."

His hand fastened around mine, tight but not crushing, and his eyes grew liquid. "Do not dare to turn my tie into a frog again."

"But it's *so fun*."

"It is not fun for me," he said. "And we have not discussed payment."

"Nope," I said, letting go of his tie. He didn't let go of my hand, so I pulled it away gently to avoid jolting his injured torso. I shoved it in my pocket instead and added, "Told you: I'm not going to pay you. You either do it or you don't."

I stood there and looked up at him, wondering if that Jin Yeong really did exist: the one who could do things for me without there being loyalty to Zero behind it. Just because I asked him to do it.

Jin Yeong looked around at the tunnel, avoiding my eyes. "My silence is valuable," he mumbled.

"If we're talking about people *owing* other people you still owe me for pretending to be my friend," I told him. I hadn't meant to say it, and it wasn't really fair to say it in the same tunnel that was still sticky with his blood from earlier in the day. But I wanted to know that I could trust him.

He huffed an exasperated sigh up at the tunnel roof, then snapped his gaze back to me, canines showing. "*Ya*. I thought you didn't want to talk about payment."

"You brought it up first," I pointed out. "And I'm not going to let you nearly die for me and then stab me in the back again, so don't try to get on my good side, all right?"

There was a brief silence while Jin Yeong muttered to himself in Korean without translating it for me. At length he said in a cross voice, "I did not follow you to the house of the zombie because *hyeong* ordered me to do so. He gave the order *after* I was already in the house. I followed you because we had become—become *allies* and I *wanted to*. I stayed with you because I trust you at my back in the fight."

I stared at him, and at last repeated, "He gave that order *after* you were with me? Why did he say—why did he tell me—why did he make me think it wasn't like that?"

Jin Yeong's eyes grew stormy and he said, "I wonder." Aggrievedly, he added, "I even once trusted you and didn't fight."

"When did you trust me and not fight?" I demanded, bewildered as to why it was a grievance or even important. I still wanted to know why Zero had deliberately tried to make a wedge between me and Jin Yeong—because there was no way he hadn't done it on purpose, or without at least realising what would come of it.

"That one," Jin Yeong said, pointing accurately at the hillock of what looked like moss in the human world but was the body of the golden fae when seen through Between.

I frowned, but I did remember trying to stop him going for the golden fae's throat once before when we were in the house. He must be talking about that, but for the life of me, I couldn't see why that was so important to him. And it was, evidently, very important: his eyes were unwaveringly, almost unnervingly, fixed on me. I was the one who looked away first, my thoughts tumbling and pinwheeling over each other.

He said, "If I had fought then, it would have been trouble. I *told* you that I have very much emotion."

"Oh," I said. There was an imbalance inside of me that tipped back toward the sense of companionship and trust I'd once felt toward JinYeong, and I wasn't sure if I wanted to let it do that.

"I followed you to the house of the zombie because you are not my pet but my—my—"

I watched his facial contortions, and asked with an attempt at flippancy, "Is it 'cos I'm a human that you can't say *friend*, or what? Spit it out."

Even before, he'd stumbled through saying *allies*.

"Friend is not correct," he said stiffly. "We have fought together. We are...allies."

"Don't think that works," I said, thinking of the vast difference between the worlds to which we owed loyalty. Still, for a while it really seemed as though we'd been facing the world together. "Blood siblings?"

"No," he said, with finality.

"All right," I said. "We're allies or whatever. But why'd you keep reporting to Zero if you were only coming along to Morgana's to be with me?"

"It is easier to do things with *hyeong*'s blessing than without."

"That's true," I had to admit.

"And I did not tell him everything I learned. Just enough to prevent him removing me."

That, I also had to admit, I knew to be true, even if I didn't do so aloud.

"We are friends, then?" he asked, and this time he didn't stumble over the word.

"That's what I thought for a while," I said. The imbalance was swinging more and more to JinYeong's side, and I was still half afraid to be convinced again. "How do I know you're not lying about all this?"

He grinned at me, startling me with the suddenness of it. "I do not lie well," he said. "I speak before I think—you have not noticed? I told you—"

"Yeah, too much emotion," I murmured, my mind reeling. Because it was true. JinYeong had always been quick to act and speak under the impetus of his immediate emotions. Which meant that the mosquito had been telling the truth all along.

I heaved a very big sigh.

"You're really annoying, you know that?" I told him.

"Yes," he said, and he was still grinning. "You are also annoying. What is it that I have done now?"

"It means I've got to apologise," I explained. "I don't like apologising to you."

JinYeong shrugged, pulling at the tear in his shirt. The wound beneath it was very nearly gone, I saw. He said, "I also have some things to apologise for. We will call it equal."

"Dunno about that," I said. "Hang on, if I do apologise, are you gunna apologise as well? 'Cos I want to know what you think you've got to apologise for."

"You think I...don't need to apologise?" he hazarded, confused.

"Nah, I just wanna get your perspective on what you did wrong," I explained. "But also I don't want to apologise so—"

"Another time," he said, "we will apologise. Today, we will be friends for a little while first and go home."

. . .

ZERO AND ATHELAS WERE IN THE LIVING ROOM WHEN WE GOT back, sitting in their respective chairs and each reading: Zero, a book, and Athelas, a file. Zero looked me up and down, past me to Jin Yeong, and said, "You smell of bridge troll."

"*Nae mari*," Jin Yeong said accusingly at me. "You shouldn't make smells like that."

"It was trying to stop me from walking under a bridge," I said indignantly. There was a little niggle of happiness in me; I turned and nearly opened my mouth to threaten him cheerfully with another tie change, but my eyes fell on the tear in his shirt once again.

Oh heck. There was more to tell today.

"That's what bridge trolls do," Zero said briefly. "They like bridges. They don't like people walking underneath their bridges."

"Well, I don't like kids being eaten because they have to walk under a bridge to get to school," I said. I should be mentioning the golden fae *any time now*, but my mouth didn't want to cooperate.

Zero actually put down his book. "Pet, did you kill a troll?"

"I *tried* to work out a payment plan but he wasn't interested! And for the record, he had a go at me first: I was just trying not to die."

Athelas exchanged a glance with Zero and said, as if it was an amelioration, "At least the troll is dead, my lord."

"Hang on, am I in trouble for killing it, or not?"

"You would have been in trouble for fighting it," Athelas said. "Since you've killed the thing, my lord has no issue with it."

"Makes perfect sense," I said, layering my voice with sarcasm. The bad thing was, it actually did make sense to me, these days. Fighting a bridge troll was something that would call attention to myself if both I and the bridge troll lived to tell about it. Me dying because of fighting a bridge troll would also bring about more scrutiny than Zero and Athelas thought comfortable or sensible. The bridge troll dying, on the other hand, brought about no such scrutiny.

Behindkind weren't supposed to mess with humans, and although the Behind authorities wouldn't necessarily stop it, they certainly wouldn't interfere if someone else did. The death of a bridge troll who had been troublesome to both worlds was a convenience.

That gave me an idea that I hoped was correct.

I cleared my throat and said, "Yeah, about dead things."

Athelas looked at me over the edge of his file, eyes amused, and Zero, distinctly wary, said, "What is it, Pet?"

"I killed that golden git," said Jin Yeong, pushing past me and throwing himself down on the couch to show the state of his shirt and chest in one grand gesture. "He stabbed me, so I bit him. He is not our problem now."

"Good heavens," said Athelas, his file dropping an inch. He must have been pretty startled. "How delightfully brief. Could you elaborate a trifle more?"

"What he means," I said, "is that the golden git has been following me for a while by the sounds of it. He saw me kill the bridge troll and started talking about how he and your dad were wondering why I was being kept, and then he went to stab me and stabbed Jin Yeong instead."

"I do not like being stabbed," Jin Yeong added. "It *hurts*."

Zero said sharply, "Witnesses?"

"No one, as far as I know," I said, hoping to sooth the terrible worry that had etched itself between his brows. "He said he was going to tell your dad about me—about me pulling stuff out of Between, but he's dead now. If he's dead there's no problem, right?"

I saw Athelas press his lips together on a smile, but it didn't do anything to suppress the amusement in his eyes. "There are perhaps a few problems remaining," he said. "But they're minor compared with the problem of someone informing my lord's father that you can affect Between. Very minor, wouldn't you say, my lord?"

Zero let out a short, exasperated breath. "Minor," he agreed dryly. "And nothing that need concern us if we're not implicated. His lieutenant will no doubt take his place."

That idea perked me up a bit as I drifted off to make everyone a late breakfast: Palomena was a far better liaison than the golden fae, and I had a feeling that she wasn't quite as much in Zero's dad's pocket as the golden fae had been, either.

Much to my surprise, Zero stepped silently up into the kitchen a few minutes after I started frying bacon. I tried not to look at him, but he was watching me steadily, and at last I said, "What?" as I turned over the bacon.

"Injuries? Troll dandruff tends to infect wounds quite easily."

That made me realise I hadn't stopped to check for injuries either before or after I got home. Was I getting so used to being bloodied and bashed about that I didn't even check myself if there was no actual blood dripping?

"Reckon I'm fine," I said doubtfully. "Nothing's bleeding, anyway. Jin Yeong was pretty rough for a while, but—"

He said shortly, "I'm not concerned for Jin Yeong. Make sure you check properly later."

I could check for bruises and that sort of thing later, in the shower. Athelas would be able to help with healing those if I didn't want to go through the trauma of getting vampire spit to speed things up.

"Did you kill the troll alone, or did Jin Yeong help?" he asked, rounding the bench to fill a glass at the sink beside me.

"Did it myself before he got there," I said. "It was mostly acci-dental, actually. The troll tripped on the ground and impaled himself on my sword."

"Sword?"

"Yeah," I said, carefully casual. Don't tell Zero about the sword. Not yet. Not when the golden fae had looked on it as proof definite that I was an heirling. So far, Zero had been able to protest with some strength that I wasn't one, and I didn't want that to change. "Could only manage one this time."

"Good job, Pet," said Zero, laying his hand briefly on my head. "Make sure you see Athelas about any bruising."

"You're acting weird these days," I told him, my head still warm from the touch. If it hadn't been for that stupid, lingering memory of Morgana's voice saying "He *likes* you!", it wouldn't even have felt weird. It would only have been a definite sign that he did actually care about me, even if I didn't always appreciate the way in which it was shown. "Patting me on the head and stuff. You've been doing it for a couple weeks now."

"You're the pet," Zero said briefly. "I was told that one should pat pets."

I mean *yeah* but also why start now? He'd been fending off any sign of physical affection since I'd known him, and I wanted to know why he was starting to figure it out now.

I was still wondering that when I went upstairs. A whole different mess waited for me up there, but at least it gave me something to do with my mind other than wonder about ridiculous eventualities.

I slipped through the hidden door that led to my room and made sure it was properly shut behind me. None of my psychos tended to come into my room unless they were waking me up, but I didn't want to run the chance of them seeing what I had out there lately: the mixed flurry of copied images, bills, purchase deeds, and other apparently unrelated documents. I'd given them to another friend of mine—Five-Four-One, a leprechaun—to tell me what they were all about, but so far, all he'd done was make copies and be mysterious about the fact that they were all connected.

It sounded like garbage, but Five knew what he was doing when it came to finding patterns and following the money. Once someone taught him how to use a computer, he'd be unstoppable.

There was an idea. Maybe I'd have to introduce him to 'Zul.

In the mean-time, all I could do was sort through it all and see if anything made sense to me. So far, I'd been able to find four pieces of information that were directly or tangentially related to me: an old copy of my mother's driving license, a page from some-one's address book that had both mine and Morgana's addresses on it, a bill for the power to be paid at my house and a little note that didn't make sense with my great grandmother's name on it.

But for the life of me, I couldn't work out how those four pieces joined together—or how they fit the rest of the pieces of the information Tuatu had gathered for me. I also couldn't work out why Athelas had set Tuatu to find the pieces. But even if I couldn't work it out, I knew that I had to try: Athelas had been up to something for the last year at least, in my opinion. The fact that he was up to something that concerned my past, or maybe my present, wasn't something I wanted to let go. Like Athelas, it was a like a puzzle: a puzzle where there were no straight edges, made up of myriad smaller images and no box to tell you what the whole was supposed to look like. You'd think I'd get used to dealing with things like this, living with my psychos, but it was still a pain in the neck to follow their twisty thinking.

I'd had the stuff out on my floor for the last couple of weeks, just sitting there to be sorted through and obsessed over, and yeah, maybe it was a bit unhealthy, but it wasn't like I had anyone else to share it with. I didn't want to let Athelas know I knew he'd been giving Tuatu jobs, and I didn't want Zero to know I was investigating things on my own. I could talk about it with Jin Yeong, but he'd probably just sit on the floor and make remarks, then tell me I had to pay for his help.

That day, fresh from beating a bridge troll and visiting a merman, I picked up the same thing I always picked up first: the copy of my mother's driving license. It wasn't that I thought it was particularly useful, it was just that I liked to look at the photo and remember her that way. My last sight of her hadn't been anything as nice, and it was pleasant to have one picture of her solemn face with just the hint of a smile hiding away.

Today felt a little bit different. I hadn't yet done more than cursorily glance at the information on the license—my mother's picture had drawn my attention first, and the fact that I'd never seen another photograph of her in my life reoccurred to me as I sipped the coffee I'd brought up with me.

I looked a bit closer at the license, and for the first time, a couple of details jumped out at me. First was the nearly type-writer font they'd used to input the information on the original: I hadn't seen a lot of driver's licenses, but I was pretty sure they didn't use typewriters for that anymore. Weird official font choice, or what?

Mum's height wasn't right, either—and her middle name had been misspelled as *Anne* instead of *Ann*, which was pretty sloppy.

I frowned. Sloppy, or purposeful? And why did this license look so different? I'd assumed it was different because it was an older license, but it hadn't occurred to me until now that the person on this license might not be mum at all. Just the height alone could be wrong, and perhaps the middle name being wrong might not be so odd—on its own. Anne with an *e* instead of without might be a small difference, but add that to the height difference and it was a different beast.

But if not mum, who? The photo was mum, I was sure of it.

And yet, as I gazed at it, I began to be less sure.

I put down my coffee and for the first time, I went through the information on the copy line by line, until I came to the smudgy date of issue.

April 20ᵗʰ, 1925

Flaming. Heck.

I'd assumed that it was just mum's maiden name because it was a photograph taken before she met dad, but with that kind of date, the wrong middle name suddenly made sense: mum had been named after her grandma, minus an *e*.

That made more sense: mum and dad had never been happy with photographs being taken, and as far as I'd known until finding this license, had never had official ID.

But it still left me wondering what the heck was going on. If it had been weird to find a photocopied driver's license that belonged to my mum in a bunch of papers that Athelas had been gathering, it was even weirder to find one that belonged to my great grandma in there. How did Athelas know about something even I didn't—and why had he been gathering the information?

Was he gathering it for Zero or for Zero's dad, more to the point? I'd be annoyed if it was for Zero, but I'd be downright terrified if it was for his dad. I still remembered what it felt like, having him in my head. I didn't want him interested enough in me that he was looking up ancestors and driving licenses. What exactly was Athelas up to?

I took another look at the gritty black and white picture, and ran my finger over it thoughtfully. Something had happened to great grandma: that was why mum was named after her. What had mum said happened? *She went out of state and no one saw her again.*

I had always assumed it was my dad who made the rules—no photographs, nothing around the house that you can't leave be and never come back for, only cash jobs—because he had been the most careful, the most worried. Now I began to wonder, what if that had come from mum's side? And if so, what had they been so worried about that it had affected our whole life?

I hadn't ever thought our life strange until well after mum and dad were murdered. My leprechaun friend Five-Four-One had suggested something of the kind a little while ago. I hadn't wanted to hear it. Now, with my texts to former friend and current zombie Morgana sitting on read and a copy of a driver's license belonging to my great grandmother between my fingers, it seemed to me that I was going to have to begin thinking about it. Morgana had locked herself away from the reality of being a zombie by refusing to acknowledge the world outside her house. I was no better: I had focused on the outside world that had gone mad to avoid looking at an inside world that was not as normal as it had once seemed, and had now kaleidoscoped beyond recall.

It was time I began seriously investigating my own past.

I mean, not today, obviously. But soon.

Soon never comes, said a whisper in my head, prickling me with discomfort. I tried to push away the voice. I was *going* to do it. I had been planning to do it for a long time.

I had even gone so far as to take that USB to Marazul behind Zero's back—that wasn't nothing. There might be something on there that had to do with my mother.

Planning, planning, never doing, accused the same voice.

"Shut up," I said to it, and hurried out of my room again.

CHAPTER THREE

I SPENT A DISTURBED NIGHT, WAKING IN THE WEE HOURS WHEN someone left the house—Athelas, I decided sleepily, since I could still feel Zero and Jin Yeong somewhere around the house. *Sneaky fae stuff*, I thought, and went back to sleep, but I didn't wake until late the next morning, feeling odd and sideways.

Jin Yeong was lounging on the couch in a soft green shirt that could have used a few more buttons done up when I finally went downstairs. Despite waking late, I'd been going over my papers and pieces of miscellany for an hour or two, trying to convince myself that I was really doing some good—really making an effort to start finding out more about my parents and what web it was that had been woven around them. I didn't dare to stay upstairs for longer than that, though. It was bad enough that Zero didn't know I'd taken his USB to 'Zul before I had to hand it over.

Perturbed and sleep-deprived, the last thing I needed to see was far too much vampire chest as Jin Yeong lounged gracefully on the couch, soulfully reading a book. Good grief. First Zero wandering around in nothing but a towel, and now Jin Yeong playing a Korean Lothario. What was next, Athelas wearing beach shorts? Weren't they all getting a bit too comfortable around my house?

"Heard the jug," I said, finishing up my braid. Were we expecting a guest? I was pretty sure Jin Yeong wasn't looking soulful for no reason. "S'pose you lot want tea and coffee and breakfast?"

Athelas languidly waved the paper at me. "It is a pet's job to fetch these, is it not?"

I stared at him for a bit, trying not to grin. He didn't need the paper—had no use for a paper. He just liked to have it there as a method of obfuscation, I was pretty sure. I said, "You know you can get those online?"

Not that he'd ever do it that way, the tricky old dinosaur. Nope. He preferred to have something physical—mostly to hide whatever else he was doing. Why was it so hard to dislike him when he was such a dodgy old bloke?

"You heard the kettle?" he reminded me gently.

"You and Blackpoint should have a word," I told him. Tricky old fae, both of them: always slipping out of this and that. "Reckon you'd get along real well. And maybe he could teach you how to interact with modern technology."

"Thank you, I'm sufficiently acquainted with Blackpoint. However, considering what he did to the computer upstairs, not to mention Jin Yeong, I think we'll have to ask a few questions of that merman friend of yours rather shortly."

I felt my cheeks go a bit warmer, but that couldn't be helped. Athelas probably already knew that I liked going to see 'Zul: hopefully that was all he would think of the blush. I'd prefer him not to know about my visit there yesterday.

"Oh yeah?" I said, in my very best carefree voice. It wouldn't fool him, but I wasn't trying to: I was just trying to misdirect a little bit. I turned to go into the kitchen and asked over my shoulder as I went, "Zero already sent me to ask about Blackpoint. 'Z'at what you mean?"

"Indeed," he replied, as I went to deal with the freshly boiled jug.

It would have to be toast today, I decided, preparing the tea tray. Toast was quicker than yesterday's breakfast, so we could start the day a bit sooner. I'd come downstairs far too late.

In the living room, I heard Jin Yeong say, "You irritate me," and Athelas' affable answer of, "The feeling is entirely mutual," and wondered what they were trading barbs about this time. Usually they fought about things that involved Zero.

"Reckon I should try to tell the human group about where the bridge troll was?" I called. It wasn't that I thought it would do much good—I didn't think Abigail would even agree to meet with me, let alone Zero agree that it was useful—but I was hoping to forestall a fight. I wasn't against the psychos fighting each other these days, mind you: it seemed a bit less potentially deadly than it once had. But it was still a pain to clean up the house after they'd gone tumbling through it if they didn't make it to the back yard before starting. "And other thinner places like that where it's easier for Behindkind to get through?"

"It would certainly free us up for more important things if the humans were agreeable," agreed Athelas' voice, to my surprise. "My lord? Do you have a preference?"

A faint whisper of movement by the kitchen doorway made me jump and look up, and I found Zero looking at me quizzically, his eyes very blue.

"Heck!" I said. "How long have you been there?"

"Contact the humans," Zero said, answering my first question. Heck. That was another surprise for the books.

"I'll try, but they might not want to talk to me after what happened last time," I said gloomily, approaching the doorway to include Athelas in the conversation. "I'll do it, though; even if Abigail only reads the text, she'll know about it. Then she can decide what to do."

Zero nodded and, absently it seemed, laid his hand on my

head properly rather than just touching it briefly. I flinched a bit but managed not to shy away completely, and looked across the room rather consciously to see an expression of amusement on Athelas' face. Luckily, he was looking at Zero, not at me, so I could duck back into the kitchen and make myself busy getting the tea tray together. Tea first, then breakfast.

I could have sworn I heard the gibbering of banshees faintly as I came back into the living room. Jin Yeong must have heard it, too, because he frowned, looking away from the book he was reading, and opened his mouth.

He shut it again when I sat down beside him and put the tea tray on the coffee table, but that might have been because I was side-eyeing his stacks of books. It was unusual enough to see Jin Yeong reading a book, but the fact that the stack closest to me had a series of covers in lurid colours and scarcely less lurid couple clinches was enough to make me say faintly, "Good grief! What are you reading those for?"

I saw Athelas flick a look toward the staircase—was he wondering about the banshees, too?—but he explained, "I believe that Jin Yeong is conducting a species of inquiry into the female mind. Human female, of course."

"What, through those?" I had a quick gander at the other stacks, and said doubtfully, "You'll only get a very partial insight if man-chest covers are all you stick to. Where did you get these, anyway? They have library tags, but you can only get out ten books at a time."

"The librarian was verrrrry helpful," said Jin Yeong, looking at me unblinkingly over the top of his book.

Still checking out the stacks, I grinned. "Female, was she? All right, at least she got you a few others—there are some classics in here as well as the man-chest, so you'll get a bit of variety. Didn't she tell you that there's different kinds of romance?"

Something very small twitched in the house, and Zero said faintly from the hallway, "Athelas?"

"Right away, my lord," Athelas answered.

"You two are as good as a movie sometimes: all hidden signals and double-speak. You could do a stage show like that," I said, going through another stack of books. To Jin Yeong, I said incredulously, "Oi. Are these *all* romance?"

"*Maja*," said Jin Yeong precisely, as Athelas rose and padded away upstairs, no doubt on whatever mysterious business he and Zero had been talking about.

I had more important things to concentrate on. "You can't just read romance if you want to get insight into the female mind!" I told Jin Yeong. "We care about other stuff too, you know! Anyway, you're always biting women—why don't you ask them?"

Sulkily, he said, "They cannot answer properly when I am biting them. I am a distraction too great."

"You're a mosquito, you mean," I said, though he had a point. "How's your stomach, anyway?"

He patted it in some satisfaction. "I am perfect again."

"Right," I said, trying not to snort. A muffled bump from the upstairs landing made me yell, "Oi! Are you all right up there, Athelas?"

"Certainly," came his voice, as calm and matter-of-fact as usual. "Do pour out, Pet; I'll only be a moment. I trust there are shortbreads?"

"Got you some special ones," I called back, pushing a small plate of shortbreads toward his side of the coffee table. I poured a cup of tea, shooting a look down the hallway, where I could see Zero's hulking shadow lurking around the umbrella stand near the front door.

That immediately sent my stomach plummeting as I remembered all that had happened yesterday—the Heirling Sword, the golden fae... I should tell Zero about the sword, but I knew I wasn't going to do it if I had another choice. There was a more immediate problem to deal with, anyway, I told myself: Jin Yeong's piles of romance books.

Goodness knew why he was reading what he was reading, but I refused to deal with a romantically confused JinYeong when he was already more monster than human. It didn't seem safe. So I went through those piles of books, stashing away the seedier options and keeping the more healthy ones for him to look over once he'd finished with the one he was reading. He watched me with a jealous eye from behind the book he was pretending to read, then eventually gave up the pretence and hung over the edge of the couch to make sure he knew which books I was taking away from him.

Athelas came back while I was still going through the piles. He picked up his teacup and the file he had been looking at when I first came down from my room—a familiar file that I remembered from a few weeks ago.

I leaned my arms on the nearest pile of books to gaze up at him, and asked, "Still looking in odd corners for our murderer?"

"Always," murmured Athelas, crossing one leg over the other and opening the file to sort through its contents. Whatever he'd been doing upstairs, it had put him in what was his version of a mischievous mood: he sipped his tea and asked JinYeong gently, "And what has your reading hitherto taught you of the effects of biting stray women—or perhaps pets?"

That made me chuckle, a small, deep sound that drew JinYeong's immediate attention. I said, partly to him and partly to Athelas, "That's just business, though, isn't it? You need blood and you have to bite to take it. There shouldn't be any effects that aren't covered under *side effects of vampire spit.*"

JinYeong stared at me. "My bites," he said frostily, "are *soft* and *warm* and—"

"If you start talking about how warm you are again, I'm gunna—"

"Athelas," said Zero from the hall, in a voice that rumbled and couldn't be ignored. "I'd appreciate it if you took a look at this."

Athelas closed his file and put it tidily beneath his teacup on the coffee table, which was an interesting thing to do. It made me think that, in the quietest and most natural way possible, he was trying to protect what he didn't want to be seen. What was the suspicious old tea-drinker up to *now*?

"A bite is not a transaction!" snarled Jin Yeong, shuffling himself and his book until they were directly in front of me and unignorable. "Would you say a kiss is a transaction?"

"With you, it is," I said, distracted from Athelas. "Sometimes I need extra speed and strength, and you need to not feel like I'm gunna die every five minutes. Of course it's a transaction! What else would it be?"

Jin Yeong's eyes widened in outrage as Athelas padded softly down the hallway. "With me? With *me*? *Yah! Noh!* Who else are you kissing, then?"

"There's something wrong with you," I told him. I plucked the book from his hands and made a bit of a grimace at the front cover. Trust Jin Yeong to go for one of the most lurid covers to start with. "What the heck is this?"

"That woman," he said, pointing at the vaguely regency-esque woman and then the shirtless man who had his arms around her, "does not trust this man. There is a misunderstanding. So now he is kissing her."

Some people might have said that the way I laughed was rude. I didn't mean it like that, exactly, but the snort that came out didn't seem uncalled for, either. "Well, what's the use of that?" I demanded. "If she doesn't trust him, how is kissing her going to change anything?"

Jin Yeong narrowed his eyes at me. "The book says she falls in love with him. He kisses her; she falls in love."

"Then it's a stupid book."

"Kissing is stupid?" He looked personally affronted, which was probably more because he was the one I usually kissed than because he disagreed.

That needs some explanation. When I say that he's the one I

usually kiss, I mean he's pretty much the only one I kiss—and the only reason I do kiss him is because vampire spit makes me somehow faster and stronger and much harder to kill, without giving me much of a desire to bite anyone else. Temporarily, at least. It's either a kiss or a bite, and sometimes a kiss is the quicker option. It's also a lot less painful.

"Heck," I said, worried by a sudden thought. Was Jin Yeong doing research because he was keen on a human woman? That would be...weird. What was she going to think about me kissing him every so often for vampire spit, if so? Or him biting me for the same effect, if it came to that? I was pretty sure I wouldn't be happy if I was the one dating him and some other woman was kissing him.

What a pain in the neck.

"*Mwoh?*" demanded Jin Yeong. "What now?"

"Nothing," I said. "Just thinking about how weird it would be to date you."

If I'd thought about it before I said it, I would have expected him to be even more offended than he had been by having his kisses described as transactional. Instead, he sat very still, as though he was trying to figure out exactly what I had said, and why; or maybe just how to respond to it.

Before he could, I said, "Anyway, if you're thinking about dating, you better think really good. Zero won't like it, and you know how icy he goes when you do stuff he doesn't like."

"You can't tell me not to date," said Jin Yeong, putting up his nose.

"I'm not telling you that you *can't*," I argued. "I'm just saying that—heck. What's that?"

Something stirred at the back of the house, toward the bathroom. Something prodding at the house, or picking at it; and that made the second or third time this morning. What was going on?

I ignored Jin Yeong, who had leaned forward and was saying

something about Zero and dating and *teeth*, and tried to let myself feel what was going on in the house. Almost immediately, I sensed something like a twinge from the toilet room.

"Oi!" I said. "There's something fishy going on in the toilet!"

"It is a toilet, not a fish-bowl," muttered Jin Yeong in exasperation. I've already mentioned that he doesn't like being ignored, haven't I?

I jumped up, heading for the bathroom and toilet, following that odd little pull and aware of a flurry of movement in the hall from Athelas, who came along behind me. I pushed through the door and tipped up the edge of the toilet seat with the tip of my forefinger, slightly worried about a banshee sortie from the depths. Instead, I saw a tie—no, a frog that had once been a tie and now wasn't quite one or the other—hunched up and clinging to the bowl below the rim of the toilet.

"There you are!" I said to it, spluttering a laugh as Athelas caught up with me. "I've been looking for you!"

Last I had seen it, it had been hopping around in the security room of Blackpoint's house. I couldn't help the grin that spread across my face. So that's what had been wrong about the house this morning! Zero and Athelas had some pretty good spells up around the house, and the tie frog must have been trying to get past them to come home. The question was, was it looking for me, or Jin Yeong? If you went by the fact that the tie had once been Jin Yeong's, it made sense that it was looking for him; if you went by the fact that I was the one who had turned it into a strange mix of frog and tie, it was just as likely that it had come looking for me.

"Really, Pet!" expostulated Athelas.

"Don't worry," I told him, removing the tie from the toilet bowl. "I'll wash my hands—and the frog, too. Can't let it go hopping around in the outside world for people to see, can we?"

"I fail to see why it should hop around the inside of the house, either," Athelas said. His voice sounded vaguely pleading, which gave me an odd little tickle of fun deep in my throat. "It would be far better off outside and more frog than tie, or turned back into a tie."

The tie frog must have been able to understand what he said, because it made a hasty leap away from me and for the doorway.

"Heck!" I said, grabbing wildly for it and catching it by the pointy tail. I curled my fingers around it and murmured soothingly, "No, don't worry, I won't let them turn you back into a tie!"

Athelas sighed faintly. "Very well, Pet," he said, his voice pained. "But if you must keep it in the house, you'll need to take care of it."

"What, you mean you're not gunna feed it and take it for walks?" I said. That was the fault of that little tickle of fun: I couldn't help it.

Coldly, Athelas said, "I shall certainly not bother myself to take care of it."

"Yes, dad," I said, grinning up at him.

"Becoming attached is a very bad habit of yours," he said, and I heard approximately three layers of meaning. "You should fix that."

He meant that I was too attached to him—to Zero, even to Jin Yeong. That I got too attached in general. That being attached was dangerous because people took advantage and that even a tie frog could take advantage of such an attachment, in the most innocent of ways.

It wasn't that I thought of it as love, exactly. It was about as close as I thought Athelas could get to it, though, so I kept grinning unrepentantly at him and said again, "*Yes*, dad."

He looked away first, which was a delightful victory. He also left me there with the tie frog, so I took it with me into the kitchen to start on breakfast. It was a bit late to be doing anything fancy, so I just went with the toast and beans I'd planned on, but my psychos must have been pretty hungry because Athelas and Jin Yeong presented themselves at the dining table while I was still buttering toast despite the simplicity of the food.

I put the toast on the table along with some jams for Athelas, and as I went back for the beans, the tie frog sidled across my shoulder and down my arm a little. Maybe it was trying to get a look at its former owner, because I'd just walked behind Jin Yeong. For a moment, I was very tempted to slide it down the back of his collar, just to see how he would react. Maybe he felt my gaze on his bare neck, because he looked around suspiciously.

"*Hajima*," he said.

"I'm starting to think you know me too well," I told him, very slightly grumpy.

Jin Yeong grinned, sharp and fierce. "*Kurae.* I will not have beans down my neck, either."

"Suspicious little mosquito," I said. "Oi. How's the book going? How'd it go, him kissing her?"

"She ran away," said Jin Yeong, after a very slight pause. "But the book says she enjoyed it, so—"

"That's because she's in a paradigm where what the author wants, goes," I said, grabbing the electric frypan full of beans. "It's not like that in real life. In real life, women punch you in the face if you try to force kisses on them."

"They do not punch me in the face," Jin Yeong said, insufferably smug.

"Only because they're buzzed out of their minds on vampire fumes," I said. "You can't call that a real connection, can you? What's the use of kissing someone like that?"

Scowling at me, he said, "*I know that.* Who else would know it like I do?"

"Oh," I said, taken aback. "Sorry."

It hadn't occurred to me that he might feel lonely in his vampiric ability to make pretty much everyone fall in love with him on sight. I'd spoken thoughtlessly, but it was true that any connection he might have formed with a woman would be completely undermined by the fact that she was attracted to him in the same way that a moth was attracted to the light that could kill it.

No wonder JinYeong didn't understand how a relationship ought to work.

I wondered suddenly how long it had been since he had been a human, and if he'd been in love before that. I'd have to check the internet to see when the Korean war was, but I was pretty sure it was a while ago. He'd have had to have been a vampire at least sixty years by now. Heaven help any woman he was keen on in the future.

"Oi," I said. "Don't force kisses on women, either. It's wrong. It doesn't matter if they're doing it without a fuss because they're hopped up on vampire fumes; it's still wrong."

"I was speaking of *the book*," JinYeong said coldly. "I am only *curious*."

"'Course you were," I said, sitting down. "'*Course* you are. For your information, you can't build trust by kissing people, no matter what your book says."

"Then how can he make her trust him?" demanded JinYeong.

"Not *make* her trust him—*build* the trust. You can't force someone to trust you."

"Nonsense," said Athelas, cutting into his toast. "That's the basis for every cult and confidence trick in the worlds Behind and Human."

JinYeong, disregarding this interruption, said as if wronged, "That takes *longer*. Why should it take so long?"

"Longer books are better," I told him. "Anyway, what's time to a vampire? It's not like you haven't got lots of it."

JinYeong muttered something in Korean beneath his breath, evidently not for the understanding of anyone but himself, but that might have been because despite his bravado, he wasn't eager to talk about such things in front of Zero, who had at last entered the dining room again.

"Made you boston beans," I said to Zero, pointing with a knife that dripped sauce on the table. "What are you doing in the hall, anyway? The house is getting twisted around whatever it is."

"Checking on something," he said shortly, sitting down.

Oh. Well then. That made things much clearer.

"What's with the sword these days?" I asked him, instead. I was pretty sure that's what he was tinkering with.

His blue eyes pinioned me. "Did you take it out yesterday?" he asked.

Ah heck. I hadn't expected to be asked outright. Zero doesn't usually ask stuff outright: he usually tries to hide stuff from me as he tries to figure out what's happening. He must be really confused about the sword if he was prepared to ask outright.

"Not exactly," I said, reluctantly. "I just grabbed for the first thing I saw, and the Heirling Sword came out. Did it really disappear from here at the same time?"

"Yes," said Athelas, delicately ladling boston beans onto a new piece of toast. "And yet, it is impossible! It should not be able to come to anyone who is not an heirling, through any random object. So very interesting, isn't it, my lord?"

"I told you not to needle me," Zero told him, looking very icy about the eyes. "Didn't I?"

"I am merely suggesting that although we have hitherto decided that the pet wasn't likely to be an heirling on the strength of drawing the sword from its actual, physical position, it is much harder to argue against it when the sword is effectively coming to her."

There was a brief silence that it seemed Zero would have liked to have filled. At last, he said shortly, "I know it."

"I don't believe I've heard of the sword making itself available to anyone but an heirling, as a matter of fact," continued Athelas smoothly. "And if I might be so bold, my lord, it is, in fact, a part of the Heirling Trials."

I made a very small protest, but Zero, tiredly, only asked, "What do you want from me?"

"It seems abundantly clear that it would be wise to take the pet further into our confidence regarding what is now her obvious status as an heirling."

Zero briefly pressed his eyes shut and opened them again. "Give me reasons," he said.

I saw the look he shot at Athelas: it wasn't a look that said *give me reasons* but one that said *your reasons had better be good, or I will ignore them.*

"I very much fear, my lord, that should we not, the pet is very liable to die from an excess of ignorance," said Athelas gently. "And perhaps it would be good to ask if the golden g—good heavens!—our past liaison had occasion to see Pet with the Heirling Sword?"

"He saw," I said glumly. "Reckon that's why he was so excited to tell your dad. He said your dad would be sure to want to kill me, so he was gunna do it first and get the thanks later."

"You," Zero said, fixing his eyes on me in a way that felt as scorching as the summer Tasmanian sun, "did not tell me about this yesterday. Why?"

"I was pretty sure you'd say I had to be an heirling," I said, sighing. "And actually, I don't want to rule Behind, so—"

"There is very little chance you would ever rule Behind," Zero said, with crushing frankness. "If—*since* you're an heirling, you would be inducted into the trials, and then you would die."

"Thanks," I said. "Very cheerful."

Flamin' rude. It wasn't as though I wanted to be an heirling, either: there was no need for him to be so annoyed that he hadn't been able to stop it being true by the sheer force of his denial.

"I wish you would attempt to appreciate the difficulties of—"

"It's hard to appreciate the difficulties if you never *tell* me anything!" I retorted. "You've been trying so hard to convince yourselves *and* me that I'm not an heirling that you haven't spent any time teaching me what to do if I am one!"

"Very well!" snapped Zero. "If you're so intent on knowing every dribble of information about Between and Behind now that the sword has started to come to you, let's begin!"

I stared at him for several seconds, trying to figure out if I'd misheard, or if he'd actually said what I thought he said.

"Hang on," I said. "You're going to tell me stuff? Behind stuff? That actually worked?"

"Since it seems it's the only way to have you cooperate with us, yes," Zero said, in something that was very close to exasperation. "First, did you really pull the sword from Between as a matter of happenstance? You absolutely didn't take the umbrella with you?"

"Pure accident," I said caustically. Even when he answered some questions, he still couldn't help himself from side-stepping others. "I told you: I didn't take it out with me when I left, but when I went to grab something from Between, it came out as the Heirling Sword."

Suddenly frowning, he asked, "Is this what happened while you were with the leprechaun the first time, too?"

"Yeah. Same feeling. Why? What's it mean?"

"It means," said Athelas, "that the King Behind is reaching the end of his reign and the cycle has begun again."

"I'm pretty flamin' sure I'm not that important," I told him. "So you're gunna have to explain a bit more than that."

"She does not have to compete if she does not wish to do so," Jin Yeong said abruptly. "Put the sword away again."

"It's no use trying to hide the sword again," Zero said wearily. Heck, he really had given up. He had finally admitted something he'd been fighting for probably longer than I realised, and now the flood-gates—such as they were, with him—had opened. I would have felt guilty if it wasn't for the fact that this was stuff that he should have told me about two or three months ago, no matter how unwilling he was to believe it could be true. Maybe I would have been able to be more careful, and yesterday's fight need not have happened. "It will simply come back out again when she needs it, as it once did for me."

It was my turn to stare at him. "Wait, the sword popped up suddenly for you one day, too? Why? And where was it before that?"

"Those are all questions to which we would very much like to know the answers," Zero said.

"Yeah?" I stared at him for a bit and then added accusingly, "Pretty sure you do know the answers. You just don't like 'em much, do you?"

Zero, his eyes suddenly very blue with rueful amusement despite the weariness, said, "Bad pet."

"We have surmises," Athelas told me. "But from my lord's perspective none of them seem particularly felicitous. Why? Do you wish to be a contender to the Throne Behind?"

"Heck, no!" I said, in horror. "Is that really what the sword means when it comes to someone who needs it?"

"It means that there are enough heirlings around for the sword to be more active than usual, and that it has, for whatever reason, picked you to wield it should you choose," said Zero.

"You should pick up two blades," Jin Yeong dictated. "Do not pick up the sword when it wants to be picked up."

"Yeah, I'll be sure to take the time to think about that next time a bridge troll's about to knock my head off my shoulders and play cricket with it. Are you saying I'm *encouraging* the sword?"

"The sword," said Athelas, very gently, "is inclined to make itself available to heirlings."

"I told you I don't want to be an heirling."

"I've yet to find that the Heirling Sword cares very much

about what people do and don't want," Athelas murmured, his eyes meeting Zero's with a faint touch of amusement.

"He's talking about you, isn't he?" I said to Zero at once. No use backing down when they were actually talking about stuff at last.

JinYeong muttered, "If you *talk* about it, it will *happen*," in an impatient sort of way, but I didn't think I could stop now. I just sent a friendly sort of kick his way beneath the table and shrugged at him when he looked at me.

To Zero, I said again, "He's talking about you, right? You said the sword kept coming to you once, too."

He nodded. "Just like it does to you now."

"Reckon that would have annoyed the king a bit."

"The king," said Athelas, "was not informed. My lord's father took very swift steps to hide the sword once he realised what was going on. No doubt other steps were taken as well, since the cycle did not start anew and the king remains on the throne to this day."

"Once he realised what I was using it for, he took *very* swift steps," said Zero, and the smile on his face was cold and worrying. "If I had been trying to make a play for the throne, no doubt he would have approved."

"Is that when you were trying to help humans last time? Hang on, is that why you were so surprised when I brought out the sword the first time?"

"Yes," Zero said baldly. "But this is worse: you brought out the sword from something that isn't its own human world form. You twice picked up a random item that had no connection to the sword, and brought it to yourself through Between, anyway. The first time, you only brought the sword out of its other physical form, but a human shouldn't be able to do even that."

"Not a full human, at the very least," added Athelas. "And it is certain that only an heirling can bring the sword out through an unrelated item—someone with a touch of Behindkind to them as well as human."

"You said that the cycle is starting again." Daniel had said something about that once. I could give him a call—ask him how Morgana was going, casually slip in a few questions about the Behind version of Ragnarök—and see what he had to say about it, too.

"We can only suppose so, with the way the sword has been reacting. It's possible that other heirlings are stirring, too."

I frowned. "That mean someone's gunna start coming after Zero?"

"I shouldn't think so!" Athelas said, rather startled. "I imagine we're among the first to realise that the cycle's started again, and even when word does get out, the other heirlings will go for outliers first. My lord is far too strong to take down without quite some thought. The other heirlings might try to form alliances first, but only if there are enough of them and they know who they each are."

"Yeah, but what about the king?"

"The king has reached the end of his cycle," said Zero shortly. "He'll soon die."

"Like he did last time?" I saw the look they exchanged, and said accusingly, "You already told me that he killed all the heirlings last time and stopped the cycle. What's to stop him doing it this time?"

"It's too late to do what he did last time," Athelas said. His eyes rested on me meditatively for a moment before he added, "Rather fortunately for you. He killed every heirling before most of the world Behind was aware that the cycle had started, even perhaps before it did begin. Barring my lord, he killed every child Behind that had a drop of human blood to them, too."

"Well, my parents are dead and I nearly was, too, so I don't think I was that fortunate." So the killing itself had been enough to stop the cycle? What was stopping him from doing it again, then? What made it too late now?

Beggar all, probably.

"How come it's too late?" I pressed. "Why can't he do the same thing again?"

"Because my lord is grown and can also use the sword," Athelas said.

"Even if he forces the issue and starts killing other heirlings, it won't matter," Zero explained. "My father will call for the heirling trials to begin, with the evidence that the Heirling Sword is now active to prove that the cycle has started again."

Great. I mean, at least if the king had me killed, it wouldn't be any use to him, but I still didn't particularly want to be killed. As an heirling, I was much more likely to die horribly in any number of ways and at the hands of any number of people. "Fine, so we're not worried that the king will try to kill us, just yet, but we're worried your dad will start making announcements on your behalf and also kill me if he finds out I'm an heirling, too."

"Exactly," Zero said coldly. "So perhaps you could try to be a little less obvious if you must fight bridge trolls."

"Got it," I said. "But that still leaves me wondering about something."

"What would that be?" he asked. He was still annoyed with me, but he wasn't willing to leave me alone with thoughts he didn't know about, where they might do damage one day. I could sympathise, but at the same time, he'd had long enough with his secrets and they hadn't helped anyone by the keeping.

"Well," I said, "the king has to be behind the killings, doesn't he? If I'm an heirling and someone tried to kill me ages ago, the murderer you're after is probably one of the king's men. He was probably trying to get the jump on this years ago. Do it before it got to this point."

"We suspected at one time that the killings were related to the succession, but never proved it," Zero said. "Now that we're sure you're an heirling, we'll adjust our investigations accordingly."

"Which is why you're getting Athelas to show you the file he has about that boy, yeah? The one whose parents died like mine?"

"Since my lord was doing nothing of the kind, may we assume that you wish me to do so, Pet?" enquired Athelas dryly. "I have the file in the other room."

Zero, a bit on his dignity, said, "There are enough links to make it worthwhile. We'll concentrate on that one for now: at this point, peripheral cases like yours may provide more information than the main cases."

"That is not the important thing," Jin Yeong said impatiently. "The important thing is that she is an heirling."

I shifted uncomfortably, but it wasn't like I could really do anything about it. I asked, "What are we gunna do about it, anyway?"

They all spoke at once.

"*Kyesok ssaum baewoyahae.*"

"Discover how widely it's known."

"Send in notice of your cession."

"'Course I'm gunna keep learning to fight," I said to Jin Yeong. "Even if this specifically doesn't kill me, I don't see Behindkind stopping trying to kill me."

"Your position in the worlds will open you to more of that sort of thing, Pet," Athelas reminded me. "My lord is not incorrect about the dangers of your situation. If it were not an inescapable conclusion at this point, I would not have advocated for telling you anything further."

"Thanks," I said, a bit sarcastically. Of Zero, who had advocated cession, I asked, "What about you? You gunna send in your notice of *No thanks I don't wanna be king?*"

"I already have," he said briefly.

"Oh, is that what you were doing while you were helping humans? Teenage rebellion?"

Athelas' lips twitched. "You have a wonderful way with words, Pet," he said.

"That was a message for my father, not the king," Zero said shortly. "We'll send in notice of your cession once we're sure how widely this is known. Athelas is correct: we need to know how many people could be aware of the cycle. If my father doesn't know it's doubtful that anyone else knows, but we can make careful enquiries."

"If your father knew of it, I rather fancy we would have received a visit from him, my lord."

"Yeah, and I'd probably be dead," I said, more quietly.

I found that Zero was watching me, but all he said was, "I'm glad to see that you finally understand the ramifications of your situation, Pet."

"Ramifications, heck!" I said indignantly. "You're the one who wouldn't tell me anything about anything—if you'd been more honest about everything from the start, maybe I would have tried to be a bit more careful!"

"If you'd just obeyed instead of questioning everything—"

"—I'd be a lot deader," I interrupted. Heck if I was going to take the blame for not obeying him when he'd never tried to explain why he wanted me to do stuff. "I know now that I can trust you, but I didn't know that for sure until pretty recently, so you'll have to excuse me for not obeying every word that drops from your lips. You threatened to *kill* me to get a USB."

"That was you," Jin Yeong said, pointing at Zero. "I was helpful. I am trusted."

"The heck are you talking—"

"I'd love to think that this means you intend to obey me without question from now on," said Zero dryly, interrupting, "but I can't afford to trust as much."

"Of course I'm not going to obey you without question," I said. "Even if I do trust you. I'm still not sure your conscience is fully functioning and even if it *is*, I've got my own I need to worry about. Maybe we can work out a deal where I obey you like sixty percent of—"

Zero sighed and Jin Yeong grinned, his eyes dark with malicious laughter.

"All right, all right, no need to snigger," I said resignedly. "I obey you most of the time, anyway. You're really hard to please, you know?"

"I have been *trying* to keep you alive," said Zero, and there was a note of exasperation in his voice that was also very slightly hurt.

"I know," I told him. I'd been telling him for ages that he needed to be more demonstrative, but the emotions that were currently making their way out of his cold shell were uncomfortable. It was easier to deal with him when I didn't have to worry about hurting his feelings. It wasn't fair of me to think that, so I said, "I'm thankful for that. Really. But it's part of the problem—I still want to have a say in how I get protected. I want to know what I'm going into, and what the possible outcome is. It's easier for me to do what you want me to do when I know it's the right decision."

"Someday," Zero said, his blue eyes dwelling on me with that same expression of mingled frustration and hurt, "there is going to be an occasion where there isn't time for me to tell you everything. I'll tell you to do something and you'll either do it or be dead."

"Makes it easier if I already trust you because I have past experience," I said. I wasn't going to let him get away with that. "And if we're talking about Jin Yeong's sister now, you're going to have to remember that I'm not her."

"Of course it's nothing to do with Jin Yeong's sister!" snapped Zero. "You're nothing like her!"

"All right," I said politely. "Never said it was. I was just pointing out that no matter what's happened with you and humans in the past, it isn't necessarily going to happen again."

"You can't promise that," Zero said. "You can't promise that I won't have to kill you because you've turned into a monster. You can't promise that you won't be torn to pieces by Behindkind while I'm out of reach and unable to protect you, and you can't—"

"Perhaps we should return to this conversation later?" suggested Athelas as Zero stopped and caught his breath, looking away.

"*Hyeong*!" said Jin Yeong, appalled. Then at me, he said, "*Ya, noh! Mwoh hanun kkoya?*"

"Pet," Zero said, through his teeth, without looking at any of us. "Stop pushing buttons."

"I'm not pushing buttons," I said quietly. "I'm just saying that it's never been your choice to decide who lives and dies, and you can't choose for me, either. But if you can remember to keep talking to me and letting me know what's going on, I can promise I'll do my best to obey you when I should."

"How will you know when—" Zero stopped, and said in exasperation, "I'm not sure why I bother."

"Me either," I said, shooting an apologetic sort of grin in his direction. "But thanks for saving my life all the time, anyway."

He actually laughed then, at first just a spurt of laughter and then a full head-in-hands laugh that shook the table while Athelas looked on in what seemed to be fond amusement and Jin Yeong stared with his mouth open.

I shrugged when Jin Yeong turned his open-mouthed look on me, and waited for Zero to gather himself again before I asked him, "What now, then?"

"First," said Zero, sobering, "sword practise. Secondly, if your human friends answer you, try to find out if they have any idea about other similar cases to yours—ones that may not have made it to the police station or my notice."

I sent a sharp look in his direction, but before I could open my mouth, he bent a very clear, cold look on me. I grinned.

"All right," I said, instead of the cheeky *oh, so you think we need help from the humans!* that had nearly come out. He'd already laughed today: I didn't want to break him. "I'll tell 'em about the bridge troll at the same time. *If* they talk to me."

"And Pet?" The slightly-damaged Zero was gone again, but there was still a touch of softness to him when he said, "For now, try to pull anything from Between *but* the sword. No need to spread word before we need to."

"Okay, boss," I said. I would have said more, but Jin Yeong was already behind me with a finger hooked into the back of my t-shirt collar. He pulled me up and across the room, ignoring the table that needed clearing and the dishes that needed doing.

"Oi!" I protested.

"Practise!" he said, and dragged me out with him to the back yard.

He didn't let me go until we were fairly outside, either, which prompted me to remind him, "There's a tie frog upstairs that could do with a little friend, you know."

He stripped his tie from around his neck and rolled it up to shove in his pocket. "Do not turn my clothes into other things!"

"You're no fun."

"Clothes," he said firmly as I looked around for anything to use as a weapon, "are to be respected. My tie—"

"I'll call it sir when I give it dinner."

He glared at me. "We will begin."

"No. Fun," I said pointedly, slipping between the fence and a clump of hydrangeas.

Jin Yeong, circling sideways with all the grace and silence of a panther and something of the eyes, asked suddenly, "You. Why did you mention my sister?"

"Athelas told me about her," I said.

"That old man!"

"He didn't say anything nasty about her," I protested, keeping a wary eye on his hands. He hadn't reached for anything, but it wouldn't be long before he did. I knew better than to try and face him when he was weaponless, these days: Jin Yeong without weapons was a Jin Yeong who would leap for the throat without caring what weapons his opponent had, because he was quicker than it was possible to attack or defend. And because apparently he would allow himself to be stabbed for a chance to tear out his opponent's throat.

"I will remind him not to discuss JiAh with people," he muttered, but he seemed slightly less annoyed than he had earlier.

"He didn't really discuss her with me," I said, reaching into the hydrangea bushes and feeling the brief roughness of a growing stake beneath my fingers before it smoothed out into a grippy leather handle. "We were talking about something else and she just sorta came up."

His head turned slightly to the side, eyebrows winging up. "You were talking about me?"

"Good grief, no!" I said hastily, drawing out the slender sword that had been a stake and passing it to my left hand to reach again with my right for the second. If he was annoyed at having his sister discussed, Jin Yeong was sure to be annoyed at the thought of me asking questions about him. "We were talking about Zero."

He scowled. "Why do you want to know about *hyeong*? I am more interesting."

"I was gathering intel," I said, and that seemed to placate him, because he drew two swords from goodness knows where and began a quick, precise attack that didn't push too hard but left me scrambling to keep up with the pace.

The lack of heat gave me space to think while my body countered the attacks in a series of almost instinctive block-and-attacks. Could Zero be conflating me with Jin Yeong's sister? Morgana had really seemed to think that he was falling in love with me, and certainly he had been more approachable, more touchable recently—as if he was making an effort to connect. But was it possible that rather than being in love with me, he was simply remembering things he didn't particularly want to remember?

"No thinking," said Jin Yeong chidingly, tapping me sharply on the side of the wrist with the flat of one blade. "Only fighting."

"Thought I was supposed to think when I fight," I panted, retreating to reset my guard. "Thought that was the problem."

"No purposeful misunderstandings," he said. "Only fighting."

And so we fought.

CHAPTER FOUR

I texted Abigail after training but left my phone on the coffee table when I went to shower. I still had the number she'd given me, but I had no real expectation of her answering my text. The last time I'd seen her, she was snarling at me for giving her up to the fae—Zero and Athelas, to be precise—and suggesting that I couldn't be trusted.

Not the best result for a relationship that had looked promising at the start. My psychos might be anti-human, but Abigail and her humans were also very much anti-fae. I mean, I couldn't really blame them: I was pretty much anti-fae for any fae who weren't Zero and Athelas, and though I'd never met another vampire, I was pretty sure I'd like 'em even less than I liked Jin Yeong. Not that I hated him, exactly. Could you call a vampire a frenemy? Probably. I didn't think I'd want to put up with that from anyone but Jin Yeong.

But to my surprise, there was a text waiting for me when I got out of the shower, and with Zero's permission I was very soon walking down the street to follow the terse meeting instructions I'd been sent, Jin Yeong almost prancing alongside me.

"What are you so happy about?" I demanded, staring for the

tenth time at the text that had popped up during my shower. There had been a *discussion* in the living room while I was in the shower—one that had had me banging on the wall and yelling *knock it off!* and made a new hole in the wall between living room and kitchen, just where the front hall began.

By the time I got out of the shower, Jin Yeong was on our couch with his clothes torn and bloody, sucking on a blood bag, and the gaping hole in the kitchen wall was fermenting away with bubbling Between trying to fix it. Zero had already left and Athelas, sitting in his chair, seemed more urbane than usual.

If I'd expected anything from a beginning like that, it would have been for Jin Yeong, who had obviously gotten the worst of the fight, to be sulking like a child.

He was not sulking. In fact, as we walked down the street, he was prancing.

I looked up from my phone again and glared at him. "Stop frolicking. People are staring."

"People are staring because I am beautiful. Where are we going?"

"Elizabeth Mall," I said. I put out my arm to signal to the bus just trundling up, and shoved Jin Yeong toward it when it pulled up and opened doors with a startlingly loud hiss. "Reckon Abigail doesn't want to meet us at home base, which means she's trying to make a point."

"What point?"

"Well, we already know where they hide out. They're just being petty and letting us know they don't trust us to come there anymore."

Jin Yeong shrugged and sat down in the back seat. "Let them play their little games. I shall meet them at their headquarters if I wish to."

"That's exactly what we *don't* want to do," I reminded him. "We're supposed to be getting them to trust us again. We're lucky they're agreeing to meet with us at all: it's pretty flamin' hard to work with people who don't trust you. Well—just look at me."

"What are you talking about?" Jin Yeong asked.

"It's not like you lot trust me—not really. Zero's always got at least one plan on the backburner, and I wouldn't be surprised if he's still got a tracking spell on me, too."

"Pft," said Jin Yeong, lifting his nose and looking away out the window. "I did not bite that golden idiot when I might have. What else is that but trust?"

"If you're saying that you trust the golden git, that's even more insul—hang on. You said that before, but I still don't understand it. You didn't have a go at him because you trusted *me?* How does that work?"

"I was very emotional at that time," he said matter-of-factly. "I trusted you to know the right thing to do. *Mulleon*, for some time now I have trusted you—but not with my ties."

"Maybe if you'd spent less time glaring at me and complaining about me spending time with Zero I would have *realised* that," I said coldly, ignoring the bit about his ties. That was just good sense. "It's not like you don't have a go at him whenever you feel annoyed at life in general, so it's a bit dog-in-the-manger of you to object to me spending time with him, but whatever."

"Yes," he said stubbornly, "but that is my *right*."

"You thought I was pinching your big brother," I said. I'd wondered that before, but now I was sure. "You want to be able to fight with him whenever you choose without someone else distracting him."

Jin Yeong's eyes flicked across to me with a hint of storm to them. "He is not my brother. That is not what it is."

"Good grief," I said. "Sorry I asked. Let me know whatever it is when you find out, okay?"

He grinned at me so suddenly that it startled me, and then he was back to being ridiculously prancy, just in time to saunter down the aisle and alight in a way that might have been described as sprightly.

"Heck," I said, jumping down from the bus to catch up with him. "Oi! Come back here! They still think you're my boyfriend, don't they?"

"I will have bubble tea," JinYeong said, gazing up Elizabeth Mall. "We will have bubble tea. *Everyone* will have bubble tea."

He was definitely high and happy about something. I only wished I knew what.

"We can have bubble tea afterward," I told him.

"If I am your boyfriend, we will have bubble tea."

"You're really weird today, you know that?" I said, dragging him away by the sleeve from the two bubble tea shops on opposite sides of the mall. He allowed himself to be pulled up the mall, but made sure I *had* to pull to move him. We were supposed to meet Abigail at the further end of the mall, nearby the spot where buskers always set up, and although I was happy for them to have time to scope out the place and feel comfortable, I didn't exactly want to be late.

We stopped before we got there, ourselves. Maybe JinYeong resisted just a little bit more, or maybe it was just that I was growing in caution; whatever the reason, we sort of dwindled to a halt just before the flower cart, between the sushi joint and the shoe shop. No sign of Abigail or any of the kids I knew by face, and it didn't look like anyone else was behaving particularly suspiciously, either, but there was something not quite right about the mall this morning.

Everything was exactly where it usually was, but was there something a bit extra? Or was it just that the space felt stretched out, somehow: a lot more distance between us and the flower cart than there should be?

Or was it, perhaps, the way the open doorway installation to our right was rippling with something that definitely wasn't the alley and the sushi shop that should be visible through it?

"Ah heck," I said quietly, twitching his sleeve gently. "Jin Yeong."

He had already stiffened, his eyes liquid with danger and fixed on the flutter of movement in the rectangular space. Flowers sprouted first, all up the sides of the rectangle and then outward along the installation and the paved floor of the mall as well. Grass leaped up between bricks and thicketed around fixed seats and the poles that held up the waving decorative rain cover above us, and as it formed a path directly from the doorway to us, an advanced guard of armoured fae stepped through the installation.

Their master stepped through behind them, towering over them head and shoulders, his skin as pale and glowing as the moon, and I knew at once who it was. Zero's dad had come to check up on us again at last. Oh heck. What did he know?

"Is he allowed to do that in public?" I mumbled, throwing a look around the mall. People were staring, too; I don't know if they saw what we saw, but they were definitely looking at the installation that blossomed with flowers.

"It's Shakespeare in the Mall!" said someone. "I didn't know that was on today! How are they doing the flowers, do you reckon?"

I supposed that was something. Zero's dad *did* look distinctly Shakespearean if you were talking about Oberon: white hair flowed behind and around him on some scented breeze that almost overpowered even Jin Yeong's cologne. Cobwebby trousers clung to leonine waist and legs, and the blue of his eyes was almost blinding.

Don't look in those eyes, I reminded myself.

I mean, at least if there was going to be violence in the mall, the actual people around would think it was all part of the act. It wouldn't stop us from dying, though—and it wouldn't stop bystanders from dying, either—so the best we could hope for was concealment.

"*Ah, jjajeungna!*" said Jin Yeong in annoyance. If I'd been with Athelas, it would have been a sighed, "How very irritating!"

"If you're gunna tell me to get behind you, I've got some bad news for you," I told him. I could feel the coldness of the fae's eyes on me from across the pavement and had to fight hard to keep my own eyes from his. The first step he took that brought him fully out into the mall made me cold to the very bones.

"*Kuroliga obseo,*" Jin Yeong muttered. "He would just plant an idea in your mind to stab me in the back. I am wearing my *best suit*."

"You really need to stop wearing your best suits when you come out with me," I said, but there was a trembling deep inside me because I already knew how well Zero's dad could get into my head, and even if he couldn't make me do things, he could definitely roam around and pick answers out of my mind. He could also start to wonder why he couldn't control me, and that was probably about as dangerous as being able to make me do other things.

"It is true. Why do I do that? You don't appreciate it. *Son*."

"What?" I said blankly, even though he was holding out his hand and I knew with absolute certainty that he had just said *hand*. There was no reason for him to be asking to hold my hand except—

"I can't protect you like *hyeong* would," he said, eyes never wavering from the disturbance of Between that continued ruffling up through the mall around us. "So I will do it my way. *Son*."

"Pretty sure Zero wouldn't approve," I grumbled, but I gave him my hand and he slid his fingers through mine, holding tighter than his casual stance would have indicated. "He's been trying to make it look like you lot *don't* care about me. If you're gunna make his dad think I'm your little blood toy, what's to stop him having a go at you?"

Jin Yeong made the smallest *click* of teeth together, a small, savagely joyful noise. "Vampire spit is *verrrrry* good for you," he said. "For the fae, it is *verrrrry* bad. They will not like me to bite them, and they cannot make me do what I do not wish to do."

"Flamin' heck," I said, in the deepest respect. I already knew how dangerous vampire blood was to the fae, but it was still a risky play. "What about if he calls some goons who don't have fae blood, though?"

"Then we will both have to fight," said Jin Yeong. "*Noh*. You will have to fight very hard."

"Never known a bloke who can make the word *you* seem like an insult," I muttered to myself, but there was no time to argue with him.

Zero's dad was only twenty feet away and he had started walking toward us, his fore-guard splitting and moving around to flank him instead. You know about that song that talks about cool gales fanning the glade wherever some sheila walks? Well, when Zero's dad walks into a place, this is what happens: everything sprouts grass and flowers and stuff—his own personal carpet to show how flamin' important he is. Kinda makes me wonder what happens when the King Behind walks around the place. Who knows, maybe the King is too important to do the walking himself. Maybe he floats on a cloud of his own importance.

I swallowed, and forced myself to lift my phone and tap out a very short text. *Abort. Big bad nearby. Don't approach.* I had to press send on it twice because my fingers were cold and the touch didn't register the first time, but I put my phone in my back pocket as casually as I could. Hopefully, Zero's dad was about as ignorant as most Behindkind when it came to human inventions; I didn't want to field any questions about who I'd been texting.

Why was he here? Why? The golden fae was dead: he didn't know about me being an heirling, right? But if not, why the heck was he here?

"I find it strange," said Zero's father, stopping a couple of metres away, "that a pet is allowed to roam so freely."

He might have stopped, but the carpet of flowers and grass

didn't, bubbling up underneath our feet and sweeping up and over the nearby red wombat statue that kids loved to climb on. It velveted its way up the white posts that supported the wavy plexi-glass above, too, turning them flower-spotted green. A few people gasped and applauded, and a few more gathered around.

"What I do and where I go with the *petteu* is my business," said Jin Yeong purringly.

The fae's eyes met mine in a shock of ice-blue, holding them. "What does your master think of this, human?" he asked, and I could already feel the little questioning worm that he had set wriggling into my mind.

Only this time, instead of burrowing for stray truth, it talked to me.

Little Pet, it said. *Why are you so important? There is so little in your mind, but I have been keeping an eye on you and that has been...fascinating.*

The memory of the golden fae's torn out throat nearly popped back into my head before I could stop it, so I hastily let out the next thought that would have followed it: *So you were the one who set up the café with Marazul!*

I already knew it, but it was truth he would acknowledge. The derisive laugh I heard was too full-bodied for a worm. It took me a while to realise that it was the fae's laughter out loud in the real world, and that realisation gave me the sense that maybe I could break free if I really tried, because for a while I'd forgotten about the real world.

So little in here, the worm said again, as if it knew what I had just realised. It probably did, and that meant trouble. *Just dead parents and a vampire. Shall I bring you in and see what use I can make of you?*

Not much use, me, I thought. *Just a human, doing human stuff.*

Are you refusing me?

I couldn't help the indignant, first thought that came out. *Heck, I don't know what you're asking!*

If that wasn't just like someone related to Zero! Tell you nothing, then get snippy because you don't know stuff. The little worm started to chew away at the idea of parents, terrifying a fluttering, unfamiliar memory into dreadfully new life, but something warm gripped my chin and turned my whole face away, breaking the eye contact.

I shuddered in the relief of that release from visions of glittering blood, and looked into narrow, liquid eyes instead as JinYeong's voice said caressingly, "Do not listen to his wriggly little voice, my *Petteu*. Only listen to me."

"Only you," I said, holding his eyes. The worm was gone as if it never had been, and I wondered if its momentary hold had left me more susceptible than usual, because it didn't seem possible to look away from JinYeong. I didn't want to, because right then I felt safe and I was still cold from the fear of that little worm that talked and ate. From fear of the dark, unfamiliar memory that had fluttered into view for a sick moment. What was that memory? How was it in my head? Why couldn't I remember exactly what it had been now that my mind was free?

JinYeong looked away first, his hand dropping from my chin, but his other still had a good grip on mine, and I was thankful for that. I might usually be proof against JinYeong's wiles, but it was obvious that he was proof against those of the fae, and that also made me feel oddly safe.

Maybe there was some justice in this world, after all.

"What," demanded JinYeong silkily, "do you want?"

"I have something I wish to say."

JinYeong stared at him. "Lord Sero is not here."

"Then it is fortunate," said Zero's father, "that I have not come to speak with him."

Flaming heck. That was all we needed. Maybe I was just feeling particularly sensitive today, but any reason Zero's father wanted to speak with us was a Bad Thing, and it was hard to believe that it was a complete coincidence, him turning up right after we killed one of his henchmen and then had a big discussion about who was definitely an Heirling and needed to be Far More Careful about everything.

"Stop growing flowers on me," said JinYeong in cold dislike, scraping a few, trailing flowers from the inside of his pants leg with the side of his shoe. "This is *my best suit*."

"The world moulds itself around me," the fae said, with an insolence far more annoying than JinYeong's. "You are barely of this world or that; why should it concern itself with you?"

"Thought you said you've got something to say," I reminded him, avoiding his eyes. "Or did you just mean you've got insults to throw?"

I definitely shouldn't have said it, and the fact that JinYeong's lips curved very slightly when I said it was absolute proof of that. That brief smile made me feel less cold, though, even though it wasn't wise to be cheeky. This is what happens when pets go out without their owners: they get cheeky and start running wild with no one to stop them with a forbidding, icy-cold "*Pet!*"

"I have heard," said the fae, with a cold look that didn't lose any of its potency for the fact that I wasn't looking right into the eyes of it, "that my son is again working with the Enforcers. Is it so?"

"That's a question," I pointed out. It was a question, more-over, to which he definitely knew the answer—which meant it wasn't the question he'd really come to ask. I would have liked to have looked properly at him to see his reaction when I added, "He's working for them, not with them."

"Is there a difference?" he asked, but there was a distinct grit to his voice that suggested Yes there was, and that the difference very greatly irritated him.

Maybe because the idea of his son working *for* anyone else stuck in his elegant gullet, which was a nice thought. I could understand it if Zero had chosen to defy his father only to make him choke a bit, because if I'd been able to do it safely, I would have taken the opportunity with alacrity.

What had he really come to ask? It couldn't have been just to put a little worm in my brain—he couldn't know what had happened yesterday, could he? We had killed the golden fae, and there hadn't been anyone else to see.

Worried and wondering about that, I looked up at Jin Yeong and found his eyes on me. They were slightly questioning, and I shrugged fatalistically. Might as well ask, that shrug said.

His eyebrows quirked a bit, but he looked back at Zero's dad and said clearly, "You already knew this. Why ask us?"

"I would have thought that my son knew better, after what occurred last time."

"These days, *hyeong* has friends around him," Jin Yeong said lazily. "You know this too. Why ask about it?"

There came a low chuckle that almost had me looking straight at him. "Still friends? How very noble of you! I would have thought that after he took off your sister's head with his sword my son wouldn't have been much endeared to you."

"Think he's more annoyed at the people who were responsible for turning her into a vampire in the first place," I said, clear and angry, my hand tight around Jin Yeong's because his had just gripped mine convulsively.

Jin Yeong looked down at me again. I tried to make sure that my gaze was full of very obvious *Don't do it* warning, and it seemed to work. Either that, or Jin Yeong was just better equipped to deal with his rage this time. At any rate, he didn't leap for the throat of Zero's father, and he didn't even snarl, which was truly impressive.

"Don't get attached, little human," said the fae to me in amusement. "For his kind, you're a bite and a sip and then dust. Or if you're amusing, perhaps you'll be a fledgling. Would you like that, filth? Your own fledgling?"

Jin Yeong gave a small, bloody chuckle that sounded truly amused. "I will never have this one as my fledgling. *Hotsori.*"

"Rude," I mumbled, beneath my breath. "You're just saying that 'cos you don't want me around forever to mess with your ties."

A small *pft* was directed at me, and Jin Yeong said beneath his breath, "Am I *hyeong*? I will not have you as a fledgling."

"I am curious to know if the rumours I've heard about a certain sword reappearing are true," said Zero's father, quiet and sudden enough to give me a nasty startle that I hoped I hid well.

Flaming heck. He knew about the sword, but *what* did he know about the sword?

"You should talk to *hyeong* about this yourself," Jin Yeong said, but his fingers had gripped mine in return. "I do not care about the Throne Behind, or the succession."

The fae flicked a few fingers dismissively. "It would be too much to expect of filth like you to care about the purity of the Throne."

Jin Yeong surprised me considerably by laughing aloud, dark and dangerous. "Purity? Someone once told me you stole a human woman to bear your son. There is no purity in the Throne Behind; just human blood running through everything. *Everything.*"

There was a silence as deadly as anything I'd heard from Zero, and then someone in the group of humans around us applauded.

"Shakespeare," said one of them, elbowing the one next to him and nodding knowledgably. "Good stuff, isn't it?"

"Shut your mouth, filth," Zero's father said, so softly that it would have been hard to hear had it not had such a vicious edge to it. "Or you will end your life in a field of flowers, at my feet."

"I am already a flower," said Jin Yeong, shrugging one shoulder. "What. Do. You. *Want?*"

The swift sound of the fae's indrawn breath in cold, deadly anger made me feel far too squishy on the inside, like a spider soaked in bug spray, melting from the inside out. I expected his anger to make itself obvious in his speech, but instead, he took a moment to gather himself and smile. It didn't make me feel much better, but maybe I've just got a bad attitude.

"I want your word," said Zero's father, "that when the time comes, you will stand beside my son and help him win the throne."

"*Hyeong*," Jin Yeong said, with scathing amusement, "does not wish to take the throne. I shall not force him or assist him."

"It would be very much the better for your health if you did so," said Zero's father, and now his smile appeared to be pasted on, for all the warmth of it. "And for the health of that little human you've made far too cheeky."

"This is my *petteu*," said Jin Yeong, silky voiced, "and I do not permit you to touch it. I will kill it myself when I am no longer enjoying it."

If Athelas had said it, I might have had a momentary worry that he actually meant it; with Zero, I would have felt a chill as he said it, even if I didn't believe he meant it. This time, despite the very real danger in front of me, I had to work not to roll my eyes.

Jin Yeong pinched my hand warningly, and I realised belatedly that perhaps I hadn't done as good a job as I'd thought at not rolling my eyes. Good thing I was already avoiding Zero's dad's eyes.

"Your loyalty—"

"My loyalty belongs to me," Jin Yeong said, with finality. "You said it before: *hyeong* has not endeared himself to me. I shall not help him to a throne."

"You are chattel with a longer than usual life," said Zero's father, with ice-blue anger. "You should remember your place."

"I choose my own place," said Jin Yeong, his gaze roaming over the crowd around us and finally resting on me once more. "And I choose who I will stand beside."

Oh heck. The cow pats were about to start flying.

"That's a very great pity," said Zero's father. He didn't look as though he found it a pity. He looked as though he was furiously glad—as though this was what he had expected all along, and now he could deal with it as he had wished to do from the start. "I dislike having to deal with filth, but if the filth does not know its place, it must be taught."

"Ah heck," I muttered. Jin Yeong's fingers pressed mine, but his expression didn't change. Oh yeah. That was right. I was supposed to be pretending that I couldn't see or feel the huge disturbances in the layers of the world all around us.

"And you, little pet—" he looked at me and I managed to stare at his left cheek to avoid his eyes. "You will regret the company you keep before long."

Whatever he had been trying to offer me earlier, he was definitely annoyed that I hadn't taken it—or that Jin Yeong had interrupted before he could elaborate.

"I will say neither fare you well nor the human *see you later*," he said in Jin Yeong's direction, the expression sitting oddly within his deliberately formal voice. "I trust that you will fare exactly as I intend and I do not intend to see you later."

He turned on his elegant, bare feet and left, cobwebby trousers legs whispering elegantly against each other as he walked, shirt fluttering softly behind him; and as he went, the entire circle of humans applauded like they'd just seen the end of the act.

It was hard not to watch him go, but it was easier to refrain than to keep pretending I couldn't see the Things segueing from Between through the formerly poles of the weather shade above us. The crowd began to disperse, but between the flowing movement of people separating here and there, Things pushed through the flowers that had grown from every white pole and carried the flowers along with them as they came.

Things that were flowery and smelly and not quite alive even though they were moving.

"Ah heck," I said once more. Tall, broad-shouldered, and whispering like a breeze through flowers, these petalmen didn't look really solid, but I was pretty sure they would pack a decent punch despite that. Or, I realised, as one of them grew a needle-like thorn of green, sappy wood, a decent sting.

Nobody nearby seemed to do more than give them the odd, sideways glance and then look hastily away: I suppose they could have looked like shadows if you didn't look properly at them. Flower-laden, stalk-encrusted, and grass-thatched shadows.

And even if humans couldn't see them properly, it wouldn't stop them from being hurt by the creatures.

"Come, *Petteu*," said JinYeong, drawing me away by the hand and swiftly toward the nearby flower cart.

I thought he meant us to pass by it and escape by way of the alley and into Wellington Court.

I protested, "There are people there too!" but he dragged me directly toward the cart itself, and we were only a few steps away when a couple of petalmen segued from there as well, blooming from flowerless buckets of water with the decaying stench of dead flowers clinging to them as they came.

They might have been made of dead flower petals; they might have been made from rotting plant matter scraped from the bottom of those same buckets of water. Whatever it was, they were the same kind of thing as those behind us, just slightly different in makeup and significantly more smelly.

JinYeong snarled at their appearance and loosened the button on his suit-coat to free up his shoulders.

"Gotta keep moving!" I said sharply, because there were still far too many humans around the place. If they got caught up in all of this—

A plastic cup sailed through the air, arcing over my shoulder and sloshing milk tea and boba as it went, and splattered against one of the petalmen. A gaping, soggy hole burst right through the creature, milk running down and taking out its legs as well, and the whole creature collapsed into a mess of petals and leaf mould.

Someone chuckled in a high, gleeful sort of way that was very familiar, and I caught sight of the old mad bloke, chortling madly as he scuttled from wombat to fixed seat, lobbing another full plastic cup of bubble tea as he darted for it. The old mad bloke: once my neighbour, now a permanent shadow in the corners of my life. Supposedly dead at least three times now but somehow still alive.

Jin Yeong said something in Korean that was probably as rude as it sounded, and we ran for it through the open space toward the alley as another volley of milk tea met flower petals and collapsed them utterly. At least in the alley, we might have a chance to fight back without hurting anyone—without anyone seeing. And now that there were a few less petalmen to deal with, we'd have a better chance of coming out of this with all of our limbs. I saw them in the reflections of the papered-up windows, following us with their single brain cell and pursued, themselves, by a final volley of bubble tea. The old mad bloke, on the other hand, was now nowhere in sight.

Find somewhere empty, said my brain, sharp and urgent, just as I saw the glass door and dark stairway vanishing into the ground that had once belonged to an opshop and was now in the process of being fitted out for a karaoke bar.

"Here, here!" I panted, and this time it was me tugging, tugging us right through the glass and into the storefront. Down the stairs, with the smell of mildew and dust suffocating us and the thunder of our footsteps surrounding us, we ran.

We stopped briefly at the bottom of the stairs, and Jin Yeong made a small, throaty noise of satisfaction.

"*Johah*," he said exultantly. "There are many weapons here."

"Yep," I said, snatching up two of the closest: a pair of wall brackets painted white that were easily persuaded to be twin swords a little shorter and sturdier than I usually used, with a slight curve to the end of them. I didn't have time to persuade them that they didn't need to be white, because a skirl of petals and sticks and wind brawled above us on the stairs and swirled at the top of the landing.

"Heck," I said, in a sudden coldness of remembrance, as we darted further into the darkness of the store. "You haven't bitten me in a while."

"I have not," he said, as if he was to be congratulated. Maybe he was. It must have been hard for the bitey little mosquito.

He hesitated, a small swaying movement back and forth, and I said, "Hurry up, then."

"You did not give me permission," he said, putting his nose up very slightly.

"Good grief!" I said, staring at him. "Did you actually listen to me the other day?"

"I always listen," he said coldly. "I do not always *obey*."

"Yeah, but—never mind that! If I need vampire spit, it's not like a real kiss anyway and—"

Stubbornly, Jin Yeong began, "It is—"

I transferred the sword in my left hand to my right, grabbed his tie, and pulled him down to a more convenient height. I'm not sure if I kissed him or he kissed me, because all I could hear was the tumble of Behindkind petalmen barging onto the litter-strewn shop floor from the stairs.

Whichever one of us it was, Jin Yeong was the one who snaked an arm around my waist when I would have let go at the first tingle of vampire-induced accelerated heartbeat and continued the embrace until I heard my own heartbeat above the sound of the Behindkind charging across the floor at us.

He released me a few moments before they reached us, and I tossed my second sword back into my left hand from the right, where it rested, ready and warm in my grip.

"Ah," said Jin Yeong, throaty with satisfaction, "this will be *fun*."

"You've got a flamin' warped idea of fun," I said, but a fierce, dark sense of enjoyment grew in my heart as its beat accelerated again, and I felt as though I could almost laugh. Vampire spit works *quick*. "Where are your weapons?"

"I have told you—"

"Right," I said, automatically swinging back and around until we were back to back with a few paces between us as the Behind-kind curled around us in a slow, wafting sea of decay and leaf mould. "Your body is a weapon. I'm circling left; mind my swords."

A thorn lunged from my right and I stepped swiftly to the left, sweeping with that hand to clear my way while I smacked the thorn away. I smacked it hard, but it must have been attached to the petalman's hand, because although the creature spun away from me, he didn't lose hold of the thorn sword.

At my back, JinYeong stepped swiftly to the left as well, keeping my back covered, and a flurry of blackened petals and sharp wind tore into the fight just past that. I was too busy with my own monsters to pay attention to his, but I felt the stillness and security of that buffer between me and them, and I took pains to stay aware enough to keep up my side of it. I didn't think I could bear the idea of him being stabbed for me *again*.

If I thought at first that we would have a brisk, if uncomplicated fight for it, I was soon proved to be disastrously wrong. The petalmen were quick to be decapitated, or lose an arm or leg, but they were also very quick to hurl their remaining pieces into a kind of mulchy whirlwind and emerge again whole, without stopping, to lunge back into the fight, thorns foremost.

I heard JinYeong snarl in frustration behind me as he took a stab to the side from the creature he had just beheaded a moment ago, and a whirl at my left took the scattered pieces of two recently de-limbed petalmen and threw them at me again, reformed and re-thorned.

I was already tired, my heart beating too quickly in my chest, and there was still a *lot* of fight left in these creatures. We couldn't run for it because they were blocking the stairs, even if we had risked them in the crowds outside; we couldn't run Behind because that would give them the home advantage.

In fact, the only thing I'd seen disintegrate the creatures for good was the bubble tea the old mad bloke had thrown at them. If I'd thought about it, I would have taken the time to throw a few of those buckets of leftover water and dead petals at them before we ran down here, but it was too late now.

Problem was, I thought, rather dizzily avoiding a thorn on one side by catching a scratch on the other side instead, I couldn't just pull water from Between. I would have to pull somewhere Behind that had water closer to the human world, and if I did that—who knew what else would come?

JinYeong fell back against me, and I stood still just a moment too long in the fight to let him catch himself; a thorn went through the flesh of my upper right arm, drawing a shuddering breath out of me.

Heck. Even if I could get to my phone, Zero wouldn't get here in time to help. Our only choice was to play at silly beggars with Between and hope that nothing worse than the petalmen came out.

"You see water anywhere?" I panted, to JinYeong.

"Turn," he said curtly, and when we had made a half-circle, back to back, he said, "Look ahead."

This time, my indrawn breath was one of relief. If I looked carefully, the change rooms weren't just dripping with water along their back walls, they were fairly rippling with moisture. That, I was pretty sure, betokened a waterfall somewhere Between. A waterfall meant that there was a pool of water for it to fall into, and a pool of water was *exactly* what we needed right now.

I stamped my foot into the floor, willing it to pass through carpet and wood to the grass or dirt that was Between the human world and the world Behind, and heard the hollow sound of wooden floorboards instead. But that impact also threw up water, as though the carpet were sodden, and I grinned victoriously.

"Right, you lot," I said savagely, whipping my blades in a swift, vicious semi-circle in front of me. "Time you went back *home*."

I stomped again, and this time instead of the hollow thump of foot meeting carpet-covered floorboards, my foot squished down in damp grass. That damp grass ruffled its way through the carpet, and over by the change rooms the floor sank and became a pool of water, misted with the spray of falling water that now poured noisily from rocks too high to see, softening the sound of our fight.

As soon as the spray misted over the petalmen nearest to the waterfall, they slowed down, sticky and tarry with damp.

"Get 'em all back toward the water," I yelled, slashing wildly at one of the petalmen and sending it tumbling into water that was still faintly, hairily blue like the carpet had been. The petals disintegrated and spread themselves across the surface like fish food, and the water smoothed and grew ripples instead of carpet.

Beneath my feet I felt alternately wet, squishy carpet and damp grass, and the remaining petalman still fought sluggishly and determinedly to get to us.

Flower petals and mould fluttered in the air and choked damply in our throats as water misted on our skin, and the stinging of thorns still whipped across shins and forearms, but now there was something of a clearness to the room. Side by side now instead of back to back, Jin Yeong and I pushed the petalmen toward the bog behind them with quick, slashing movements rather than any kind of advanced technique.

I began to think that we might possibly get out of this without dying—maybe even without worse than a few stab wounds.

Then something started singing in the shelving beside the change rooms, high and wailing.

Jin Yeong snarled, and I saw him shake his head in my peripheral. *Banshees*, that snarl said.

Banshees. I knew what banshees were, but why were they singing at us? The ones at home wailed a bit, but they didn't do the kind of singing that made your ears feel as though they were going to burst and dribble down the side of your face.

"Cut it out, you little ratbags!" I yelled, slashing a thorn in half and sweeping the head from the shoulders of the petalman it belonged to with my other sword. The head rolled away, disintegrating into petals as it travelled along the wet ground, but I swayed, a buzzing in my ears where there had been the sound of singing before.

Those little beggars were messing with our heads! And the last few petalmen, without ears or eyes, simply pushed forward, unshaken. One of them thrust too short to pierce my stomach but caught me with a thorn across the wrist, barely missing the artery, and my defensive slice was just a bit too drunken.

"*Choshimhae!*" snapped Jin Yeong, but I saw a slight stagger to his step, too.

"You sort out the last two!" I called to him. "I'll get these little ratbags."

I heard his short *Ne!* as I lurched across the floor toward the big industrial-sized vacuum that had been left to gather dust by the counter, its cord snaking across the carpet and unplugged. I grabbed the nozzle in one hand and went for the cord with the other, but a zap of something that was almost Between but maybe not quite shocked me as I snatched up the nozzle, and the vacuum roared into life of its own volition.

And when I say roared, I mean it fairly *howled*, even above the sound of the waterfall. I heard the faint, panicked gibber of banshees in the shelving and saw white legs and tartan flying as I hauled the vacuum cleaner across the room again, but it was too late for them. I brandished the nozzle threateningly in their direction and yelled, "You lot better belt up if you don't want to go head-over-heels into the dust catcher!"

I didn't actually intend to vacuum the banshees up: I was just planning on using the machine to scare them and dull the sound of their wailing. That sounds really smart but would have been, as

Athelas told me later, as entirely ineffective against that sound range as the waterfall had been, so it was lucky for me that they were so scared.

Only then the vacuum stretched eagerly and *grew*. Faster than I could stop it, it snorkelled up every last banshee: I felt them impact against the soft piping as they tumbled helplessly inside the machine, then heard them wailing as they were thrown around and around inside the cyclonic dust catcher.

"Heck!" I yelped, and dropped the nozzle of the vacuum. It didn't stop at once, which was pretty creepy, but we were more than halfway Between by now, so it wasn't really surprising.

Maybe vacuums roamed free-range in certain areas of Between.

I would have felt sorry for the banshees if it wasn't for the warmth that I was pretty sure was blood making an itchy trickle in my ear. It wasn't like they were dead, either: as I turned to see how JinYeong was getting on, the vacuum's roar sank and then ceased, and I distinctly heard the sound of a very small person chucking its guts inside the dust catcher.

Ha. That'd teach 'em not to sing stuff at us and make us dizzy. See how they like being too dizzy to stand.

JinYeong was standing—the last one standing, as a matter of fact—so I staggered back toward him, still a bit wobbly on my feet. The banshees could get themselves out of the vacuum.

"You're a nice mess," I said, panting, when I got closer. I was a nice mess, too; I could see myself in the darkened mirror of the changerooms behind JinYeong. The waterfall had already segued back into Between where it belonged, leaving the mirrored surfaces behind more sparkling and clean than previously.

It was nice not to have Behindkind blood on me for a change, though: all the blood on me was mine. You gotta fight to survive, but it's never fun cleaning the blood of dead things off your clothes: I felt oddly grateful to the petalmen for being so distinctly unliving, even while animated.

Jin Yeong grinned at me, still staggering a bit, and stripped off the remains of his suitcoat along with his tie. He threw them on the pile of gooey petals that was all that remained of our late enemies, then threw himself on the floor and leaned against the wall beneath the staircase, breathing deeply.

"Ah, that was interesting!" he said.

CHAPTER FIVE

"Yeah, interesting," I said, but I laughed a bit as I lowered myself onto the floor beside him, massaging around the slowly blood-seeping arm that had taken the most damage. The floor still felt a bit damp beneath me, but I couldn't bring myself to care too much. "Oi. You reckon Zero's dad really wanted you to help Zero? Or do you think he was looking for information?"

"Both," said Jin Yeong, laughing softly. "More than that, he knows something we do not. He knows certainly that the succession has begun again—he is seeking allies for his son."

"He wouldn't do that openly if he wasn't ready to make his move," I said, going cold with the knowledge of it. Beside me, Jin Yeong made a soft intake of breath when he moved, and I turned my head to look at him. "You all right? They manage to get you with those thorns?"

My own arm wasn't as bad as I'd thought, and the vampire spit was already starting to clot the blood and heal it up, but although it was hard to tell between the black muck and my own blood, there was a dull kind of pain around my ribs that suggested a wound I'd have to take a look at later, too. I patted the area absently, which exacerbated the dull burning, and found that

JinYeong was watching me, his head leaning against the wall and his eyes only half-open.

"You did not ask my permission," he said, *sotto voce*.

"What?"

"You did not ask my permission to kiss me."

"The heck? You're always biting me without permission!" I pulled my hoodie away to display the very clear bite mark from a couple of weeks ago that had just started to heal to a soft pink. It would have healed much quicker if it hadn't been exactly where he bit me *every flaming time*. "Look at this!"

"Yes, but you said—"

"Okay, okay. I *apologise*. I'm very sorry to have damaged your flamin' delicate psyche!"

"I am not damaged."

I snorted a laugh before I could stop myself. "What garbage! You're bleeding over most of your torso, including from the ear, by the way. Were those little ratbags *singing* at us?"

"They sing their prey to sleep," JinYeong explained, sitting still as I leaned over to wipe away the blood from his ears with my hoodie cuff. He let me turn his head and wipe the other side, too; didn't even snarl at me, which was a surprise. "My psyche is not damaged."

"I s'pose that's something, then. Look, we don't have time to be waiting for permission when it comes to stuff attacking us. If I'm not already pumped up on vampire spit, we're going to be in trouble. You've got open permission to kiss me, okay? Or bite me, whatever is quicker."

He seemed to think about that for a few moments before he said, "*Kurolgae*," but I had the sudden suspicion that his *malaise* was because he was injured a bit worse than I'd thought, and a twinge of worry pinched at me.

"C'mmere," I said, tugging at his shirt.

He leaned closer, but ignored my attempts to check on the slashes around his torso, and instead performed the same office for me that I had done for him a moment ago, wiping away the blood from my ears.

That took too long, and left me sitting awkwardly with my face in his hands as his eyes roamed my face.

"If you sit still, I'll check to see how bad your wounds are," I told him, shifting uncomfortably. "I know you heal quickly, but you were just stabbed through the same—"

"If *you* sit still, I—"

There was a scuttle of very tiny feet from the direction of the vacuum cleaner, and Jin Yeong's head snapped around, his eyes narrowing. My own eyes were immediately on the vacuum cleaner, and I pulled away from Jin Yeong just in time to watch a banshee stagger out of the nozzle.

"Don't even *think* about it!" I said to it, but the banshee simply leaned against the vacuum with one tiny hand, considered the world around it in a miserable sort of a way, and threw up violently. Other banshees staggered out past it, tottering here and there as if they were drunk, sending up miniscule static sparks against the dryer bits of carpet and falling on their faces. A couple more of them threw up, too.

Jin Yeong, his eyes bright with malice, said, "Ah! Now I shall have something to do at home!"

"Hey, at least at home they don't try to sing us to sleep," I pointed out. I was pretty sure that having a go at our banshees would lead to outright war, and presently we were reasonably happily co-habiting—if you didn't count the stuff they threw at Jin Yeong every now and then.

"I shall vacuum," said Jin Yeong, but he said it quietly.

He began to tidy himself up again and I cleaned off my swords with a bit of dirty newspaper. I didn't know whether they would clean themselves on the way back or whatever, but it seemed rude to use them and not clean them, even if they were only going to turn into wall brackets again. There was already enough mess around the place.

When the swords were clean and more bracket than sword, I rose, shrugging out the tenseness in my shoulders and feeling a slight pinch from the healing gash in my arm. Vampire spit's the good stuff, I tell you.

"Reckon Zero's dad really meant to kill us?" I asked, absently touching the sore spot on my ribs again. There had been a flash of memory before, now that I thought of Zero's dad again—when he had been in my head. What had that been?

Jin Yeong shrugged. "We didn't die."

"Yeah, but only because I was able to pull Between here to us instead of us going to it," I said, frowning. Flaming heck. The memory was gone, wriggling back into my mind so quickly that I couldn't even remember what had caused it to come out or what it had been about. Flamin' wriggly truth worms. "He didn't know I'd be able to do that. Those petal beasties were pretty flamin' near to being the end of us before that."

At least, I *hoped* he didn't know I could do that. Zero's dad being creepy in my head was bad enough: him knowing about me being an heirling would be far worse—I had a feeling that he would wait around personally to see that I died if it came to him knowing that. I very much agreed with Zero that it was better his dad not know.

"He knows *something*," I said darkly. "Dunno what he knows, but it feels like he's pushing buttons to see what pops out."

He gave a sniffy little laugh. "Of course you would know that."

"If you're suggesting that I'm always pushing buttons—"

"I am not suggesting, I am *saying*."

I chuckled, feeling the dull throb of it in my ribs for a moment. "Okay, that's fair. Anyway, whatever he was here for, I'm getting pretty flamin' tired of people trying to kill us."

"We didn't die," said Jin Yeong again, far too cheerfully, in my opinion.

"Yeah," I said. I headed for the stairs at a bit of an amble. I didn't feel like moving, but I *did* feel like arguing. "But I feel like that's such a low bar for how a person's life should go. Broken arm? Yeah, but I didn't *die*. Lose a leg? I mean, I didn't *die*, so it must be okay!"

Jin Yeong made the little hissing sound that was his laugh once again. "Now you are just complaining."

"I know you blokes are used to this sort of thing," I said, still willing to argue, "but there isn't too much more that wouldn't actually kill me."

He shrugged. "Your fighting is better these days. And you can do things you shouldn't do. You will not die."

"The vampire spit helps, too," I acknowledged. It seemed as though I could feel the stuff doing loop-de-loops in my veins. Ridiculous, but it really did feel like that: the mainline equivalent of a really strong cup of coffee without the side-effects.

"*Maja*," he said, smugly.

And that reminded me. I was going to have to find a more suitable way of getting vampire spit if Jin Yeong was thinking about trying to date. That was a pain in the neck, but a necessary one. A bit like getting vampire spit in the first place, actually.

I huffed a sigh, looked at the stairs we still had to climb to get back up into the real world, and said, "Oi."

"Do not poke me; I have a hole there. What is it?"

"What happened to you, anyway?" I asked him. "In the war, I mean. Athelas says you were nearly dead when Zero found you."

It wasn't until the silence had stretched out for a few moments of plodding stair-climbing that I looked back to see Jin Yeong watching me suspiciously.

"What?" I protested. "I'm just curious! I'm not gathering intel to use against you later. Flamin' heck!"

Jin Yeong sniffed a bit, but I got the impression that he was quite pleased. "I shall tell you another time," he said. "First, we should meet these humans so that *hyeong* does not throw me through the wall again."

That was probably fair enough, I thought, emerging from the

stairwell with my phone in my hand to text Abigail again. Zero was pretty prone to throwing vampires through walls these days, apparently.

I'd just unlocked my phone to text when Jin Yeong gave a stifled *aish*! and covered his nose as a warm, sticky hand grabbed mine.

"G'day, g'day!"

"Flamin' heck!" I yelped, just barely stopping myself from snatching my hand away and kicking for good measure.

Reckon he knew that, because he grinned at me through a thick, tangled thatch of beard with teeth that had always been unexpectedly white for the general mess of the rest of him. It was the old mad bloke again, of course. He'd been following me around since I came to Tasmania with my family, and although I'd somehow forgotten about him for a few years a while back, he'd been around and very obvious recently.

"Bubble tea!" he said now, and giggled.

"Looks like someone else wanted bubble tea," I told Jin Yeong.

He made a very small grimace and flicked a look across at the old mad bloke, then sighed. "I will get you bubble tea," he said to the old bloke. "But you will drink it somewhere else."

The old mad bloke gave a gleeful chuckle. "You have to come with me. It costs two."

"Two what?" I asked him, as he tugged me along the alley and into Wellington Court. We emerged into bright sunshine that surprised me after the cool, musty interior of the abandoned shop below.

"Two!" he repeated, and dragged me all the way across the court and down another alley that led to Liverpool street. There was another bubble tea shop there, I knew, so I wasn't too worried about the fact that he was pulling me around.

At the very worst, I expected to find Abigail in the tea shop when we arrived—they'd used the old mad bloke to run messages before, and it wouldn't surprise me to find that they had a front somewhere else around the city.

She wasn't there when Jin Yeong and I trailed in after the old bloke, though. He marched up to the counter, said, "*Two!*" in a fine spray of spit, and then dashed for the back of the shop, leaving me and Jin Yeong to pay.

That was fair—he'd used up a good amount of bubble tea helping us fight off the petalmen—so I made Jin Yeong pay instead of just charming the drinks out of the cashier like he looked as though he was about to do.

I elbowed him at the first sign of his smoulder and said, "Oi. You can't be charming other women while you're out with one. Haven't you learned that in your books yet?"

He blinked a bit and said, "It is *necessary*."

"One," I said, pinching his wallet from his pocket without asking, "it's not necessary. It's just bubble tea. Two: of course it doesn't matter when you're on the job with me. But if you're actually thinking about dating—*especially* someone human—"

"Are you teaching me right now?"

"Only a little bit," I told him. "I'm not going to get involved if you actually end up dating someone, but you shouldn't scupper your chances first thing."

I left him behind, muttering that he was not *going* to scupper anything, and went back to find the old mad bloke before he did something too bad. I didn't get there in time: he had made a neat circle of sugar around the table he sat at, prompting one of the servers to glare at him, and he was unweaving the weaved basket chair he sat in when I got there.

"Good grief, it's like being out with two kids," I said, plopping myself down in the chair next to him.

"*Hotsori*," said Jin Yeong. He sat beside me and said to the old mad bloke with a distinct undercurrent of threat, "Do not do useless things."

The old mad bloke crossed his legs beneath him without

acknowledging either of us, and sat solemnly until the server brought us our two drinks. He grabbed both drinks with a crow of glee, and started slurping one up straight away. JinYeong, as if he couldn't quite help himself, tidied the curve of the sugar circle where the server had disturbed it, and that made the old bloke mumble a laugh into his drink.

"Bitey bitey," he said, dribbling milk.

JinYeong threw me an irritated look, but at my grin he just sat back and folded his arms, raising his eyes to the ceiling for a brief moment.

"Oi," I said to the old bloke. "You're looking pretty flamin' good for a bloke who's died so many times. Who are you, exactly? You can't tell me you're really my neighbour because I'm pretty sure that if I tried to check the name on your deed—"

"No names, lady," he said solemnly, at once. "I am man. Homo sapiens. That's why they can't touch me. I'm an important person."

"'Course you are," I said. If he was the Harbinger like Zero and Athelas suggested, he was a very important person. In that light, his repeated brushes with death made perfect sense. Trying for an easier question, I asked, "Where are you staying these days?"

"I'm free!" he said, eyes brightening at once. "Once I was captive but now I'm free!"

"Yeah, you got taken by the fae, didn't you?"

The old bloke exhaled explosively into his straw, slopping milk tea over the top of the cup and onto the table. JinYeong moved his arms back fastidiously and shot him a warning look, but the old bloke only said, "I am a ninja. I go nowhere I don't want to go."

"Okay," I said. The suspicion that he was the Harbinger—the one meant to usher in the new cycle and support a particular heirling—left me feeling distinctly edgy. He'd been hanging around me for a bit too long, and I wanted to be the King Behind even less than Zero did. "No offense, all right? What are you up to at the moment?"

"You have to come with me," he said. He finished up his first tea in a death rattle of boba, and burped loudly before he pushed away the empty cup and slid the second cup closer.

"We are with you," I said, because Jin Yeong was muttering in exasperated Korean that he hadn't bothered to translate and didn't seem willing to engage further. "What do you want?"

"You have to come *further* with me."

"Further *where*? 'Cos if you're talking about going Between with you—"

"We are not going Between," Jin Yeong said flatly. "I do not wish to, and *hyeong* would kill me."

"There's a lot of that going around lately," I said, throwing him a narrow-eyed look. For some reason, that made him grin and regain some of the jauntiness he'd had earlier in the morning. "If you bunch are going to be knocking down my house bit by bit, we're gunna have a pro—"

"Time to go!" said the old mad bloke suddenly, darting out of his seat with the second bubble tea still in his hand. He shot out the door, leaving me and Jin Yeong scrambling to keep up, and trotted back the way we'd come, through to Wellington Court.

By the time we entered the court again, there was no sign of the old galah, just people milling here and there as usual: kids yelling and chasing the pigeons, teenagers jeering at each other, adults fastidiously cleaning off the fixed tables and chairs before sitting down.

And standing with her back against the pole topped by a mosaic-covered sailing ship in full sail, was a girl, watching us. She was nondescript: brown hair in a long bob, jeans that fit in with pretty much every girl her age around us, and a camo hoodie.

"Reckon Abigail sent someone to meet us," I told Jin Yeong, catching the girl's eyes.

"*Kurogae*," he murmured.

She must have been one of the few that find Jin Yeong unaccountably terrifying, because she looked at him once and dropped her eyes; but she didn't run away when we approached, and that meant she was brave. I mean, brave *or* stupid. I'm still finding out where the difference is, myself.

"You waiting for us?" I asked her.

"Yep," she said, pushing away from the pole. "I'm Cadence."

"Pet."

That made her frown. Then, with a frankness that gave me a cold start, she asked, "Name, or function?"

It was my turn to stare at her. "What do you know about Pets?"

"Had an owner once—it makes you appreciate your own name a bit more, doesn't it?"

"Yeah," I said, even though I wasn't sure that was true. There was a kind of safety and anonymity when people—fae—didn't know your name. When you were just a pet, they didn't pay as much attention to you—they also tended to very badly underestimate you.

"Anyway," said Cadence, hunching her shoulders a bit. "Abigail sent me to meet you."

"Too busy to meet up?" I asked, even though I knew it wasn't that.

"She wanted to make sure your other friends weren't with you, this time," Cadence said. "She knew I'd recognise fae when I saw 'em."

I jerked my thumb at Jin Yeong. "What about him?"

"Your boyfriend is fine. Humans are allowed."

"You weren't with the group last time."

"Had a thing. You ready to go? I'm just the fore-guard to make sure we weren't going to encounter any fae."

She started off without waiting for a yes, and I followed her with Jin Yeong, cutting through the dead-end road that ran alongside the TAFE, leaving the giant red fish mural in our wake.

"If you'd been around a bit sooner, you would have encountered a few," I said, gazing longingly at the motorbikes that lined the old red-brick alley wall on the other side.

Jin Yeong must have seen that, because he gave a derisive *pft* of laughter. I mean, yeah, if you can travel via Between, the thrill of a motorbike might lose a bit of its lustre, but they still looked pretty good to me.

"I saw that," Cadence said, her voice edged with respect. "You should think about joining us—we could use people like you."

That…was interesting. I had expected for Abigail to simply not reply, or to reply with a distinctly short and sharp negative. At the best, I'd expected her to do exactly what she was doing with her precautions, or to have even more precautions than before. I was not expecting casual offers of employment. It was the second time today that someone had done something for a reason I couldn't fathom, and even if the urge wasn't quite so strong when my life wasn't so likely to be in danger, I did want to know why I was being practically welcomed back into the fold.

"Like what, exactly?" I asked, since I couldn't meet that offer with a suspicious *why are you lot being so friendly again all of a sudden?* From all that Cadence had seen, we'd run for it as soon as we were attacked, even if we'd faced the petalman out of sight.

"You faced up to one of the flower-growers," she said, stopping at a door between two motorbikes. "I've never seen a human do that before—haven't even seen many fae do it. *And* you tricked his little flowermen into following you away from the other humans so that no one got hurt."

Interesting, I thought, looking at that door. I knew that there was only another alley on the other side of that door: this alley separated from that by a brick wall with a door that went nowhere you couldn't get by just walking around the end of the wall.

Still, I wasn't surprised to see the inside of a furnished room when she opened it. Jin Yeong's eyes met mine, one of his brows rising, and I shrugged slightly.

"Be careful when you step across," Cadence said, stepping into the room herself. "It can be a bit disorienting if you're not used to it."

"We'll be careful," I said solemnly, since it would be rude to laugh in her face. The desire to laugh faded again as it occurred to me that far from being a fob-off from the headquarters that Jin Yeong and I already knew about, this was showing us another sensitive place. Heck. What was going on? "Is Abigail in here?"

I'd already seen the answer to my question: she wasn't. The entire room was maybe ten feet by ten, with a couch and two chairs, and a coffee table. Unless Abigail was hiding behind the couch, she definitely wasn't here.

"There is no door," said Jin Yeong in dissatisfaction.

I was about to remark that I'd seen that, when it struck me exactly what he meant: there was no other door than that by which we'd entered, and when Cadence shut it, that one disappeared as well.

Oh. Maybe this appearance of friendly hands shaken in forgiveness was an actual trap.

"What is this?" I asked Cadence, in a friendly sort of a way. There were a lot of weapons that I could grab from here: I could still see the underpinnings of the room that were actually part of the alley it was in the human layer of the world. No need to get nasty just yet.

"Don't worry," she said quickly. "It's just a waiting room. If you want to leave, you can; I'll open the door for you straight away."

"No worries," I said, plopping down on the couch. Ridiculously, I was uneasy again. Jin Yeong sat beside me, slinging one arm around my shoulders, and grinned at Cadence with enough tooth to make her distinctly uncomfortable, if I was any judge. "Have you blokes noticed the bridge trolls and goblins that have been popping up around Hobart more often lately?"

"We noticed," said Cadence, after a moment. "We've been having a bit of trouble with them ourselves; we've got an idea why, too."

"'Zat why Abigail agreed to see me again?" I asked, but I didn't really expect an answer.

Cadence began readily, "Nah, that was because—" and then stopped short. More carefully, she said, "I mean, I think Abigail has a favour to ask."

"*Taebak*," said Jin Yeong, for my ears only. "I thought she would try to kill you."

"Thanks for the warning, then," I said to him. At least I wasn't the only one who found it surprising to be welcomed back. "Nice to know you're looking out for me."

"I came with you. Do you think I'll let her kill you?"

"Thanks," I told him, with more sincerity. To Cadence, I said, "What sort of favour?"

She shifted a little bit. "I'll let her tell you."

She wouldn't be swayed from that stance, either: I had the feeling that she felt she had slipped earlier and was afraid to say too much more. It was another stiff five minutes for us all before Abigail arrived, pushing through the wall as if it wasn't there and then closing a phantom door behind her.

"Strike a light," I said, impressed. "It looks different from this side!"

"Only someone entering can see the door," Abigail told me. She looked a bit tidier than last time I'd seen her; her red hair was in a ponytail, plaited, then wrapped into a bun, but her clothing was just as plain as ever. The real difference was the fresh scar that ran down her left arm, still puckering as it healed.

"Someone had a go at you?"

"A few goblins," she said, shrugging. "I got careless. You had a bit of trouble on your way here, too; I saw your text."

"Came through all right. Just met an old acquaintance and had to run for it. Thanks for sending the old bloke to bring us to the right spot."

"Turned up, did he?" She looked relieved. "Sometimes he does what he's meant to do, sometimes not."

Cadence, bouncing on her toes, said, "Abs, she said they've noticed more incursions than usual, too. Bridge trolls and that sort of thing."

"Thanks," Abigail said. "You didn't have to come all this way to tell me that, though. You could have texted that much."

"Didn't think you liked leaving a trail of texts and stuff," I pointed out. "Actually, I didn't think you'd answer."

"We don't like trails," she agreed, ignoring the second part of my answer. "Where have you been having the most trouble?"

"North Hobart, going toward Lenah Valley. There's been a bit of trouble up around the old brewery at the bottom of the mountain too, though; and we had some excitement in the Huon Valley, but that came back to an office in North Hobart. Zero suggested that you lot could take care of that sort of thing if you had time."

Maybe it was a bad way to bring up Zero again, but I had to address the elephant in the room and get it over with before we could get down to business. Maybe there was also a part of me that wanted to poke and see how much I could get away with before something jiggled loose and made it obvious why I had been allowed back in again.

She did stiffen, but that was about all. "That's kind of the fae lord. Throwing us a bone, is he?"

"Not a bone," I said. "Reckon he thought you'd do a good job. And I told him it was your right: humans helping humans."

"I'm flattered," she said dryly. "We'll do our best to live up to his expectations."

Heck. She was just going to take that on face value. I wished I could get rid of the niggling sense that there was more to things than just Abigail being a forgiving sort of person.

"That's not exactly why I came, though," I told her. There was time to figure out everything else. "We need a bit of info."

Abigail looked at me quizzically. "A bit unusual for fae to be asking humans for information, isn't it?"

"Some humans have been murdered, and we're trying to figure out who did it. We reckon there are more cases out there, but the cops don't know about all of them. Zero figured you might know about cases the cops might not."

"Did he," said Abigail rather grimly. "So that's what he wants? I wouldn't have expected it, but no doubt he has an angle of his own."

That didn't sound promising, and her posture wasn't really encouraging either: arms folded across her chest, hands tucked under her arms, and head down, frowning. I hoped it just meant she was listening.

I pushed on. "You ever hear about a kid whose parents were killed with a series of murders happening in the neighbourhood beforehand? The kid might be dead or not, but the parents are almost definitely dead."

That made her look up and gaze at me for a very long time. "Why would you ask about that?" she asked, at last.

"Met someone like that," I said, hardly daring to breathe. "Heard about more than one. And maybe someone who escaped it."

"If you know someone who escaped that, they're more fortunate than the other cases I've heard of," she said. "I've seen, oh, four of those, I think? in our records. And none of them has escaped it yet. They're not normal deaths, though: no bodies are ever taken to the morgue, and they don't always find the kid, even though they know there should be one."

"Yep," I said, my throat dry. "Those are the ones. Can I see whatever information you've got?"

"We'll discuss it," she said, which was better than the outright negative I'd half expected. "But it's not fodder for those other two."

Jin Yeong shifted impatiently in his seat, and said, "Who else will do the work, then?"

"You remember they're the ones investigating the deaths, right?" I said at the same time, poking him gently in the ribs to remind him not to go all toothy on the humans. Luckily, he hadn't translated any of that. He sniffed and settled back down, his arm settling more heavily on my shoulders. "If you've got physical files or evidence, I can look at the stuff and tell them where to go, but why double-handle it if we don't have to?"

"We'll discuss it," said Abigail again.

I had a feeling that it wasn't the dismissal it seemed: there was more here to discuss than I was seeing at present.

I asked her, "Where are you getting your info about these cases from? I mean, is it stuff I can find on the internet? Because then you wouldn't have to feel like you're compromising by actually giving me physical files to look over—you could just point me in the right direction."

"Maybe if you're someone who knows where to look and how to find hidden stuff," she said. Then, after a few moments of what seemed to be a severe struggle with herself, she added, "You'd only find a bit, though. There are a few records—paper records that aren't on the 'net as far as I know—of cases like that. Other cases, too; other information. We're not the first humans to band together like this in Tasmania, even if we're the only ones still alive now. I don't know about the rest of Australia, or the world, either; but there was a group here in the mid-eighteen hundreds, then again in the twenties, fifties and eighties. None of them last longer than five or ten years, by all that we can make out, but they always seem to make sure they keep the records in a safe space."

"We all know this is a game of time," Cadence added. "You know, a game of how long until they get us, one by one—how long until they find us and wipe us out. So we do the same thing: make a cache of records and proof. Then when the cycle starts again, the information is out there for people to find when they band together to fight the fae."

"What cycle do you mean?"

"We don't know," said Abigail shortly. "Whoever came before us didn't know, either; there are just periods where everything gets worse for no reason that we can tell. More human deaths, more monster sightings, more fae snatching children. The human cell is usually stamped out whenever each cycle gets to its height."

"That's...interesting," I said, exchanging a look with Jin Yeong. I'd have to ask Zero about when the last trial for a new king Behind had started up, because things running in cycles was too much of a coincidence to actually be one. "So you've got access to those documents, and you might or might not give me access to the ones I want to look at?"

"I'll give access to you under conditions," she said, and there was that pause again. Whatever it was, she didn't like what she was about to do. "And it'll still have to go to a vote first."

Encouragingly, and to remind her that she had something to bargain with, I said, "Cadence said you had a favour to ask."

"Yes," she said, but she was silent for another minute or so before she continued. "I wouldn't ask you if I had anyone else I could ask. I don't like that you're connected to the fae, and I don't like that you're letting them boss you around."

"Thanks a lot," I retorted, but I grinned, because I couldn't help feeling sorry for her. She hated fae *a lot* and while I couldn't really blame her for that, she also had a few bitter pills coming to her. For example, her glorious leader that she had tried so hard to save from the fae, *was* fae. That she apparently needed me to do something for her, and that I was very much involved with the fae, was not as bitter as that fact was likely to be when she learned it.

"You know I'm negotiating my contract with them, right?" I said. "They don't hold all the cards."

She stared at me. "What do you mean, you're negotiating? You can't negotiate with them."

"Everything is negotiable. They give; I give. They take, I take. Not gunna lie, though: you gotta make sure you've got flamin' good leverage, and you've gotta make sure they're halfway decent fae."

"There's no such thing," she said flatly.

"I do not negotiate," Jin Yeong said directly to Abigail, sounding far too pleased with himself. "I give freely. I chose to do so."

"That's what a boyfriend is supposed to do," Abigail told him. She didn't sound impressed, though she smiled as though she couldn't help it. Vampire voodoo: can't do anything about it. "I thought you didn't speak English?"

"He just prefers not to," I said, glaring at Jin Yeong. He wasn't supposed to use Between to translate himself around the humans.

"I bet she puts up with a lot from you, too," Abigail said to him, as if she perfectly understood how annoying he was.

"Here and there," I agreed. "What's the favour you want me to do?"

"I told you about the records," she said, sober at once. "But we've got more than that. We've got stuff that's useful for people who can do the right kind of magic. Artifacts, I suppose you'd call 'em: rings, necklaces. We've never been able to get much good out of them, but we don't want anyone else to get use out of them, either."

There she went again, telling me sensitive information that you shouldn't tell to people you don't trust.

"We've got 'em," explained Cadence. "But we already told you that stuff tends to happen to humans like us."

"And you already noticed that things are starting to get worse around here—the cycle is starting again, which means there's a good chance that in about a year or two, we'll all be dead."

"You want me to keep your trinkets for you so that the fae can't use 'em?"

Jin Yeong gave a small, delighted chuckle that made Abigail redden with what looked like a combination of annoyance and flustered consciousness. "Today is a very enjoyable day," he said, for my ears only.

"Your boyfriend needs to learn that it's rude to deliberately speak so that others can't understand," Abigail said.

He sent her his most dreamy, sparkling smile, and she took only a moment to crack, laughing ruefully.

"He already knows," I said sympathetically. "He's just a generally awful sort of person."

"I am a beautiful person," said Jin Yeong, his nose in the air. "I should be forgiven."

Abigail considered him for another few, rueful moments. "It looks like you usually are. How about it, Pet? Are you willing to keep them for us?"

"I can do it," I said slowly. "But I reckon I know someone who would be a better fit—and safer."

"I'm not very fond of introductions," she said. "And the more people who are introduced to me, the more patterns we put out in the world. We've stayed alive by staying small. Your friend would be in danger if you introduced them to us—is that a risk they'd be willing to take?"

"You don't need to meet him," I said. "I could pass the stuff onto him. You might already know him: Detective Tuatu, at the Hobart cop shop."

She stared at me. "You know him? He knows about us?"

"He doesn't know about you—not yet, anyway. He knows about...well, pretty much everything else. He tries not to get too involved, but he gives me info from time to time. He'd be safe, and he's...protected. He has a few less ties to the other world than I do, too. No fae to stick their fingers into a bit of jewellery they shouldn't be touching."

I was being very strictly truthful, but although Tuatu didn't have any *fae* friends, he did have a very interesting sort of relationship with the North Wind. As far as I was concerned, that just meant he was a bit safer than most humans who knew about Behindkind.

"I've heard of him," said Abigail. "We were—that is, a friend of his was part of our group a while ago. He died just before he was going to bring Tuatu in on it: we had him staking out a location from someone's house."

"Still haven't managed to get someone else in there," Cadence added, with a twisted smile.

"It's a hospital," I told them. So that's what Tuatu's friend had been up to at Morgana's house!

Her voice was disappointed. "What? A *hospital*?"

"Yeah. A sorta prison hospital: it's where Behi–fae keep prisoners who need to be recovered before they can be sentenced or imprisoned. It's nothing important."

"What a waste!" she muttered. "Resources, life—what a reason to die!"

"It caused a bit of a problem for the detective, too. They tried to pin the death on him."

Abigail's eyes fastened on me sharply. "And he escaped?"

"It was a bit hard for them to keep framing people for stuff from the inside of the police force after we kicked them out of there," I pointed out. "They still try to have a go at him every now and then, but he's pretty well looked after, these days, and they can't mess with the cops too much at the moment."

"Level of incidents around the Central Business District went way down a couple of months ago," Abigail said, as though she didn't quite believe it. "That was *you*?"

"It was us," I said. "Us and the two fae. They'd made a nice little rat's nest in there that we had to clear out, but once it was gone, they had a harder time using police support. They've still got a few roots in the police force, but nothing like it was."

She drew in a deep breath, and behind her, Cadence shook her head in wonder.

"You should think about joining us," said Abigail. "If you're trying to do good around here and you don't want to be compromising the good you do, we're an option."

"I'll think about it," I said, and I said it with absolute honesty. I was still eager to know exactly why Abigail had chosen to meet with me again—why she even thought to trust me with her artifacts—but I'd wondered, now and then, what would happen once my three psychos found their murderer and went back to wherever they'd come from, leaving me alone in my house. I didn't think I'd be able to go back to normal life—didn't know that there was a normal life waiting for me. I didn't even really know if I'd had a normal life to start with. If everything with Abigail checked out, it might be a good option for me.

Abigail nodded toward Jin Yeong. "What about him?"

"I go where she goes," said Jin Yeong, shrugging.

"I see." With an honesty that cut right to my heart, she said, "I've got the feeling we'll survive a bit longer with you around, too. We're good, but we're only as good as our talents and our experience. You've got more experience and you're somehow stronger and faster, too."

"Yeah," I said ruefully, "you probably don't really want our experiences."

"Probably not," she said. "I'll get back to you about those files, all right? And I'll think about your friend, too: he's already pre-vetted, even if we'd prefer it was you."

Realising that this was the end of our meeting, I stood up and tugged at Jin Yeong's sleeve until he got up, too. "I'll think about it," I said, since she seemed to expect an answer to that.

Something scratched away in my brain, wanting to be asked, and as we stood there awkwardly, I added, "There was something else."

Might as well go for it. I looked across at Jin Yeong, and he met my eyes briefly before looking away, smiling faintly. It wasn't a promise that he wouldn't tell Zero, of course, but it was a sign of slightly exasperated resignation. "Cadence says she was a pet, and you've got other humans here that you rescued from the fae."

"It's our *modus operandi*," Abigail said, grinning at Cadence. "Find a fae with a human, free the human. Find a human in danger from otherworldly Things, save the human."

"Ever deal with people who just...disappear?"

She shook her head. "Can't. We don't know where they go: it's like they disappear off the face of the earth. Sometimes they come back, sometimes not. We only deal with the ones that we can see."

"Right." Not much good asking them about my great grand-mother, then, I supposed. I said quietly, "Reckon that's it, then."

Abigail hesitated for a moment, then said with a speed that suggested she was trying to get it out before she thought better of it, "You might want to check up on the Standforths. Mother Aileen, son Ralph."

"They're in one of your files?"

"It's the only name I remember outright," she said, "and I don't remember much about the case other than the names. If the group agrees, we'll go fetch the files and go from there. For now, you get one name, and if they decide not to give the rest to you, that's all you get."

"Thanks," I said, and I meant it. She was helping, even if she was doing it rather grudgingly.

"It is *very interesting*," said JinYeong below his breath and untranslated. "So useful. I wonder why!"

"All right. Make sure you keep remembering to leave your friends at home when we meet again, and I'll probably be nice then, too."

"I'll get the door," said Cadence.

Definitely a pet once. I shot her a grin and she grinned back, then opened the door for us. No door, then a door: very nifty, that.

"I'll message you if they want to ask questions or speak with you," I promised Abigail. "And if you say you don't wanna talk, I'll tell 'em that, too."

She stared at me for a few seconds, and I wondered suddenly if she disbelieved what I said. I added, "I wouldn't have done it last time if there had been another choice."

"That's what I meant about being compromised," she said, as if she couldn't help the words tumbling out. As if she'd been wanting to say something the whole time but had been holding herself back. "If they force you to do something—"

I shook my head. "You don't get it. I made the decision that there wasn't another choice. They didn't make me do anything."

"That's what we all think at first," she said, rather sadly. "I'll get back to you about the decision, Pet. Get home safely."

I wanted to say more, but what would she believe? We'd already done better than I could have hoped for. I let Jin Yeong shuffle me through the door and left without trying to convince her further, emerging into the noisiness of Wellington Court on one hand and the busy road on the other.

"C'mmon," I said to Jin Yeong, even though he was the one who had propelled us gently back outside. "Let's get bubble tea for Athelas. I wanna see his face when he gets a mouthful of boba."

It would probably have been a bit of a subdued walk home if it wasn't for the fact that Jin Yeong was still very much strutting along the street; both of us were tired from our fight earlier, and I just considered myself lucky that I was still hopped up on vampire spit. Apart from a bit of stiffness, I was no longer injured.

"What are you so pleased about?" I asked him, but now I was more amused than irritated by his bounciness and there was a bit of a swing to the hand in which I held the bubble tea bag.

"I am a good boyfriend," he said, buttoning the first button on his holey suit-jacket before coming across the missing one and abandoning that particular effort at dignity.

"Yeah? Where'd you get that from?"

"I am doing what a boyfriend is supposed to do. The woman with the red hair said so."

"She meant that it's the base level of what you're supposed to do," I told him. "Not something to be boasting about. But here you are, boasting about it."

Jin Yeong slid me a sly, sideways look. "I think you don't know anything," he said. "When did you have a boyfriend?"

I couldn't help the laugh that escaped me. "That's rude and also true," I said.

I mean, what did I know, really? I knew that I was still thinking about the smile of a merman even though I'd never been on a date in my life, and my only kisses had been with a vampire for the purposes of getting drugged up to fight. What would I expect if I were to go out with someone? What would I expect if I went out with someone who wasn't even human, if it came to that?

Did mermen even ask people out? Would I have to ask him? Heck, was that even something I was capable of doing?

I was still wondering about that with some interest when Jin Yeong took the bubble tea bag from me with a quizzical look and stuffed his other hand in his pocket, swinging the bag between us. He was still sauntering a bit.

"What about you?" I asked him. "Did you go out with someone before...all that?"

This time he answered without suspicion. "I went into the military when I was eighteen: I had no time to date."

"There's a compulsory draft over there, isn't there?"

"Not then," said Jin Yeong. "Then, we were poor and needed food and a house. My sister was working, too, but she was delicate and the work was too hard for her."

"That's a bit rough," I said. No wonder Jin Yeong enjoyed

receiving smiles and admiration and wide-eyed looks: he hadn't had the chance for any of that before he went into the military, and then he'd been turned into a vampire while he was there. "What about afterwards, when you were turned?"

"*Ani*," he said. "Then, it was too dangerous. I was young in blood and it was too easy to make mistakes. I travelled with *hyeong* instead."

Mistakes, hm? The sort of mistakes that left young women dead, I wondered? Probably. It was a good thing Jin Yeong had met up with Zero at that point, I supposed. If you preferred to be a vampire rather than dead, anyway. And if you wanted to learn how to not kill humans.

I nearly asked him if that was when something had happened to his sister, but he was still swinging the bubble tea bag—still sauntering and enjoying the sunshine like no self-respecting vampire ought to do—and I didn't have the heart to bring up unpleasant thoughts again.

"Oi," I said, jabbing him in the side with my elbow, "you'd better stop telling me *I* don't know anything, then. It's not like you've ever dated someone."

He grinned, sharp-toothed and bright. "I learn *verrry* quickly. You will see."

It sounded like a threat, but that's vampires for you: say anything with sharp enough teeth, and you get a bit of bite to it.

"Yeah, we'll see," I said.

CHAPTER SIX

"Pet," said Athelas in pained tones. "What is *this*?"

"Bubble tea," I told him. "Got you the brown sugar one because it had a tiger on it."

"I'm sure that makes sense to you, my dear—"

"I could have gotten you an earl grey," I continued, "but the tiger won me over. It looked just like you."

"I'm eternally grateful."

"Yeah?" I grinned at him. "You haven't tried it yet."

"I'll try it in a moment," he said, without looking any less pained. He'd even forgotten to cross one leg over the other, so he must have been perturbed. "I assume that you didn't return home merely to ply us with—" he looked down at the plastic cup, mildly bemused.

"—bubble tea," I reminded him.

"Bubble tea. Yes. May one ask what the bubbles entail?"

"Boba, apparently. They're all heavy and squishy with brown sugar syrup, too!"

He looked appalled. "Did you *taste* this before you gave it to me?"

"Nah, I stole some of Jin Yeong's."

"That was very understanding of him," Athelas said faintly.

"I gave him some of mine!" I protested. "It's not like we weren't exchanging saliva earlier, anyway."

"What a quaint way you have of expressing yourself, Pet!" he marvelled. "May we assume that you met with some difficulties in your expedition, then?"

"One or two," I admitted. "Where's Zero? He needs to hear this, too."

I could sense him around the place, but I couldn't see him, and if he was downstairs, I should be able to see him: he's too flamin' big and white to be hidden.

"In the backyard," Athelas said. "He's been doing some work with the Heirling Sword—and shaking out a few cobwebs, too, I shouldn't wonder."

"He's really worried about this Heirling cycle, isn't he?"

"I imagine that he would prefer not to die, yes," agreed Athelas. "I rather fancy he is trying to persuade the sword to be less... obliging when it comes to you."

I threw him a rueful look. "He really doesn't like having to tell me stuff, does he? He'd prefer to shove all of this back under the carpet if he could, I reckon."

"It would behove you to keep up with your own training, too, Pet," he said, without answering that.

"Yeah, I don't want to be dead, either. Good grief, do you *ever* take clothes in with you?"

This was an appeal to Jin Yeong, who had just exited the bathroom wrapped in a cloud of scent and a towel and nothing else. He was apparently feeling just as jaunty as he had been earlier, too, because he clicked his teeth at me and sauntered across the room toward the kitchen to fetch a blood bag.

His trip back across to the stairs and—ostensibly—his bedroom upstairs, was just as leisurely, and he was only halfway across when a huge, pale figure loomed in the hallway leading from the back door.

"Jin Yeong," said Zero's cold voice. "Get dressed or I'll send you through the wall again."

"If you do that," Jin Yeong said, taking his blood bag away from his mouth with the wickedest grin, "maybe I will lose my towel."

I heard Athelas murmur, "Life holds few joys in general at my age, but I admit that I am finding it distinctly enjoyable, these days."

"Got you bubble tea," I told Zero.

He ignored me. "I won't tell you again, Jin Yeong."

"At this rate, you're the only one I haven't seen shirtless," I said to Athelas, since it looked like the other two were about to start fighting any minute. "You should work on that."

He gave a surprised choke of laughter and managed to turn it into a cough. "I shouldn't like to enliven the atmosphere any further than it has already been enlivened," he said.

"Can you lot drink your bubble tea and stop threatening to chuck each other through walls or take towels off?" I said loudly. "We've gotta report and all you're doing is arguing."

Jin Yeong put his blood bag back in his mouth with a half-shrug and strolled mockingly past Zero, whose cold eyes didn't acknowledge the provocation by the smallest flicker. I chucked a plastic-wrapped biscuit at Zero and he caught it, too, so he must have been paying attention.

"Thought you said we shouldn't be using the sword," I said as he gingerly opened the tiny biscuit packet and pinched the wafer biscuit between his fingers. I wanted to know if what Athelas suspected was correct.

"I said that you shouldn't pull it out when you're looking for a weapon on the run," he corrected, gazing at the biscuit. He tossed it into his mouth and it disappeared. Didn't even see him swallow; it was just gone. Maybe I'd have to skip the tiny biscuits and get the extra large ones next time.

"You been in contact with your dad lately?" I asked him, by way of a poke in the ribs.

Zero stepped out of the hall and crossed the room to sit in his usual chair. He smelled sweaty, which he didn't usually when he practised with me—that was a lowering thought. He must work harder when he was training by himself, than he did fighting with me. At least I could get Jin Yeong on the back foot every now and then.

"I don't speak with my father if I can avoid it," he said. He looked very tired, all of a sudden. "I've managed to avoid it for some time now. Why?"

"He came to say hello to us today."

The rumble of his voice fairly shook the room. "*What?*"

"Well, he says it was Jin Yeong he came to see, but since we were together—"

"What happened?" he said sharply.

At the same time, Athelas murmured, "Good heavens! Will wonders never cease?"

"Reckon he knows a bit more than you lot will be happy with," I told Zero. It was more than I felt happy with, myself. "He came to tell Jin Yeong to support you in a play for the throne. Spent a bit of time threatening us, and when Jin Yeong said he'd support who he wanted to support, he got pretty stroppy—sent some things made of flowers after us."

Zero gazed at me for quite some time before he said, unexpectedly, "You don't look injured."

"Yeah, we did all right," I said. "I've had a bit of vampire spit, too, so I healed up pretty quickly. Look, I don't wanna say nasty things about your family, but he's being pretty chirpy at Jin Yeong considering the fact that a bit of vampire venom would see him laid out on top of his own flamin' flowers."

"My father has never thought much of vampires or humans," Zero said, with a very slight smile. "I'm glad to know he underestimated you both."

I nearly made a cheeky remark about how underestimating humans, at least, seemed to run in the family, but this was probably one of those times when it would be a bit of over-egging to do it. Let him catch the implication himself.

I saw Athelas direct a small, prim smile at the ceiling, and grinned at him when he looked back down again.

"It would seem, my lord," he said to Zero, ignoring me, "that we made the correct decision by further initiating the pet into Behindkind politics."

Oh, so they'd been discussing that, had they? And Zero had still been complaining about telling me things. Flamin' typical.

Zero made an unconvinced sort of grunting noise, and said grimly, "We can congratulate ourselves when she makes it through the year alive."

"Cheerful," I said. "It's not like I'd be likely to live any longer *not* knowing stuff."

"That is the only reason I agreed to tell you anything of this business," he said.

"Especially now that your dad's poking his nose into stuff," I said gloomily. "He got in my head again and I don't like little worms in my head talking to me."

That made the two of them exchange looks.

Zero asked, "What did he say?"

"Nothing much: he had a few remarks to make about how there wasn't much going on in my brain, but he was leading up to something when Jin Yeong pulled me out of it."

There was silence in the room for nearly a full thirty seconds while Zero passed a hand back and forth over the white stubble on the top of his head and Athelas watched him in what felt like fatherly affection. I remembered again, briefly, the darkness of a forgotten, bloody memory flitting across my mind, and pushed it away. Home was warm and that memory was cold and sharp-edged.

"Would you stay at home if I asked you to, Pet?" Zero asked, abruptly breaking the silence and making me jump.

I stared at him. "What?"

"If I asked you to stay at home: go nowhere, do nothing but stay here safe until the trials are done with, would you do it?"

Part of my brain wanted me to do it: agree and be done with it. Stay at home, be safe, never have to venture for real into the representative messiness upstairs that was my past life and my parents' past lives. Never really do more than poke at little bits of paper and decide every now and then that I *would* investigate properly—tomorrow, next week. Make a little nest for myself again and sink comfortably into it while stronger people than me did the heavy lifting.

"Can't," I said, before I could agree. It scared me how much I wanted to agree. It scared me how similar I was to Morgana, and it scared me to think that I could end up more dead than alive, never more than a shadow on the outskirts of life and forever hiding in my house. "Sorry, can't. There's...there's stuff I gotta do. Stuff I need to know."

It sounded weak, but I knew I had to say it now, with or without actual reasons.

"Very well," said Zero, and there was a hard edge to his voice that was expected, even if it made me sad. "Then be it on your own head."

I opened my mouth to ask exactly what he meant by that, but Athelas asked, "How went it with your human friends, Pet? Or was the *fracas* enough to cause them to abandon the scene?"

"Nah, they hung around and waited for us to get rid of the petalmen," I said, relieved to escape the heaviness of the previous moment. "They said they've noticed more Behindkind popping up here and there lately, too, and they have a theory for it that's pretty flamin' interesting. They also gave us a couple of names to go nosing at to see if we turn up anything—ones like that file you've been looking at."

"Go on," said Zero, and a flicker of cool humour had returned to his blue eyes. "And if you can refrain from cracking jokes about how useful the humans are when you get to know them, that would be useful. I have already acknowledged that a working relationship with them may be expedient."

Relationship, he said. Not partnership. Still, it was a good start, and I couldn't help grinning at him, too, because I *had* been planning on waxing a bit cheeky to remind him that Abigail and her crew were looking like they'd turn out to be very useful.

"I would never," I said solemnly, instead. "But actually, I reckon you're gunna be pretty interested in what they said about why Behindkind are popping up more than usual lately. They say that this sort of thing happens in cycles."

That got their attention at once, the fact betrayed by a faint flicker of dismayed understanding in Zero's eyes that was quickly masked by his usual, cool exterior, and a glow of sudden interest in Athelas' eyes.

"Dear me," said Athelas. "I do wonder what else they know!"

"So do I!" I said frankly. "And it looks like they might be willing to share a bit of info with me, at least. Don't reckon they know about the King Behind and the Heirling cycle, but they did say that whenever it goes into one of the cycles that they noticed, more monsters come out, whatever cell is trying to go around and fight those monsters tends to die pretty quickly, and then everything resets itself."

"They have information," said Jin Yeong, prowling down the stairs. He was still barefoot, but he'd put on a pair of loose trousers and a likewise loose shirt. "They will share with *her*."

It's hard to explain how irritating it is when he says it like that. In Korean, pronouns are different, and if I translated it as *that girl* or *that female*, the feeling and translation would be a bit more correct.

Irritating. I mean, at least he wasn't calling me just *that* anymore, but still.

He caught my scowl and returned a mouthed *mwoh?* at me as if to say "What? What did I do wrong?"

"What an interesting position in which to find ourselves!" marvelled Athelas. "My lord, I really do think it might behove us to join hands with the humans—at least temporarily."

"What sort of information do they have that we can't get elsewhere?" Zero asked.

"Technically, I don't know that it isn't anywhere else," I said. "But Abigail said she's got records from previous groups: apparently they keep them in a safe place because they know they're likely to die, and then whoever finds the cache starts a new group until the next cycle. They've got records from the eighteen hundreds, twenties, fifties, and eighties. Hard copy, and she doesn't seem to think much of it is on the 'net."

"And?" Zero's eyes rested on me, considering and not yet satisfied.

"And she reckons she might have seen a couple of casefiles that are similar to the one we're looking at now—kids who disappeared with their parents, or whose parents were murdered, in a neighbourhood where there were a series of other murders first. Says she'll share 'em with us if the others agree."

I waited for him to ask why it had been so easy; to ask why Abigail was willing to share with us on such a small condition after our relationship had soured. But he didn't. He took it in his stride and merely asked, "Did you tell her why you were asking?"

"Not specifically," I hedged. "Just said we were looking at solving the murders, that's all. I told her the information would be put to good use, and she seemed to be willing for me to have a look at the stuff if the others agree. She just doesn't want to let you lot paw over it, apparently."

"How appallingly bigoted," said Athelas smoothly, his grey eyes mocking.

"I know!" I said straight away, matching his affability. "Can't understand how someone could just lump all of one race together and always talk garbage about 'em like that."

"How delightfully subtle you've become, Pet!"

"Haven't I just?" I held his eyes for just a moment longer, then looked at Zero. "What sort of partnership were you thinking of?"

"I'm not sure yet," he said. "I'll meet with them if need be."

"Yeah? How you gunna do that, then? They don't like you much."

There was a slight beat while he took a moment to get his exasperation under control before he said, "See if you can set up a meeting with the humans for me: somewhere they feel safe."

"I'll try," I said. A while ago I would have said it was impossible, but I felt safe to only mention, "I reckon it's going to be a hard sell, though."

"Do the best you can," he said. He didn't seem particularly perturbed. Must be nice to be so confident all the time.

"What are you gunna do about your dad?" I asked him tentatively. "Seems like he knows or suspects that the cycle is starting again, and I dunno what else he knows but he's not real fond of me and Jin Yeong."

I saw the look that passed between him and Athelas, and wasn't surprised when he said, "Leave my father to me. If he approaches you again, run as fast and far as you can."

"Jin Yeong kept me safe," I said. "Kicked your dad out of my head."

"Then Jin Yeong did one good thing today," said Zero shortly, but the look he shot Jin Yeong was far from friendly.

Jin Yeong received that attention with the sunniest of smiles, which was a turnaround for the books. Usually it's Jin Yeong needling and glaring and snarling while Zero takes it all without any sign of being goaded into a fight.

I wriggled myself off the couch and said, "I dunno what's up with you blokes lately, but if you're just gunna glare at each other, I'm going to get lunch. Happy with corned beef sandwiches?"

"Double stacked with seeded mustard," said Zero immediately, and then looked faintly ashamed of himself. "I mean—"

"Hungry, eh?" I said, grinning. There's no way he'd admit it, but despite everything Zero says about humans, there isn't a better way to his heart than through his stomach, and with human food. I don't know what they get by way of food Behind, but it must be pretty flamin' bad. "Double stacked it is. I got some mustard the other day, so I'll load it up. What about you, Athelas?"

"Seeded mustard, but I *implore* you not to double stack mine this time. I greatly dislike depositing my lunch on my lap midway through a bite."

"No more double stacks for you," I agreed, and trotted off to the kitchen. Jin Yeong had already eaten, so there wasn't really any need to get him food, but there also wasn't much of a likelihood that he wouldn't demand food, either.

When I brought the tray back out, I heard Athelas say as I crossed the room, "Does it strike you as odd that there is so little time between cycles according to the humans, my lord?"

Oh, we were back to talking about *the humans*, were we? I managed to bite my tongue and made myself busy unloading the tray on the coffee table so that I'd stay that way. I had a lot of things to ask and a lot of information I wanted shared, and it wouldn't help my case if I antagonised two of the Behindkind at the table before we were fairly begun.

"Kindly don't elevate your nose at me, Pet," said Athelas, amusement in his eyes. "I refer to *humans* in the basest, most factual way."

Mollified, I gave him his sandwich *and* a cup of earl grey with two biscuits on the side. Zero got two double stacks that would probably last him about two or three hours before he was wandering into the kitchen silently when he thought no one was looking and helping himself to whatever was left in the fridge.

"We can't verify that each of them was an actual cycle," Zero said, ignoring Athelas' aside but not the sandwiches. "To be recognised as the beginning of the changing of a monarch, we have to reach a point where the Harbinger is clearly visible and the Heirlings start appearing."

"Like the old mad bloke running around and chucking bubble tea at Behindkind who are trying to kill us?" I asked.

Zero's eyes flickered shut and open again. "That's all it needed," he said, beneath his breath; a man overcome by circumstances and flamin' tired of it. "I suppose at least that's a good sign: those the Harbinger tends to favour often make it out alive, even if they don't become king."

"Yay for me," I said.

"That aside, for a *past* cycle to be recognised as an actual changing of the monarch, we'd still need to see heirlings that are clearly visible and aware of their function. There would be preparation to compete in the trials, for example."

"Hard for 'em to appear if they're being killed off as soon as someone realises they're likely to be heirlings," I muttered. "Reckon your king has been up to his old tricks more often than you lot realised."

Zero scrutinised at me for long enough to make me worry that I'd said something unintentionally cheeky. Don't get me wrong: I don't mind being cheeky, but I like to be able to do it purposefully.

Eventually, he startled me by agreeing. "*If* you're correct about the murders, and *if* the cycle wasn't completed satisfactorily, a new cycle could begin sooner than the accepted norm."

"Behind itself trying to slough off the old skin that was kept?" mused Athelas. There was a malicious kind of amusement in his eyes. "What a shame, if the King Behind has been expending so much effort to maintain his throne and prevent the cycle, only to have them recurring every thirty to sixty years instead of once every few centuries!"

"You talk about Behind as if it's a person," I said. I plopped down next to JinYeong with my own double stack of corned beef sandwich, narrowly avoiding dripping seeded mustard on his trousers. He glared at me but was mollified by the coffee I passed him as soon as he got a good whiff at what was in there. A bit of cinnamon, a bit of clove—a hecka lotta blood. Vampire spice, I call it.

I took a bite of my sandwich and said through the mouthful, "You know: alive with a mind and a will, picking a king and kicking him out when he's done. Do you mean there's an actual person, or group of people that decide this sort of thing? Like little gods or something?"

I'd never fully understood what the whole thing was, but then, no one had ever really explained it to me properly. I'd learned in dribs and drabs that I picked up from Athelas and Zero—and sometimes from other Behindkind I met along the way.

"There is no such organisation, little gods or otherwise," said Athelas. "The land itself precipitates the change—think of a human equivalent such as an earthquake or a volcano eruption. Perhaps a tsunami. Through a series of seemingly unrelated and vastly separated happenings, the entire earth contracts itself and throws up a wave, or lava."

"Yeah, but natural phenomena don't prompt people to spontaneously give birth to kids who might one day take over the worldwide throne," I told him. "And they don't give the old king the boot, either."

"The natural processes of Behind are different from those in the human world," said Zero. "Behind, the changing of the Kingship is a process as natural as the tides following the moon."

"Unless one decides he wants to stay on the throne."

"*Maja*," said JinYeong. "I also don't understand that."

"Nor does anyone else," Zero said. "That's probably how he got away with it. No one expected it because no one knew it was possible."

"Dunno why you lot didn't just band together and overthrow

him," I said into my sandwich. "If he was doing stuff he shouldn't do."

Zero said evenly, "No one can defeat a king but an heirling, and they were all slaughtered. By the time it was safe for me to be born, and I was allowed to do so, even I could not officially challenge him."

"Bet that's what everyone said before this bloke killed all the heirlings and did another term. *No one can serve more than one term as King Behind. No one can defeat a king but an heirling.*"

"If one was inclined to wonder why a King Behind must have at least a drop of human blood, perhaps this exchange might clear that up," murmured Athelas. "This charming way of thinking is no doubt common to humans."

"Rude!" I said. "You fae are the ones with the rep for being tricky and making the best of your bargains! I'm just saying that Behindkind spend a lot of time saying *Nah, can't be done; isn't possible* to stuff that's actually happening, and—"

"Calm yourself, Pet," said Athelas, laughing softly. "I do beg your pardon! I had no intention of insulting your race, believe me!"

"Heck," I said, staring at him. "It was a compliment, wasn't it?"

"I hesitate to claim it as such, given your reaction," he said. "But yes, it was. I'm really very much in awe of the King's *coup*, and I am likewise constantly in awe of your thought processes."

"Yeah? 'Cos that definitely sounds like an insult."

"That is because you are a suspicious person," Jin Yeong said.

"If I may continue," Zero said suggestively.

"Oh yeah. Sorry. Go ahead. The changing of the kingship is a natural process like a volcanic eruption."

"Exactly," said Zero. I was pretty sure he was fighting a smile, because his eyes were very blue. "So it's not surprising that my father is looking for allies. As soon as it occurs to the King Behind that the cycle is trying to begin again in earnest, I've no doubt he'll look for the heirlings to slaughter them again quietly before they can come out in sufficient numbers to be obvious to Behind at large."

"I should imagine that he'll have a rather hard time of it," Athelas said. He seemed amused. "It will be hard to find heirlings when no one has seen hide nor hair of them since the last official cycle, even if two of them are sharing a roof here. The distinct lack of swarming heirlings seems to suggest that it will be difficult for the king to do what he did last time."

"Which means he'll probably just come after the obvious ones to make sure it's not gunna happen," I said gloomily. "Heck. Doesn't look like being too healthy to be you right now, boss."

"Thank you for your concern, Pet," Zero said, in mild exasperation. "As I mentioned before, that is no doubt why my father is trying to drum up support for me wherever he can."

"Perhaps it really is time for us to seek support where we can get it," suggested Athelas. "And the more unexpected, the better."

Jin Yeong nodded decidedly. "The humans. I agree."

"It's one thing to share information with them and receive information in return," Zero said. "Involving them in the problems of succession will likely lead to their deaths."

"They know the risks," I said. I knew I'd want to have a say in it if I was Abigail, especially when it came to something this big. "But if you're going to bring them in, you'll need to tell them a bit more than they currently know about Behindkind and the rule of the land."

"We'll see," said Zero, and that was a surprise in and of itself. I'd expected a very quick no.

Things really were changing, these days. Maybe I'd even be able to talk them into taking a look at Morgana's case as well—it wasn't like she was eager to accept any help, but it wouldn't hurt to dig into her parents a bit, too.

It's a pretty big life change when someone tells you you're a zombie, and that's exactly what had happened to my former friend Morgana—hence the *former*. Brains, for instance: apparently that's true. Morgana had spent decades living in her room with only ghosts and her barely-there parents to keep her company, and while the person who had almost-killed her parents had arranged for her to feed off their remaining essence, she would need to eat brains if she was ever to leave the house.

She wasn't willing to do that—but then, she didn't know that she was essentially feeding off what was left of her parents, either. She didn't know a lot of things about her new life, and she'd thrown me out before I could tell her very much. Morgana hadn't exactly taken the news that she was a zombie very well. Until then, she'd been the closest thing to a real female friend that I'd had.

At least she still had Daniel: turns out that werewolves who let you boss them around and don't tell you you're a zombie are more welcome to stay around than humans who tell you you're a zombie.

That sounds like I was angry. I wasn't: not really. I was just sad, and horrified, and aware that I couldn't do anything to help other than find a good morgue for brain supplies. Until then, I just messaged Daniel every couple of days to see how Morgana was going, and vainly checked to see if she had answered any of my previous texts sent straight to her. Today was my day for messaging Daniel.

My earlier text of *How's she going today?* had been answered by a pretty pointed, *I'm fine, Pet; thanks for asking.*

Sorry, I replied. *How's the boys and everyone? Morgana kicked them out yet?*

The boys are fine. I sent them to the morgue for supplies, so you don't need to worry about that. We've got what they could find in the freezer and we'll be ready for when she comes around.

OK. Reckon you know how soon that'll be?

Pet.

All right, but you lot better be looking after her. She might be someone.

What does that mean, Pet?

I nearly didn't answer that, because I'd already said too much.

Two minutes later, another text buzzed. *Pet! You better answer me or I'm coming to see you.*

Just be careful, I had texted back. *I don't know anything for sure, but there could be some people after her. Just look out, ok?*

I had no proof, but I had been certain for a few weeks now that Morgana's parents had been killed by the same murderer who had killed mine. Now that we were convinced I was an heirling, that left too many connections between heirlings and the murders, and me and Morgana. If Morgana was an heirling too, having to eat brains would be the least of her problems: she'd have to either avoid the succession fights or learn to fight. Judging from how she'd handled the news of being a zombie, I was willing to bet that she wouldn't want to fight. Maybe it was safer if she stayed in her house for now.

That was a chilling redux of my own thoughts earlier, and I hunched my shoulders a bit. It would be safer for her, maybe, but not necessarily as good for her as facing the reality of her new life. And it wasn't up to me to keep her safe, either. She was in the world Behind, whether or not she wanted to be; what she made of that and how she dealt with it was up to her. If and when she wanted my help, I'd be there. For now, at least she had Daniel.

My thoughts went back to the file Athelas had been looking at for the last couple of weeks: another boy he said was one of the murderer's peripheral victims. That boy and Morgana had a lot in common, and it would be helpful to the investigation if my psychos decided to have a poke around her parents and her past, too, right? Anything to either qualify or disqualify her from being an heirling. She shouldn't have to deal with being a zombie *and* an heirling if it could be avoided.

I took another few mouthfuls of my sandwich, and maybe they were all waiting for permission to eat without being bothered, because there was a silence until I got to the last bite of my sandwich.

I didn't notice that until I was brushing the crumbs off my fingers and it became obvious that Zero was watching me quizzically, his huge arms folded across his chest.

"What?" I demanded defensively. "You need more corned beef?"

Athelas laughed softly as Zero said, "Ask."

"Ask what?" I said guiltily. For a bloke who didn't say too much, he certainly made sure that what he did say counted. He could leave a pet wondering if he knew what she was up to with a certain USB and was encouraging her to open up about it, or whether he actually did just know she wanted to ask something and was letting her know she could do that.

"You've been sulking—"

"I haven't been sulking!"

"Skulking, then," he amended. "You've been skulking around the house for a couple of weeks now, and you're obviously trying to figure out how to ask something, so you might as well come right out with it."

"Why?" I countered. "Are you gunna help me with it if I ask?"

To my utter astonishment, he said coolly, "I don't see why not. We haven't been given work by the Enforcers recently, and we're between cases as regards humans. Ask; we'll help."

"Okay, but you better not take it back when you know what it is," I warned him. If I'd had another sandwich, I could have thought about how I was going to present the idea while I ate, but I didn't have another. Finally, I just said, "Reckon we need to talk to Morgana, too."

"You said we weren't to disturb her."

I couldn't figure out if he was being sarcastic or not, so I just stared at him. "Heck. Look at you blokes lately, listening to me when I ask you to do something!"

"The human girl will not talk," said Jin Yeong. "Not now. Not yet. She is angry."

Athelas lifted a brow. "I fail to see why she should need to talk."

"It's not that she needs to talk, it's that you lot need to listen," I told him. "If I'm an heirling, I reckon Morgana is, too—I think she's another one of your peripheral cases from the twenties, like the file Athelas has been looking at. Zero, you said the peripheral cases might be more useful at the moment than the main cases, so we might as well consider them all. Helps you, helps me."

He actually took it seriously. "Will the girl really speak to us?"

"Reckon she'll speak to you," I said, a bit gloomily. Morgana might have kicked me out because she didn't want to be reminded of the world she was so newly aware that she was a part of, but I was pretty sure she'd still speak with Zero or Jin Yeong. The psychos weren't human—didn't really seem human. I did. And I reminded her that she wasn't human.

Zero nodded; Athelas, now more thoughtful, gave an answering nod. So they agreed. That was nice. I was still getting used to them agreeing with me on things. Really listening.

"I don't see why we shouldn't do some digging," Zero said, wiping his mouth and going for the second sandwich. "Since we're working on peripheral cases due to their similarity, we'll do everything for her that we would do in investigating the others."

"We have more resources, these days," added Jin Yeong. "That leprechaun."

"And 'Zul," I added.

Jin Yeong sniffed into his coffee, but said, "I agree. We should look at this one too."

Athelas sighed faintly. "Must we, my lord?"

"What?" I said to him. "Don't you approve?"

I was conscious of a very faint disappointment. It wasn't like Athelas was encouraging or fatherly or anything; in fact, he had always been downright direct in his warnings about getting attached to himself, Zero, and JinYeong. But somehow he had always been there to slip me information in the most sneaky way possible, or to push me in the right direction when it came to things I was trying to figure out.

If anything, I think I'd expected him to be mildly cheering.

"Disapprove?" he mused. "No. I think not. The timing seems particularly apt."

"Then how come you're upset?"

"I really advise you not to presume too much," Athelas said, his voice sharp. "At this point, it is by no means settled that your friend is an heirling, and I am contemplating a more expedited culmination of events than any of us had anticipated if she really is one and it becomes known. I am quite certain that my lord shares the view that we expected a little more time in which to prepare for it."

"You lot have already had a long time," I told him, and poured him another cup of tea despite his tone. "I'm the one who should be complaining about not enough time. Well, me and Morgana."

"We'll investigate," Zero said, and this time he was looking at Athelas: an even, steady look that said he had already made up his mind.

I saw Athelas sigh faintly, but he said cheerfully enough, "As JinYeong says, we've got quite the support network these days. I would suggest seeing the merman about this particular case, however: the leprechaun makes a good money-finder, but the young zombie's history is some hundred years ago, after all, and I'd guess the merman is more likely to find anything else that can be found on the human internet."

"And the Behindkind one, too," I added. They all looked at me, and I said, "What? You blokes know there's a Behindkind internet too, don't you? It's like the Dark Web; you can't get in unless you know what you're doing. 'Zul told me about it."

"When did he tell you that?" asked JinYeong suspiciously. "I did not hear him."

"You weren't there. I met him at a café the other day when Zero wanted to find out about where to find that plant that burns people's insides out."

"I must once again inform you, Pet," said Athelas, "that the plant in question does not, in fact, burn people's insides out. It sets them on fire perpetually, neither burning nor consuming, and it has a health benefit wherein—"

"I don't care what it's got," I said. "I'm not gunna be eating something that's gunna set my insides on fire. Who would eat that?"

"Someone with a very bad case of internal rot," Athelas told me, with an entirely simulated severity. He was trying not to laugh. "And let me tell you, Pet, that—"

"I don't think I'd bother," said Zero, insultingly. "You know she won't listen to you anyway. Bring in Marazul and the leprechaun if you wish, Pet: you can set them to work on the case Athelas mentioned earlier, too."

"I really wasn't finished going over it," murmured Athelas, but he leant back in his chair to stretch an arm to the small table. "Did you not mention that we'd received a couple of names from the humans, Pet?"

"Yeah," I said. "Ralph Standforth and his mum Aileen. They were the only ones Abigail could remember off-hand: reckon it was a goodwill kinda thing that she told me that much, though. You reckon we're gunna find more of them alive, like Morgana?"

"*Alive* is a very strong word to use in connection with a zombie," Athelas mentioned.

"Yeah, maybe, but she's not in the ground, and neither is Jin Yeong—and you could say that *alive* is a pretty strong word to use in connection with a vampire, too."

Jin Yeong sent me a rather narrow look, but didn't protest.

"I can talk to the merman about your Ralph Standforth as well," Zero said. "Athelas, continue looking into your file and we'll see if we can match up some information; Jin Yeong, get in contact with the detective and see if you can find any information that the police have—over the phone if you must, but not via text. Watch yourself if you go out."

Since it looked like they were ready to start as soon as we finished eating, I piled all the dishes back onto the tray and took them back into the kitchen, hoping to be quick enough to sneak out and go with someone—preferably Zero.

"I'll take the pet with me," said Zero, as I came back into the room, much to my glee. "If only to keep her out of trouble for a little while."

"A hopeless endeavour, I believe," Athelas said.

"Rude," I told them both. They knew I was there, and they still said it—which ought to sound bad but I was pretty happy with it. I'd rather they say stuff where I can hear it than not tell me things and pretend we're working together.

"If my father should choose to approach again, I'd prefer him to do it when I'm there."

"Then shouldn't you be going out to guard Jin Yeong?" I asked. There was still a scent of him, but he must have already left the house while I was dumping plates into the sink. "He's the one your dad was trying to recruit."

Me, he'd just given the creeps and the cold feeling that I ought to be remembering something.

"Jin Yeong can look after himself," said Zero. "I told him to be careful. Come along, Pet."

I came along like the best of pets, and maybe he appreciated that, because he patted me on the head as I passed through the hall ahead of him. I managed not to shy away this time.

I KEPT AN EYE OUT FOR THE OLD MAD BLOKE AS WE HEADED down the street, but he was always inclined to keep out of sight when Zero was around, so I wasn't surprised not to catch a glimpse of him.

"I suppose there isn't a lot of use trying to talk to your zombie friend before we go to the trouble and expense of hiring the merman?" Zero asked me, when we got to the main street.

"Probably not," I said, a bit gloomily. "What do you mean, anyway, the *expense*? How much does it cost?"

"Nothing in human money," he said. "Well, not entirely. He'll want some human money, but he'll no doubt want some exchange of favour as well."

I don't know why that made me feel a sudden chill. It's not as if I didn't already know that 'Zul, as a merman, was Behindkind. They all do business in deals and exchanges.

"I can make the deal myself if it's too expensive," I said. 'Zul hadn't asked me anything for unlocking the USB: I hadn't even thought to question it.

Coldly, he said, "Absolutely not. It's one thing to let you find your feet when it comes to Behind; it's another to throw you to the wolves straight away where bargaining is concerned."

"Marazul isn't a wolf," I protested. There were a lot of things in life that I wasn't sure of, but I was very sure that 'Zul was both warm and kind, even if he was a bit skittish. "He wouldn't try to take advantage."

"Behindkind are taught to take advantage of everyone from their youngest days," Zero told me. "If they don't, they're taken advantage of. Either way, the lesson is learned."

"That's no way to live your lives," I told him.

"There is no other way," he said. "One way or another, we learn."

"Yeah," I said, "but you're not always doing that when it comes to me. So you guys can learn to be selfless—and don't pretend you're not always doing selfless stuff for me, either. I might not always appreciate the way you do it, but I do appreciate the fact that you want to do it."

The more I got to know him, the more I understood his outlook: being taught nothing else but backstabbery and cruelty hadn't made him exactly dark and dangerous like Athelas, but it had twisted his natural protectiveness into something to be feared —and it wasn't just something to be feared from the perspective of someone facing that protective force.

To my surprise, he didn't counter with his usual *we have an agreement*—which I wouldn't have accepted anyway because right now, technically, we *didn't*. Instead, he said ruefully, "This is exactly why I didn't want to keep you in the first place."

"Yeah, can't be having people think you're going soft, protecting humans and not looking down on them all the time, eh?" I said cheerfully.

"I don't want you to die."

"I appreciate that."

I heard him laugh softly, but there was an edge of uncertainty to it. "Pet, I don't want you to die," he said slowly, the words uneven and slightly reluctant. "I don't know why, or how, or—no, I don't even know—there is...something we need to talk about."

I shot an uneasy sideways look at him, because *that thought* had popped up again: Morgana suggesting that there was more to Zero's protectiveness than just...protectiveness.

"All right, all right, don't hurt yourself," I said hastily. "It's all right to have feelings, but you can work through them slowly; you don't have to blurt them all out at once! You don't want me to die. Beauty. That's a flamin' good start."

He gave another low laugh, this one maybe relieved, and said, "While we explore the similarities between these cases— Morgana, Ralph, the others—you're going to have to consider your own case."

"Yeah, it's similar," I said, with the smallest inkling of relief. There was already too much going on in my life to want to worry about...other sorts of feelings. "That's what made me take notice. And you know I'm an heirling now, so these other ones probably are too, which means that the murderer is—"

"Which *means*," he interrupted, "that we're going to have to look at the surrounding incidents to your parents' deaths as well. We're going to need to ask you the same sort of questions that we're asking the others—dig into your parents' lives just like we're digging into the others."

"Oh." Stupid to think, but that hadn't occurred to me. I suppose I'd thought of myself as being somehow outside of the questioning—or maybe just part of the people who were asking the questions. Was I starting to get as aloof and entitled as Behindkind? Thinking myself above the other humans who had had awful things happen to them because I understood a bit more of the world that had brought about that loss?

I shivered. I hoped not. At any rate, this was what I'd wanted, right? An opportunity to really start investigating my parents' deaths—and lives.

"Yeah, of course," I said. "We can talk about that. I don't know much, though."

"Yes," Zero said meditatively. "That's very interesting to me: you not knowing...such a lot."

"Oh," I said again. It was the first time he'd really asked me about my past: the psychos hadn't really been interested in that before. It was enough that I was there, that I was the Pet. It was like they hadn't even thought about the fact that I had a past before that.

Well, maybe Athelas had made a few allusions to it, but that was more in the way of needling, I was pretty sure. Other than that, I had been a peripheral case—best left until the important cases were looked at and lunch was served.

"It will be uncomfortable," he added. "And it might bring up memories that you'd rather not have. You could go somewhere else for a while—visit your friend and work out things with her."

"It's a bit late to be saying stuff like that when we're already heading out together to ask a merman if he can find out anything about Morgana and the others. Are you trying to back out of helping me?"

"No," he said, but I was pretty sure he meant *yes*. "It's just that asking the kind of questions we'll need to ask—treating you like a witness—"

He really didn't think I was capable of dealing with this. I hitched in a short, disappointed sigh, and managed to say without too much rancour, "I've been dealing with my parents' murders for years. Maybe it's gunna hurt, but what else am I supposed to do? Stay out of it?"

"I can handle it all," Zero said, more gently than I'd heard him speak. "You don't need to get involved. Just let me do it."

"Can't," I said laconically. It was the same question he'd asked before, and I couldn't trust myself to think about it for too long before vetoing it.

"Won't," he retorted, with an exasperated sigh of his own. "You don't trust again easily, do you?"

"It's not about trust. Would you let Athelas look into your mum's death for you?"

He stared at me as if trying to figure out exactly what I'd meant by that. "Of course not!"

"Don't you trust him?"

"I trust him enough for that, but of course I wouldn't let him do it."

"Then why would you expect me to let you do it?"

"Because I am fae, and you are human. You can rail against it as much as you like, but there are reasons why humankind doesn't live long when they encounter the fae."

"You and me have already pretty much hashed this out, and I don't think we're gunna agree on it," I told him flatly. "This is something I need to be involved in. I can't sit back while someone takes over my responsibilities."

"I'm *making* them my responsibilities!"

"You don't have that right. I wouldn't give that right to anyone who wasn't prepared to work alongside me instead of over the top of me."

"Then what about your heirling problem? Will you try and solve that by yourself?"

"Nah," I said. "I'm not that dumb. I'll listen to you and take your advice."

"I'm relieved to hear it," Zero said, his voice dry but amused enough through the frustration to make me feel a bit more comfortable. "In that case, try to talk about it by name as little as possible."

"Right, I'll just call it *the-job-that-must-not-be-mentioned*. Why?"

"Jin Yeong said it yesterday," Zero said. "When he told you not to talk about it, and not to pull the Sword from Between. Speaking things into existence is a real thing—speaking them into a more concrete form is a real thing, too. Names, words, concepts; they can all affect the world around you if you speak them too loudly or too often. If you act like they're true, they could become true."

"Heck," I said, shivering. "So don't go talking about it too much or I could speak it into existence even if I don't want to do it."

"And—" Zero hesitated. "Be careful who you give your real name to. The longer you stay as *Pet*, the safer it is for you: you're human, but you've been in our world a bit too often to be entirely safe."

"So what, if you have someone's real name, you can sorta *speak* stuff at 'em?" I stared at him. "Wait, is this a weakness of Behind-kind? 'Cos humans are taught that *sticks and stones can break my bones but names will never hurt me*."

"Yes," said Zero, with a very slight sigh. "Humans are taught that for a reason: a reason they have long since forgotten. By making a bubble of disbelief for themselves, they've cut themselves off from the kind of hurt they might otherwise bring on themselves by tossing their names out into the world every which way."

I grinned. "Who woulda thought it! Humans having a power that Behindkind don't!"

"It's a very small power—"

"Garbage!" I said frankly. "It's *huge*. I've been changing stuff Between by speaking at it—you can't say that's not a huge danger to Behindkind, especially if I know their names. What if I tried to change them into something else? Like something not alive?"

"If you did anything of the kind, they'd probably take you by force and make you king," Zero said, his eyes particularly icy.

"Oh. Right. Got it. Don't turn Behindkind into stuff, even if I know their names. But it still means they can't do anything like that to me, right?"

"They don't have to," Zero said coldly. "They can just kill you."

"Nah, in this situation I'm betting I'm gunna be behind you," I told him. "They've gotta kill you first, remember?"

The iciness vanished in a moment, and Zero actually laughed. Several times in one day. Good grief.

"I'm glad to see there's at least one piece of advice from me that you routinely follow," he said. "Very well. Have the goodness to follow this advice as well, then: when I bargain with the merman, keep out of it. It's always wiser to have someone else bargain for you when it's something you particularly want."

"Got it," I said, and gave him the thumbs up. It wasn't that I didn't trust 'Zul: I'd trusted Zero first, that was all.

CHAPTER SEVEN

WE WAITED OUTSIDE MARAZUL'S DOOR FOR ABOUT FIFTEEN minutes, this time. I had a pretty good idea what he was doing during that time, too: I'd bet a good chunk of my non-existent salary that 'Zul was in there getting himself dry and into his wheelchair. Maybe trying to calm down a bit. He definitely seemed to have a bit of a thing about not wanting to be around Zero.

When the door finally did open, it did so of its own volition once again, and we heard a voice from the deep say, "Come in."

I led the way, which was nice for a change, while Zero gazed wordlessly at the tank walls on either side of us and followed behind. Ahead, the blinds were slanted to let in the sunshine, and shadow and water reflections danced together on the walls. When we entered the living room area, there was already food on the coffee table and a flutter of motion from the kitchen—'Zul rolling around the side of the low kitchen bench with a tray clipped to his wheelchair.

He put a cup of coffee in front of me first, which was weird, considering that there was already food *and* drink on the coffee table, then put another in front of Zero and one in front of himself. That done, he unclipped the tray and stashed it under the coffee table, and sent a sort of bow, sort of head-bob in Zero's direction.

"You can drink that," he said to me.

That would have seemed weird as well, if it wasn't for the fact that the food and drink on the coffee table, at a second glance, wasn't quite...right.

In fact, it was murky and gunky with some kind of magic that might have been Between affecting stuff, but might not have been.

I wrapped my hands around the coffee mug, but didn't take a sip until Zero did, purely out of instinct. I nodded at the other food. "What's this?"

"That," he said, smiling at me quickly and consciously as Zero turned his gaze on the tank once again, "is food that you should not eat."

"Yeah," I said, smiling reflexively. "I gathered that. Why is it so sticky?"

"It's custom when doing business with fae," Zero said briefly, turning back to us. "The food is a trap: whoever eats it belongs to the person who prepared it, and must serve seven years."

"That seems rude," I said. "But whatever floats your boat."

"It's just tradition, these days," Marzul said. "That's why the magic is so obvious: it puts people at ease."

"What, like a *haha, I'd never trick you, that's ridiculous* kinda thing?"

It looked like Zero tried not to, but his lips twitched anyway. "Food is the first step in bargaining, and is a sign of trust. He agrees by providing spelled food that he is not to be trusted, and I agree by refusing to eat the food that although I don't trust him, I still want to do business with him."

"You blokes have a weird idea of what a sign of trust is," I mumbled. "Anyway, now that we've stared at the poisoned food and decided that no one trusts anyone else, are we going to get on with it?"

Zero gave me a meaningful look—the meaning being *remember what I said about not butting in*—and turned his attention on 'Zul instead. "We will begin," he said.

YOU BLOKES, THEY TOOK *SO LONG* DISCUSSING EVERYTHING that I was almost tempted to start eating the stuff on the coffee table even though I knew what it was. My coffee was long gone by the time they came to an agreement about what would be paid and the extent of the work to be done, and I was left wondering exactly when Zero had arranged all this with 'Zul the last two times I'd gone to him on Zero's orders.

I mean, it wasn't like I knew every move that the psychos made, and they left the house whenever they wanted to without telling me where they were going, but I hadn't really expected there to be such a lot involved in the deal. I thought of my loose deal with Five-Four-One, and grimaced a bit. I hadn't told Zero about it, and with this in mind, I doubted I would. I could already imagine the nagging.

The long and the short of it was that 'Zul would agree to dig into exactly three names and what Zero called *their peripherals*, and in return would be granted what sounded like a protected status. That made me grin into my empty coffee cup, because an Enforcer-sanctioned hacker was very law-enforcement-and-the-hacker stereotypical.

They finished it all up with a handshake, which would have been very civilised and human if it hadn't been for the way the entire room went murky like water in a backyard pond as they did so. Interesting, but definitely worrisome.

I started gathering up the empty coffee cups more by habit than anything else, and as I came back from putting them in the sink, Marazul said to Zero, "I was looking into something else for you," in a reminding sort of a way, his eyes flickering briefly toward me.

Much to my annoyance, this made Zero's eyes fall meditatively on me, too. More annoyingly, he said, "Wait for me outside, Pet."

"Okay, but I haven't been fed, and I'll chew through my collar if I don't get fed," I warned him, and went outside. There wasn't anything else I could do—and it wasn't as if I didn't have 'Zul doing stuff for me that I wasn't going to be telling Zero about, either.

Fair is fair.

I was a good pet: didn't even try to listen at the door. Not that it would have done me any good. I felt the fuzziness spring up around the inside of the door as I pushed it shut, muffling the feel of the door from the outside, and knew that someone had put a bit of magic out to keep unwanted ears from hearing what they said.

I waited for Zero downstairs instead, listening to the sound of my stomach rumbling. It wasn't that long since I'd eaten, but I had a suspicion that it was the vampire saliva still running around in my veins that was making me feel as though I needed to eat again. Maybe a rare steak would be a good idea for dinner tonight. Couldn't have me sniffing around after blood like Jin Yeong.

I hadn't quite finished thinking about that when Zero came downstairs and collected me from the wall I was leaning against, and maybe I was still feeling a bit bloodthirsty, because as we headed back toward home, I said, "Oi. You said you'd been in the same room as the murderer once."

There was that brief pause that I'd come to associate with Zero preparing to tell me to mind my own business and then remembering that he was supposed to be sharing information with me.

Then he said, "It was right at the start. It was what made me begin this hunt all those years ago."

There was such a stifled sound to his voice that I asked quietly, "Should I not ask who he killed?"

Another pause; this one a different kind altogether.

"Why do you ask that?" he demanded. "I know you've been keeping secrets around the house, Pet, but that is—"

"Heck," I said, startled. "Am I supposed to have an ulterior motive? You got all chest-coldy, so I got the idea I'd asked about something I shouldn't ask about. I'm not Athelas, you know."

"No," he said, the stifled sound vanishing from his voice to be replaced with amusement. "You are no Athelas. I was not chest-coldy, whatever that is—and *no*, Pet. I won't answer any more questions today. You've had more than enough. We're going home."

THE NIGHTMARE CAME BACK THAT NIGHT. IT WAS PROBABLY the encounter with Zero's dad that did it, or the chilling not-quite-there memory that still iced the edges of my mind when I thought of that earlier meeting. It could have been the terrifying reflection that I was about to have to make good on all my self-promises to really investigate my parents' death that did it, too. I went to sleep with the content knowledge that all my psychos were in the house and woke in the cold of the night, sticky with fear and a prickling shock that sank claws into every inch of my skin.

There it was: a huge, matte shadow with mass but no face, standing by the door and looming over the foot of the bed despite the distance. I already knew that Zero and Athelas must be out, even before I felt the emptiness of the house, because the Nightmare didn't dare visit me when they were at home.

I scrambled up into a crouch in bed, my heart beating madly in my chest, and there was already a sword in my hand, glowing with a warm yellow that glanced stickily off the tarry surface of the nightmare.

I heard my breath shudder in and out, though I didn't whimper, and this time, instead of remaining voiceless and terrifying in its menace, the shadow said quite clearly and coldly, "You might as well ask what you want to know, if you're so determined to understand what happened to your parents."

"What's the use of asking you anything?" I asked it, panting with the effort it took to say the words without crying in fear. "You're just a nightmare. You can only tell me what's in my own head, anyway."

"What's inside your head," it repeated, and took a step forward that *squished* against the carpet in a way that was far too wet and slick. A laugh, black and tarry as the shadow, slithered in the air between us. "Isn't that the point? So many people would be better off knowing what is in that head—and yet you would rather be dead than find out."

"You're saying I know a lot more than I think?"

"No," it said contemptuously.

I don't remember when I started crying, but my face was already wet and my voice rough with fear when I said, "Then what are you saying?"

"That you'll bring me out every time you try to find out what happened," it said. It took another of those awful, squishy steps forward. "Just like today. So stop now, while your little world is still patched together enough to pretend to be real."

"Can't," I said, trying desperately to lift the sword with shaking hands. "It's too late now. Who are you, and why did you kill my parents?"

It laughed again, sending a shudder through me that nearly made me throw up. "Aren't you asking a little much of a nightmare?"

"You're the one who said it was what was inside my head that matters," I gasped. "And you're inside my head, which means I saw you. Why can't I see your face?"

"Why would you want to see my face?"

I struggled to my feet, hiccoughing on a sob, and said as clearly as I could, "So I know I have the right bloke when I shove this sword through your actual chest."

A strand of fragrance, uncurling from the direction of the hidden door, tickled my nose. I straightened my shoulders, because even if the nightmare was between me and the door, I knew exactly what was about to come through that door and I was pretty sure the nightmare would be wishing our positions were reversed in a few moments.

"You better watch it," I said to the nightmare, and this time, my sword arm lifted without hesitation until the tip of the sword was level with that dark, depthless chest. "I've got family again, now. They don't like people messing with me."

Beyond the door, I heard Jin Yeong muttering, then a satisfied exclamation as the hidden door swept aside.

"Ask what you wish to ask," the nightmare said once more, as though my threats were beneath contempt. It shouldn't have been aware of Jin Yeong behind it, but I saw the brief glance it cast over its shoulder as he stepped into the room and for the first time I felt fear for Jin Yeong, too.

Fear that it could hurt him. Fear that he would hurt it before it could tell me what I needed to know.

I hated that I had to ask it—the monster that had murdered my parents. I hated that I had to ask it, but I couldn't help myself. "What did my parents decide?"

Jin Yeong scanned me, sharp and suspicious, and I saw his eyebrows wing up as he caught sight of the miasma between us. There was a beat of utter silence, and Jin Yeong's eyes fastened on the nightmare as it said into the heavy silence, "Your parents chose to die for you."

I sobbed, whether with sorrow or gladness, I wasn't sure, because now I knew: I knew my parents had died for me, and I knew without a doubt that the same murderer had also killed

Morgana's parents. Jin Yeong snarled and stepped forward, right through the nightmare.

"*Naga*," he said to it, flicking his hands disdainfully as he passed through, and it was gone in a moment, as if it had never been. He swept me off the bed and put me on the floor, then took the sword out of my hands. "This belongs downstairs," he said firmly, and started out of the room with it over his shoulder.

I think he was giving me a second to wipe away the tears on my face, because he didn't actually go: he waited by the door until I'd dried my face and caught up with him. He led the way downstairs, but he didn't speak until he'd put away the sword in the umbrella stand.

"You should not be pulling that thing out," he said directly. "If you do not wish to be tied to the throne, you should avoid it."

"Didn't do it on purpose," I said tiredly. "How come you came upstairs, anyway?"

"When *hyeong* and the old man are gone, it is quiet," he said, as though that ought to mean something.

"You're gunna have to be a bit clearer," I said, my voice still slightly snubby.

"Your heart was beating too quickly," he explained. "Usually I can't hear that unless I'm hunting, but in the quiet..."

"Huh. Didn't know you could do that."

"These days," he said, with a sharp grin, "I am very focused."

That made me laugh, and the sickness that had clung to me until now sloughed off. "What, on my heartbeat?"

He shrugged. "Heartbeat, words, expressions."

"Oh." I set the percolator to bubbling, and took some blood out of the fridge. Jin Yeong had scared away the nightmare, and that called for special coffee. "How come?"

"I told you," he said, leaning on the kitchen island to prop his chin in his palms and gaze at me. "I am doing research."

"Right," I said, shaking a few spices into his coffee cup: cinnamon, ginger, a couple of cloves and a cardamom pod to soak. "You know Zero's not getting any less cranky about that, right? Things are gunna get messy around the house if you're gunna start dating people."

Jin Yeong shrugged once again, and his smile was sparklingly, delightedly self-satisfied. "*Hyeong* will do as he pleases."

"Yeah, but—"

"What did that thing say to you?" he asked, so smoothly that I was certain he was just changing the subject. "Why were you crying?"

"It told me to ask what I wanted to ask," I said shortly, turning away to add the blood. I skirted around Jin Yeong and the kitchen island to return the rest of the bag to the fridge, ignoring his constant gaze. "I asked it what my parents decided when it told them to choose between killing them or killing me."

"Ah," he murmured. "So it was that. Just like the other girl."

"Yeah," I said. There was still a cold, wobbly patch in my stomach, because I knew now that no matter what, no matter how hard it was to force myself out of the safety of my house, I would have to do everything I could to find out exactly who and what my parents were. And in the doing of that, I would find out what Behindkind had murdered them and every one else, and make them pay.

My parents had tried to keep me safe, and now I knew that when it had come right down to it, they'd died to keep me safe. I couldn't stay where I was, tucked into my comfortable little house, cowering behind Zero for the rest of my life.

It might have been too much to say that the iron had entered my soul, but—actually, no. It was flamin' fitting to say that the iron had entered my soul. Just let faekind or Behindkind try to stop me now.

"Where are the other two, anyway?" I asked him. I didn't want to talk about the nightmare. Not yet. My decisions and my determinations were still too raw and new to bear too much talking about, and the nightmare itself was still terrifying.

"*Hyeong* is with his father, I think," he said. "The cupboard door was used. I do not know where the old man is. Are you going back up there?"

The incredulity in his voice made me smile a bit.

"Could sleep on the couch, I suppose," I said. Athelas, gone again? I would very much like to know what he was up to so often at night, these days. Especially when Zero wasn't at home to know he was gone. "But then I'll probably just wake up when those two get home, and I have a bit of stuff to do in the mornings before I come down, these days."

"Papers," he said, nodding. "Then we will look at papers."

"Hang on, what do you mean *we?*" I protested, but he had already swept both coffee cups out of my hands and was legging it up the stairs, swift and unhearing.

I chased after him, but somewhere between walking through the door and striding past the bedpost, I discovered that it was somehow more comforting to have a blood-sucking mosquito sitting dignifiedly in my beanbag than it was to enter the same room alone, after a more-than-usually-terrifying nightmare.

It could have been that I could see his tie peeping out of the suit-coat that he'd thrown over my bedpost, too; or maybe it was just that he'd left his shoes at the door and a shoeless vampire was somehow less worrisome than a properly shod one.

I plumped myself down on the other side of the beanbag, prompting a shift of beans that nearly upset Jin Yeong's dignity, much to his surprise, and said, "All right, but none of this leaves my room and no blabbing to Zero about the stuff that you see here, all right? It's *my* stuff until I decide to tell him."

It was going to be tricky enough to explain exactly why and how I had all this stuff when the time came, anyway.

"*Ya,*" he said, recovering his balance and attempting to recover his dignity as well. "*Noh,* you—"

I bopped him on the head with the closest sheaf of papers and said, "*Hajima.*" Gently bopped him, of course; he'd just helped me to get rid of my nightmare, after all. "My name isn't *you*."

"Then what should I call you?"

"Beggared if I know," I said. Even when mum and dad were alive, I'd usually gone by a nickname. I could give him that, I supposed, but it was weird to give a vampire the nickname my parents had used with me.

JinYeong clicked his tongue in annoyance. "Ah! This is irritating! I will give you a name."

"You can't just *give* me a name. I'm not a dog."

"But you will not tell me what to call you," he protested. He thought about that for a while, glowering, and added, "And I will not call you *pet*. You are not my pet. I have decided."

I made a *pft* at him. "*You* decided? *I* decided."

"I also decided."

I looked at him suspiciously. "Yeah? What made that happen?"

"*Hyeong* told me that I must call you *pet*."

"That's why you've suddenly decided not to do it?" It wasn't like that showed his personality in a particularly winning light. More, I felt disappointed, and that was a weird feeling to associate with JinYeong. "You just want to irritate Zero?"

JinYeong, looking annoyed, said, "That is not the *point*! You purposely misunderstand me!"

"Hang on, why are you the one getting cranky?"

He took in a deep breath through his nose, and I could have sworn he muttered something in Korean about emotions and *too hard*. I nearly asked him if he was trying to tell me that I was too emotional, which would have gone down like a lead balloon, but he got in first.

"I am *saying*," he said, "that I do not always obey *hyeong*. And that when he thinks I am obeying him, I do so only as far as it seems good to me."

That brought up an interesting question.

"When did Zero tell you to call me Pet?"

A frown moulded itself between his brows, as if it wasn't the question he had been expecting. "Last year. He...reminded me again yesterday."

This time, I was the one frowning. "Is that why you were sucking on a blood bag when I got out of the shower yesterday? Hang on, is that why he threw you through the wall?"

"Of course," he said, matter-of-factly. "Why else would he do it?"

I opened my mouth to tell him exactly why else anyone would do that, but he hurried into speech before I could, as if he was well aware of what I was going to say.

"That is not important. Today, I need a thing to call you. I do not like *Pet*, you do not like *noh*; also you object if I call you another name."

He stopped and thought, then said a word in Korean, tentatively.

In the Between-edged translation, it came out as *thou*.

"The heck?" I said, startled. "You trying to give Shakespeare a run for his money?"

"You have a real name," he said, looking at me through his lashes. "You could give me that."

Was it actually possible to give him my real name? I found myself settling into a thoughtful silence as a series of small thoughts fluttered past to be considered. Now that I'd had my little discussion with Zero about names, I wasn't sure I wanted it out there, even if Behindkind couldn't hurt me with it. There were other kinds of hurt you could get from someone who knew your name, and I wasn't quite sure I trusted Jin Yeong enough to give him my real name just yet.

"Maybe later," I said at last.

I saw him grin, and he looked satisfied. It didn't occur to me until a few minutes later that he hadn't expected me to give him my name at all.

"You testing me?" I asked him suspiciously. "Making sure I'm not going to do anything silly if someone asks for my name?"

"*Ani*," he said. "It was not a test. Not that sort of test. I want that paper—give me that paper."

I gave him the paper, but instead of settling down to my usual scattershot leafing through papers that hadn't yet yielded much useful information, I asked him, "What do you blokes usually do about memories?"

He flicked a look at me over the paper. "You already had a nightmare. Why do you want more memories?"

"The nightmare said my parents chose to die to keep me alive," I said. I was surprised at how easily it came out. "And there was something that nearly came out yesterday with Zero's dad, and I don't remember either of those things."

"Ah," he said, and although it was a small word, it was big with understanding. "You think there are missing memories?"

"Reckon so," I said glumly. "That's what Zero's dad said—he said there wasn't much there in my head but my parents and you, and that's how I stopped him from being able to see what else was there, too. I just let little things bob up where he could see them."

He gazed at me for quite some time before he said, "I have something else to say, but for now we will talk about your parents. You think you had some training—training to forget things?"

"Maybe training not to think about things," I amended. "It was—the first time I dealt with Zero's dad, it was like I already had the reflex memory to do it. Only I think I've been doing the same thing to myself..."

That was the only way I could think that the alien flutter of memory could have come from my own head without me knowing it was there.

"Ah," JinYeong said again. "Memories are...difficult. The old man will maybe help you."

"That's a good idea," I said, settling further into the beanbag and yawning. "I'm gunna do that. For real this time: I won't just pretend."

While I was still thinking about that and falling into a bit of a doze, Jin Yeong murmured, "What *hyeong*'s father said—I am in your head?"

"Yeah," I said sleepily. "It's probably because you were chucking yourself in front of swords for me again."

"Is that what it was?" he said thoughtfully. "That is interesting."

"No, it's flamin' suicidal," I mumbled. "I already told you: you gotta stop doing stuff like that."

He might have said something like, "I told you that I do as I please," but I was only half awake by then and he was a bit mumbly as well.

I don't know which one of us fell asleep first. It should have been me, because Jin Yeong doesn't *need* sleep, but I remember protesting sleepily that there was no *room* when his head dropped down beside mine on the beanbag, shoving clumsily and ineffectually at the green and grey shirtfront my curled fists had been resting against. Catlike, Jin Yeong simply stretched around the push and curled up more comfortably on the beanbag, yawning.

It wasn't like the nightmare would be able to fight through that cloud of perfume, though.

I went to sleep again.

I THINK I'D PROBABLY EXPECTED TO WAKE UP WITH THE Nightmare again regardless, but I hadn't expected to wake up the next morning with a sick feeling in the pit of my stomach. I opened my eyes to gentle early morning light and a slightly squishy warmth that was the beanbag around me; another warmth that was far tighter and solid beside me.

"Think I made a mistake," I mumbled to that muddle of early morning light and perfume. Guilt and regret bit into me, making my insides curdle. "Reckon I should have just let it all sit."

Beans squished and squeaked as Jin Yeong bent his neck to

peer down at me. "You are still asleep," he said. "Don't talk about useless things right now."

"Tell Zero," I muttered, the words sticky with sleep. "Tell him I don't want to do it. I'll just stay home and we can look at other cases."

Jin Yeong made a constant murmur in my ear that was fractions or equations, I wasn't sure which, because I fell asleep again too quickly. I didn't wake up until the sound of snarling tore me from peaceful dreams, and the warmth that curled around me was yanked away, spilling me and the beanbag sideways.

I protested my annoyance to the carpet, and sat up in time to see Zero fairly carrying Jin Yeong toward the door, one huge hand around his throat. Jin Yeong, dark-eyed but remarkably calm, snarled only a little; and with a self-control I hadn't expected, didn't bite the arm that was definitely close enough to bite if he had really fought for it.

I threw the closest cushion at Zero, hitting him square in the back of the head, and he turned around to stare at me.

"That's my emotional support vampire!" I said crankily. "Put him down!"

"Pet—"

"I was *asleep*!" I snarled. "And I was warm! Now I have carpet burn and I'm awake!"

"Don't let the vampire into your bedroom," Zero said, cold and warning. "In fact, no other men in your bedroom, either."

"First of all, *dad*—"

"Don't call me that!"

"First of all, he's not a man. Second of all, what the heck kind of a man is ever going to set foot in the house with you lot in here?"

I didn't like how thoughtful that made him look.

"Jin Yeong is still a man," he said at last. "And you shouldn't be letting him in your bedroom."

"Fine to say now!" I snapped back at him. "Nobody minded

when we were looking for Athelas. Then it was all *no, the couch isn't comfortable enough!*"

Zero, taken aback, protested, "I didn't say that! And things were very different at that point—"

"Tell you what," I suggested, more awake by the second and still very annoyed to be awake. "You put him down and we can all go downstairs and have breakfast like normal people. Or don't put him down and I'm going to kick you in the flamin' shins!"

Zero turned his back and marched out of the room anyway, and I thought I'd have to chase after him to make good on my threat, but he put JinYeong down outside the door, with a care that was as close to sarcasm as I'd seen from him.

JinYeong grinned at me, and then at Zero, who received the look coldly. The coldness seemed to please JinYeong, because he fairly sauntered across the living room and down the stairs, hands in his pockets.

That meant Zero had no one but me to glare coldly at, which he duly did.

"Had the nightmare again," I explained, taking pity on him. I still wasn't sold on the idea that he was keen on me, but he was definitely very annoyed at me having someone in my bedroom. And it wasn't that I wanted to explain myself; it was more that I didn't want him feeling bad about ridiculous things for no reason.

"I see," he said slowly. "Then sleep on the couch downstairs. One of us can wake you if it begins again."

I found that I didn't like the idea of him telling me what to do even if he *was* keen on me. *Especially* if he was keen on me.

"This isn't something to do with Behind, where I have to obey you," I pointed out. "I'll sleep where I'm comfortable sleeping, and unless JinYeong suddenly falls in love with me there's no problem sleeping next to him."

Zero, his blue eyes startled, said, "What?"

"Means there's nothing to worry about," I explained. "Jin-

Yeong gets all mathematicky when I can't sleep; does wonders when you're hopped up from a nightmare."

I started across the room while he was still standing there, and I heard him say, "What exactly do you mean, if Jin Yeong falls in love with you?"

"Well, it's like saying *if hell freezes over*, isn't it?" I tossed over my shoulder as I went down the stairs. "Nothing to worry about and all that."

"Is it really?" came Athelas' voice through the bannisters. "What a lot I'm learning this morning!"

From the sound of that voice, I would have guessed that he was smiling slightly, but when I got into the lower living room and caught his eyes, he was utterly serious.

Eyes roaming my face, he said, "I take it there was a reason Jin Yeong was keeping you company last night."

"Got a visit from an old friend," I told him. How could I go about asking him for help? Would he help? What would he ask as payment if he did? "You're not gunna scruff Jin Yeong too, are you?"

"I wouldn't dream of disturbing myself so much. Perhaps breakfast can wait a little longer, my lord?"

"I'll stretch and work out first," Zero said, and strolled toward the back door. He'd been doing that a lot more lately—like he expected to have to fight a lot more than usual soon. That was a sobering thought. Was he preparing to face his father, or was he just doing more work with the Heirling Sword to try and persuade it to stop coming to me so easily?

I plopped down on my side of the couch and blew my cheeks out. The house felt normal again, which was nice. Or maybe it just felt safe again as a result of Zero being home, I wasn't quite sure.

"You saw the nightmare again, you say?"

"Yeah," I said. "A bit different this time, though. It told me to ask what I wanted to ask."

"I rather think you must have seen our murderer at some point, Pet," Athelas said.

"Yeah," I said. "Figured."

"Did you indeed? I would be curious to know why."

"Heard its footsteps," I told him, pushing past the wobbly bit of me that tried to make me stop thinking about the memory. "They went—they were squishy. That's what my footsteps sounded like when I went—when I went out into the living room and found mum and dad. They wouldn't have sounded like that unless it'd already been out there and come in to see me afterward. Figure that's why I've got the nightmare in the first place."

"I take it the nightmare doesn't usually do so?"

"Nope. First time. Still didn't see its face though: don't know what that's about."

"So very interesting," Athelas mused. "And yet, we still can't identify our killer."

"Yeah," I said thickly. "Interesting."

Ask. Ask for help, insisted my mind, but then Jin Yeong strolled back into the living room from the kitchen, interrupting the moment. He shoved a cup of coffee under my nose, then headed out to the backyard almost without waiting for me to take it.

I said, "Heck," quietly and thoughtfully. I still wasn't used to people bringing me coffee instead of me bringing it to them.

I sipped my coffee while Athelas seemed to reflect on his own thoughts, and wondered if it would be too much to make them eat toast for breakfast again.

Interrupting those thoughts, Athelas said, "Apparently we need to have a discussion, Pet."

"Oh, is that why everyone vanished?" I said, a bit sourly. Maybe not toast, then. "What'd I do wrong this time? If it's about me learning how you do your healing thing—"

"Ah, is that what it was?" he said to himself, in quiet triumph. "I knew someone had been doing magic in the house, but there was never enough of it to be sure. No, I was not referring to your attempts at healing magic; I was referring to the fact that my lord wishes us to discuss those things pertaining to the death of your parents and your recurring nightmare."

"He does, does he?" I said briefly dipping under the influence of the same instinct that I always had when someone tried to talk about my parents—dodge, distract, dismiss. Only this time, I saw it in the cold light of day instead of just following it blindly. Zero might be pushing like this out of some hard-headed desire to make me fully understand what I'd taken on, but I was just as determined to do it and I needed to be aware of those slippery instincts that tried to stop me. And I still had something to ask, myself.

Athelas merely waited. I think he had some idea of the tug-of-war going on inside of me.

I said, "I mean, yeah, all right. Just—I don't know what I'm going to remember. Everything from the night itself is pretty slippery, and I don't think what I remember happening is all that happened."

"We'll come back to the night itself later," said Athelas easily. "For now, let us consider other matters."

He stopped, to all appearances deep in thought, and I prompted, "For instance?"

I wasn't sure I was happy with the way this was going. Surely the first step in figuring out why my parents had been murdered was to make sure we knew all that had happened on the night? If we didn't, how was I supposed to segue into asking Athelas about finding missing memories?

"For instance," he continued, as though he had never stopped, "you said that you spent some time with friends out of state. A little unusual, was it not?"

"I s'pose," I said, taken aback. This was very far from what I'd expected. "Mum and dad didn't really like me going over to visit friends, so I reckon I must have been a bit surprised when they let me leave the state."

Athelas tilted his head. "You *reckon*. Indeed. I'll move on to something else for now; we'll circle back later, I believe."

"Sounds ominous," I mumbled. I sipped my coffee again, and discovered that the wriggling somewhere in the region of my ribcage was the tie frog, struggling out from under the couch cushion. I rescued it, wondering who had shoved it in there, and asked, "All right, what next?"

"Deaths in the neighbourhood, my dear."

"Flamin' heck! You make it sound like we're the murder capital of the state or something." There was my mind doing the *dodge and distract* thing again. It was so hard not to do it! More cautiously, I pressed on. "I mean, there were actually a lot of deaths in Tasmania back then, but they weren't in my neighbourhood; they were out Kingston way, and up in Launceston, too."

"We can consider Launceston at a later point. What sort of deaths?"

"Mum and dad wouldn't tell me," I said. "They just said people had been killed, so I had to be careful to be inside before dark, and only to travel on the main roads—make sure I shake things up."

"What exactly would *shaking things up* entail, Pet?"

"You know, come back by bus if I went out walking, or come back walking if I went out by bus."

Heck. Five was right—what kind of parents taught their kid how to discourage ambush by coming back home a different way than they came out? Because that's what that was. Zero had taught me that, too, and my memory had squirreled away that little bit of my past under the heading of *unimportant* and *don't need to think about it.*

Memories, said my mind. Gotta ask about finding sneaky memories.

But Athelas was still asking questions. "Didn't you see the deaths on television?"

"We didn't have telly," I told him. "Saw a picture in the papers, though: someone had drawn a pentagram around one of the bodies and really stirred things up.

"How very interesting!" murmured Athelas. "So that's why they weren't seen as part of the pattern. My lord will be very interested!"

"What, you reckon they were the main murders?"

"Of course. We came across a few cases similar to yours and Morgana's, but not one for every set of murders, so—"

"So that's why you weren't sure it was connected." I frowned down at my toes and asked, "How come they're being killed? I can understand if someone's trying to kill off heirlings, but what about all the other deaths around it?"

"That," said Athelas, "is exactly our problem. Let us continue."

CHAPTER EIGHT

One of these days, I'd be able to walk down the street without being followed. That's what I told myself, anyway. Now that I knew I was an heirling it seemed less likely: I'd just keep getting followed until the day one of my followers managed to kill me or capture me, or whatever it was the King Behind did to people who were fated to fight for his throne.

Where was I? Right. I was being followed.

Well, *we* were being followed: me and Jin Yeong, off to check out the house that Ralph Standforth and his mum used to live in. Early that morning, Zero had knocked at my bedroom door to demand breakfast and sword practise, and while Jin Yeong and I were training in the backyard, he'd slipped away—to see 'Zul, probably—and returned with an address for us. Of course, he didn't tell us what he and Athelas were going to be doing while we were off chasing a house, and I found that I had again missed my chance to ask Athelas about how a person could ferret out sneaky memories.

I'd only got a few steps down the street with Jin Yeong before I realised that we were being followed; luckily for me, I knew who it was that was following us. Today he was wearing a singlet instead of a full shirt, his tattoo faded purple across his shoulder and the hair under his arms sticking out with a wiry exuberance that was just as disturbing as his beard hair.

"The one with the hair is following again," said Jin Yeong, faintly irritated. "I do not wish to bite it, but—"

"Heck no!" I said hastily. "You'll probably catch something nasty if you bite *him*. He's not doing any harm."

"He smells of—do not tell me that I smell also!"

I grinned at him. "One of these days I'll have you trained to insult yourself. Oi. Why did Zero say to ask the neighbours before we go in?"

"The merman said there were rumours of ghosts," he told me. He didn't grin back, but he looked less offended. "*Hyeong* thinks it will be wise to ask questions first."

"What do you think?"

"Me? I think that humans think many things are ghosts that are not ghosts."

"Well, I thought ghosts were people, so that figures," I said, shrugging. "So long as it's not another one of those shades—don't reckon I want to see one of those again."

We took a bus up toward the old brewery in silence, listening to the wheezing of the engine while person after person got off, and when the bus became empty and we were only a few stops away, I nudged Jin Yeong with my elbow.

"Oi. Reckon he's still there?"

Jin Yeong looked across at me, and it struck me that his eyes were wary. "It is a different person," he said. "It is not you. Nor the little zombie."

"Yeah," I said. "But you've gotta admit that the cases are pretty darn similar. And they never found that boy that Athelas is looking into, either."

"Human police," said Jin Yeong, with a small, derisive lift of his upper lip, "are very useless."

"Hey, you couldn't find me."

"You do not smell like a human."

"First of all, that's rich coming from a vampire soaked in cologne. Seriously, what are you, marinating? Second of all, you didn't smell that Morgana was a zombie, either, and I would have thought a dead person would be pretty easy to smell."

He shrugged one shoulder. "I told you. You are pretending you don't remember. I had not before smelt a zombie, so I did not know what they smelled like. I am not as old as *hyeong*."

"What if this kid was something else, too?"

A brief beat passed before Jin Yeong said thoughtfully, "*Ah. Kurol su isseo.*"

"That's what I thought," I said gloomily. "Oi. You reckon the murderer offered this kid's parents the same thing he offered Morgana's and mine?"

"If we find him, we will ask him," said Jin Yeong, showing his teeth very slightly.

"He'll only be around if he's been turned into something awful like Morgana," I said. There were no good outcomes here. "He disappeared somewhere in the twenties. No way he's still alive in the normal way."

"*Hyeong* says that heirlings live longer than natural humans."

"When they're not killed by the king or the Family," I mumbled, not entirely politely. That made sense: the bit of vampire spit that often ran around in my blood kept me faster and stronger, and I could well imagine what a drop of other Behindkind blood could do, especially if it actually *belonged* in the body. "Hang on, does that mean that—Whoops! this is us! Quick, press the button."

Jin Yeong disdained to touch the button, but he did stand up, and the bus stopped for him without us having to say a word. I called out a *thanks!* to the driver, but she was in her own little hazy world of vampire-glamour and would only gaze after Jin Yeong as he alighted.

"Looks like you got a new fan," I said, grinning a bit. I took a quick look around us and added, "Which one is it, again? Number seven? It's not the block of flats over there, is it?"

It wasn't that they didn't look old enough to have been around since the 20s, it was just that until now, all the kids I'd heard of in my situation had been in their own houses—nothing so much as even semi-detached.

Jin Yeong shrugged. "It is easier to talk to the neighbours like this," he said.

"Yeah, but which ones should we start with?" There was a building across the road, which might give a good view into the apartments across the street, but the flats next door would probably be more likely to have heard something.

"Start with the flats," Jin Yeong said decidedly. "People who live next to each other know everything about the others."

"Neighbours, then? All right. I never shared walls with anyone, so I wouldn't know."

It was a nice area, not far from the old brewery, and everything was old brick, even the flats. Next door to our right, an old double-story place slouched up against the brick of the flats, and maybe it was just a trick of the old timbers, but it really did look like it was slouching.

"Looks like it's about to try to bum a smoke off the place next door," I said under my breath. The house on the other side was a lot more respectable, but nowhere near as character-filled: one of those tidy new red brick things in a single story, with a bit of a jungle behind it that looked like it went behind the flats as well. Beyond that, I saw a fence rising high and battered, and the edge of an old tin shed roof behind that.

It wasn't until we got up onto the covered veranda that I saw something that made me stop.

"Hang on, the number's wrong," I said in surprise. There was a big number five on the main doors.

Jin Yeong frowned at it and said, "It is that building, then," pointing at the house next door to the flats.

"That one says nine," I told him, craning my head around the pillars. I headed back across the patio and down the stairs to get a squiz at the house on the left, and eventually found a wooden number three hidden in the bushes on the last remnants of a fence pole.

"Where's number seven, then?" I demanded. I glared at the house-fronts, as if that would do any good, and backtracked a bit more so that I could see a bit further over the back fence of the place on the left. To Jin Yeong, I said, "Oi. What's the bet that there's an old, mungery house hidden behind this lot with a number seven on the gate?"

Jin Yeong clicked his tongue. "Ah. I do not like this."

"Yeah, it's a bit Aussie gothic, isn't it? Well, we might as well knock on a couple doors, anyway—we could try the flats that overlook the back, too."

No one answered when we knocked at the first door, but I wasn't really surprised. Not only was the garden overgrown and potentially imbued with a life of its own, but the door was rusted at the hinges and if the musty smell was anything to go by, no one had lived there for quite a while. We went on to the house on the right next, wary of the bow in the sunken wooden stairs, but no one answered there, either.

Jin Yeong gave a bit of a sniff and said distastefully, "Nothing here but mould."

"Into the flats, then, I s'pose," I said. "We'll check around the block later. There's gotta be another way in from around the back."

An untidy office lady let us in when we buzzed at the main door; she didn't seem surprised to hear that we were interested in the house behind the block of flats, and invited us to take a look from the stairwell windows further up before coming back down to her office on the first floor.

"Just make sure you blur my face out if you're doing a video," she said, which made me exchange a startled look with Jin Yeong.

"Maybe they get a few documentaries and ghost hunters?" I suggested, as we climbed the stairs to the second floor. The stairwell windows were big and bright, and at the second floor we had a good view into the narrow strip of concrete that passed for a backyard, and the little house I suspected to be number seven. You could see right into the windows if you tried; big, reflective things under awnings that gave them the look of heavy-lidded eyes that sometimes seemed to move with odd shadows.

We had a quick look along the corridor there, but the hall was cobwebby and looked unused, and the four units there, from seven through to ten, all looked distinctly dusty to me. We went onto the next floor.

From the third story, it was easy to see the layout of the area behind the block of flats, though not so easy to see what was happening in the actual courtyard of number seven. It was surrounded on all sides by older houses, and had snuggled itself into a courtyard overhung by verandas, trailing vines, and overgrown trees. The only way in or out seemed to be a thin lane that vanished into a barely-wider strip that ran between five and three and stopped just before the main road.

"Looks like us going back down to see the landlady," I said gloomily. "The only places you can see in from are on the second floor, and it didn't look like there was anyone there. Not much use trying to ask neighbours when there are none."

We found the office door open for us when we got back down to the first floor. That office looked out toward the front, too, unlike the unused and padlocked office further down the main hall.

"Not many people on the second floor," I said to the office lady, by way of starting the conversation.

"Nope," she said. "Can't sell or rent those flats for love or money. As soon as someone moves in, they move out: too much weirdness from the house behind. I thought that's why you came here—you weren't looking to rent, were you? It's good, cheap rent for a couple just starting out."

"Sorry," I said. "We're not looking right now. We just heard there was a bit of strangeness about the place behind, and look into that sort of thing. What sort of weirdness did you mean?"

She shrugged. "Screaming, ghost sightings, people with special equipment going in there to investigate paranormal events. There's always some sort of a fuss going on. The last tenants from unit ten said they saw the house eat someone, and I had someone tell me that it tried to *crawl into their flat*."

"Nice," I said. "That's all we need, houses that eat people and try to sneak through windows."

"Tenants are skittish," the woman said, "and normally I'd say they're just getting overwrought about an old house, but I've seen a few things myself. I'd avoid the place, if I were you. I'm selling up as soon as I can."

"Thanks," I said. "That's...useful, I s'pose."

"If you haven't got any more questions, I'm about to head out," she said. She wasn't rude, just matter of fact. "I don't like to stay here for too long at a time; your mind starts playing tricks on you."

"Nah, that should do it," I said.

We were halfway out into the hall again when the office lady called out to us, "Wait! If you really want to talk to someone, there's the old woman in number nine."

"Thought you said seven to ten were all empty?" I said, stopping.

"All of 'em except that one," she said. "The tenant's a bit odd, but she doesn't seem to mind whatever happens over in the next yard, so I kept her there. She might be able to help you a bit."

So back upstairs we went. I wasn't particularly hopeful, and

Jin Yeong gave the barely-concealed impression of impatience, but it was our last shot.

"If this one doesn't have anything to say other than that the house ate someone or tried to sneak in over the balcony, we might as well make a go of it by ourselves," I said when we were outside the door of number nine.

"*Ne*," said Jin Yeong. "This is boring."

"Well, at least we're not being eaten by a house," I said cheerfully, as the door opened.

I'd been looking for someone at about eye height, so it took a couple of moments just staring at a yellow-papered wall in the distance before a very polite, very tiny *ahem* drew my eyes down to about chest level.

There was an old woman there, about as diminutive as her cough, and looking like the skinnier sister of Tweety Bird's owner. White hair that nearly glowed, plump bun, cheerful apple-cheeked face—even the crafty, glittery little eyes.

"I don't think you can really say *eaten* when it comes to a house, can you?" she asked, in a precise, warm little voice. "I always thought that *consumed* is more evocative in that case."

"Hadn't really thought about it before now, actually," I said. "Sounds like you've given it a bit of thought."

"I've lived here for twenty years," she told me, as if that was an answer. Maybe it was. "Are you here to talk about number seven? Do come in; I'm Vesper."

Jin Yeong, who always likes a direct invitation, looked pleased and stepped inside as soon as Vesper took down the security chain. I couldn't help thinking that if things were as scary as the office lady had made them seem, the chain might have been put to better use on the door of the patio that I could now see across the room.

"That's exactly what we came for," I told her. If she was willing to talk, there was no need to beat about the bush. I looked around the room curiously, all soft yellow wallpaper and fluffy cushions, and wondered how this obviously warm and pleasant woman had found herself alone in a flat opposite what was said to be a haunted house. I moved further into the room after Jin Yeong, and tipped my chin at the windows that faced number seven. "Bet you've seen some weird stuff, living across that place."

"The world is full of oddness," she said contentedly, shutting the door behind us. I don't know exactly why, but I was relieved when she didn't put the security chain back on the latch. "And sometimes a person discovers that the oddity is themselves."

She looked at me with her sharp old eyes and added, "But that's not what you came to hear from me, is it?"

I grinned. "I was hoping for some stories."

"What sort of stories, dear?"

"Anything you think is important to know about number seven," I said, shrugging. "Anything you want to tell us."

"I suppose you'll be wanting to get in there. People usually do."

"First, stories," Jin Yeong said. "After, we will go in."

"How pleasant, for a change," said Vesper happily. "The others would keep rushing in and we know what's said about fools and rushing, don't we? Dear, would you mind putting the kettle on? We might as well have tea and pound cake if we're going to tell stories."

"I knew we came to the right place!" I said, making a bee-line for the kitchen.

Vesper sorted out the cake and a teapot, which was nice from my perspective, and when we were all seated with a piece of raspberry poundcake and cup of tea—*sorry, dears, I don't have coffee, is that all right?*—she said cheerfully, "Well, this is nice, isn't it? What would you like to know first?"

"What kind of a house eats people?" I asked her at once.

Jin Yeong raised his brows at me, but Vesper poked him in the side of the thigh with a knitting needle that had just materialised in her hand and said, "Never beat around the bush, young man. At my age, I don't have a lot of time."

She began knitting in a businesslike sort of way and added, "What kind of a house eats people? Well, possibly it's more important to consider what kind of people would deliberately go into the sort of house that's said to eat people, isn't it?"

"Either people who are trying to disprove that kind of thing, or people who are trying to prove it," I said slowly. "You mean, the house doesn't like being bothered?"

"I shouldn't think the house cares about anything; it's a house, you know."

"Oh. Then what do you think is happening?"

"I've not the slightest idea, my dear. I can't explain it at all."

"You said you had some stories," I prompted, trying not to grin. I didn't want her to think I was laughing at her: I wasn't, but it was hard not to grin at her slightly sideways way of talking. Maybe she'd spent too many years near something that was edged a bit too much between worlds.

"Indeed I did," said Vesper, alternating double stitches in knit and purl. "Would you like to know about the ghost hunting team or the spectacled little man who visited from the Society for Debunking Ghostly Phenomenon?"

"Ghost hunting team," I said. "We'll get to the ghostly debunker afterward."

"Very well," she said, settling into her rhythm. "The ghost hunting team was three very nice young men with cameras: they told me they were doing a story on the deaths that had taken place in the house and the bad luck force it exerted on the whole neighbourhood."

"Hang on, what deaths?"

"The ones that started it all," Vesper said, knitting her way back across the row. "They were well documented at the time: deaths close by around the neighbourhood, deaths at the house itself—though no one ever found more than the body of the mother. They never found the boy."

"Any of those deaths left hanging by the neck with the entrails out?"

I could have said it in a nicer way, but I wanted to see if I could shock her. She was so comfortable with the level of weird that she'd been experiencing over the last twenty years that it seemed if not suspicious, at least odd.

"Oh yes," she said, with a sharp look at me. "Very untidy it was —right in front of the number seven's windows. How did you know about that? They tried to hush it up at the time, apparently."

"Well, how did your ghost hunters know about it?"

"They said something about a club they were in," Vesper said, making me wonder if it would be an idea to suggest to Abigail that hers might not be the only group of rebel humans in existence around Tasmania.

"What happened to the ghost hunters, anyway?" I asked. "Were they the ones the house ate?"

"I saw them moving around on the first day," she said. "Setting up lights and cameras, and plugging things into some sort of big engine they brought with them."

A generator? I wondered. That would make sense.

"It hadn't been dark for more than an hour when the yelling started. They were clever boys, bringing their own lights, but I'm not sure they thought further than illumination—it might have been wiser to think defence instead."

"Sounds like it," I muttered. "Right, so there was yelling— what about?"

"One of them screamed that the house had eaten Alex or Alan, but my hearing has never been the best. They tried to run for it with a camera each very shortly after that. One of them tried to get out by the lane but the trees got him, as I told you earlier, my dears. The other boy escaped into unit eight and…well…"

"That lady in the office downstairs said the house went into the unit," said Jin Yeong, his eyes dark and thoughtful.

"I suppose it must have," Vesper said meditatively, and for the first time, her knitting slowed. "I didn't see much, of course; but the wallpaper on my side grew scarlet pimpernels for half an hour in that little damp patch over there."

My eyes turned unconsciously toward the darker yellow patch of wallpaper for the briefest fraction of a moment, and then toward Jin Yeong. One of his brows was up, a small quirk that suggested he was trying to decide if this little old woman was dotty, or knew entirely too much.

It wouldn't have been so hard to decide if she wasn't so flamin' *calm* about it all. If she'd seen all that she said she'd seen, what gave her the confidence to stay where she was and knit?

"There were tenants in number eight at that time," Vesper added, knitting steadily. "They weren't big knitters, so they were inclined to get a bit flustered when odd things happened: it gives your hands something to do, you see."

"What happened to the people in number eight?"

"They moved out that night, of course. There's still a few of their things in there, I fancy; they left in quite a hurry."

"Reckon I'd be thinking about moving if my house got taken over by someone else's house," I opined. I found that Jin Yeong was watching me, and gave him the smallest of nods to let him know that *of course* I'd recognised the similarities between what had happened when I went to stay with Morgana and the story we were hearing. My house had followed me right into Morgana's—a circumstance that left me pretty flamin' sure that whatever Jin Yeong and I would meet with when we visited the Standforth house, the Standforths themselves were probably going to be one of those things.

"The investigations man, now that was an interesting one,"

continued Vesper. "He didn't take in a lot of equipment, but he had a better idea of self-preservation, at least: a very nice little sword-cane, if I wasn't mistaken. I've only ever seen two others, but I'm quite sure it was one of them. He also had one of those very small cameras strapped to his head. He didn't run out screaming, but he did make a very valiant effort to get to his car before the shadows got him. That was back when people could still get through the gate."

"Flamin' heck," I said, impressed with the placidity with which she said it. Maybe it really was the knitting.

"I still see him every now and then: such an eager, earnest little man, I thought. I never did get to see the documentary those three young men were putting together, though."

Well, at least the bloke got out all right after all that, I thought, in some relief. I put down my empty teacup and wandered over toward the window. Over my shoulder, I asked Vesper, "You got any tips for getting in?"

"A little determination seems to go a long way when it comes to that," she said, peering at me over her spectacles.

"Looks like the gate's locked now, though," I said, turning to look back down into the courtyard below. "Even if the trees don't go after us."

Vesper gave a very small, lady-like sigh. "You're really going in, then?"

"Gotta," I said. "There might be someone in there that we need to talk to. Don't worry about us. We're pretty indigestible."

"If you're *sure*, my dear," she said, fixing me with a disapproving look. "Your young man does seem a little too decorative to be taking into a place like that."

Jin Yeong, very surprised, said, "*Mwoh?*" and I couldn't help the gratified chuckle that escaped me.

"That's what I keep telling him!" I said. "But he keeps wearing his good stuff when we're going out to work. Serves him right if he gets his pretty things ruined."

"It's his pretty face I was worried about," said Vesper.

Jin Yeong, who looked as though he couldn't decide whether to be gratified at the praise of his looks or insulted at her appraisal of his ability to handle himself in trouble, said, "I am able to protect my face."

"And I look after the rest of him," I added, grinning a bit more widely still.

Jin Yeong met my grin with something very close to rolling eyes, but I saw one of his incisors briefly through his lips, so he must have grinned a bit, too.

"You can use my balcony to get over the fence, if you like," said Vesper, pointing at it with her momentarily free knitting needle. "If you're really going. You won't get through the door at the front, but you might be able to manage one of the windows or the back door."

"Is that how people usually get in?" I asked her curiously.

"I'm sure I don't know," she said, knitting studiously again. "I've never offered it to anyone, if that's what you mean. All I know is that they can never get through the front door—it confuses them no end."

"Doesn't it confuse you?"

"There are so many things that confuse me about this life, dear. The television remote is one of them—I never know *where* it has gone, or where it will turn up, and it has a mind of its own."

"I've got a friend who feels the same way," I couldn't help saying. "I should introduce you."

"Should we come back again the same way?" Jin Yeong asked her. "Or will the door open for us when we are inside?"

Vesper looked at him admonishingly over the top of her spectacles. "I'm sure I don't know, young man."

"What do the others usually do?"

"Once they go in, they seldom come out," she said, knitting her way back across, surprising me with her matter-of-factness.

"Did no one tell you that seven people have gone missing in that house these last ten years?"

"Good grief!" I said, startled. Ghost stories and frights were one thing—I hadn't realised that the people we'd been talking about hadn't actually made it out of the house to tell their stories in person. "What about—you said you still see the investigations man!"

"Just every now and then," she said. "Near the windows or on the roof—I've never been sure if he's a ghost or not, but he certainly seems to be busy."

I met JinYeong's eyes and found that he was looking faintly wary.

"Do you want us to wait for *hyeong* then?" he asked.

"Nah, might as well go in. You're scarier than anything we'll find in there, anyway."

I caught Vesper giving JinYeong an assessing look-over, as if trying to decide if he was actually more frightening than whatever might be in the flat. He must have passed muster, because she gave a small, decided little nod, and went on with her knitting.

"Do keep the door or window open when you go in," she suggested. "It might make it easier for you to get out, who knows. I did see someone tumbling out of the window one day, but the trees got him before he could make it to the road."

She said it so pleasantly that it was hard to feel the chill I should have felt at her words.

"Right," I said. "We'll watch out for the trees, then."

"So long as you're polite and leave before dark, I don't think you need worry," she said. "Off you go then, my dears. Just knock on the patio door if you need to come back through, won't you?"

"Sounds good," I said. I was grinning, which was stupid, but the whole thing just tickled me. Here was an old human woman who had no idea what she was faced with every day as she knitted, giving out completely sound advice on being polite to other worldly things that would no doubt use any excuse to take offence and retaliate for the offense taken.

When we were out on the patio with the door safely shut behind us, I said to Jin Yeong, "Givus a sec: I'll give Zero a call first."

"I am not frightened," he said, but he didn't tell me not to call.

"Yeah, but we gotta look out for your pretty face," I reminded him. "Can't be damaging that now that we've already ruined your best suit. Fair warning, though: if the house gets hungry, I'm shoving you at it and running for it."

CHAPTER NINE

It was a bit of a drop down from the patio to the top of the stone wall, and a bigger one from the top of the wall to the unevenly paved courtyard below, but it wasn't the sort of drop that should have given me the feeling of floating in mid-air for one brief, horrible second.

I left Jin Yeong swearing in Korean behind me and started toward the house with the rather fatalistic thought that if I didn't go for it now I would probably run for it instead.

Explore carefully, Zero had said on the phone. *If it has that many stories surrounding it, there's likely a very strong presence Between, not unlike your own house. Call me if you run into any problems you can't solve.*

I might not be as stubborn as Jin Yeong—yeah, I know, I said *might*—but his eyes had met mine when Zero said to call, and I'd seen in them the same determination not to need help.

So when the front door didn't open to either gentle or no-so-gentle persuasion, I wrestled open one of the front windows instead and climbed in that way. Jin Yeong didn't assist with the opening of the window, but he made use of it after I tumbled through into dust and floating motes that were hopefully dust and not spores.

"Oi," I said, as he slipped through the window behind me. "Thought you vampires could still get into houses without an invitation if you tried hard enough?"

"You opened the window for me," Jin Yeong said. "And what is hard for me is easy for you. Why are you asking questions suddenly?"

"It's not *suddenly*," I protested, gazing around at the room we'd entered. I didn't know exactly what interior to expect from the twenties, but the thing that most struck me was how tidy the place was in spite of the bit of floating dust. Unlike the houses beside the block of flats in front, there was no smell of decay and mould, and there wasn't even a lot of dust lying around the place if you didn't count the stuff floating in the air. Everything was decorated in deep blues in a range of ocean shades and thick gold lines; this was a house that had once been both very expensive and very expensively decorated.

We were in what looked like a sitting room, all polite couches and cushions, with a bar in dark wood at the far end of it that was sifted with a faint layer of dust. Couches and cushions both had been kept to much darker shades of blue than the walls and fixtures, almost as if they were shadowed underwater.

What I wanted to check now was the lighting. It was shadowy inside the house, but not dark, and across the room I could see a light switch that definitely wasn't twenties, though it was stylish.

To Jin Yeong, I said as I crossed the room, "I've been asking questions ever since I met you lot! I just don't usually get answers unless they're in riddle form. According to human lore, you lot are forbidden from entering houses without an invitation."

"There are a lot of ways around the rules," Jin Yeong said. "And it is not *forbidden*, it is uncomfortable. Like when you put things crooked around the house."

I tried very hard not to laugh. "What, you get uncomfortable because you're being rude?"

"I," said JinYeong, as I flipped the light switch to absolutely no effect, "am a very polite person."

This time, I didn't try to hide the crack of rude laughter that escaped me. "Yeah, why not? So you're a polite person. C'mmon, let's check the other rooms. Maybe if you're really polite, the house won't eat us."

The place wasn't huge, so it only took us a few minutes to check out the rooms on the bottom floor—sitting room, formal dining, kitchen, downstairs bathroom, and study—and all of them were both surprisingly clean and entirely unthreatening.

It was all laced with Between, of course, but nothing like as bad as my own house was. I could feel it in every corner and room, but it wasn't crawling over the walls and ceiling and making things move in the corners of my eyes.

"This is a bit of a let down," I said to JinYeong as we came back out into the receiving hall. "Reckon we should try the front door and see if it opens?"

"*Ani,*" he said. He seemed discontented, as though he had been expecting to be able to fight something and had been robbed of that opportunity.

Come to think of it, that was probably exactly what he was feeling.

"We can have a poke around upstairs first, anyway," I said, still gazing around the hallway and up the stairs. "Vesper said that not much happens until dark, usually, though: what do you reckon we could do to change that?"

He grinned. I should have known: born trouble-maker, is JinYeong. "First, you will *bother* it," he said.

"Okay, following you so far—you want me to have a bit of a go at the Between bit of it and see if I can shake anything loose."

"Yes," he said, with great satisfaction. "Then if it does not work, I will bite something."

I sputtered a laugh. "What, like a wall or a chair or something?"

"You're not to bite anything!" said an imperious, snooty little voice. "I forbid you!"

"Flamin' heck!" I said, jumping. There was a kid on the stairs now; he hadn't been there a second ago, but he was there now, all pale face and starched collar with britches that only came to his knees and shoes that looked far too shiny. I looked him up and down, wondering if I was imagining the faint red gleam to his eyes, and said, "You must be Ralph."

"Who are you and what are you doing in my house?" His eyes travelled rather disdainfully over to Jin Yeong as he added, "And why are you wearing those *awful* clothes?"

"You should not talk about other people's clothes," said Jin Yeong coldly, "when your hair looks like *that*."

The child fairly swelled with rage, his face reddening, and I protested, "Don't get your knickers in a twist, he's just a little kid!"

"And at least I do not look like an old grandfather," Jin Yeong continued, eyeing the tweedy material of Ralph's trousers and jacket with a certain amount of fascinated horror. "I am smooth and beautiful."

"Get out of my house!" shouted the child, in a rage-filled but reedy voice. "I won't have you in here!"

"No need to be like that," I said soothingly. "Just ignore the vampire; he likes to think he's the pinnacle of sartorial magnificence—"

"I am beautiful and stylish."

"Get out of my house," Ralph said, his eyes gleaming almost red, "or I will tell it to eat you both!"

"First of all, there's not enough flesh on either of us to make a good meal," I told him. "Second, does this house *actually* eat people? Because I know a bit about Between and my house likes changing around from time to time, but it's not like it actually eats people."

"My house," said the boy, in what he probably thought was a terrible whisper, "is hungry and vicious. It will *chew your bones*."

"Yeah, but with what teeth? And how does it even digest stuff?"

He stared at me, and I saw him actually thinking about it, but the house was already on the move by then. I grabbed Jin Yeong's arm to reef him out of the reach of the bannisters, which had separated and now flailed and grew like a line of sentient vines dressed up as bannisters for a fancy dress party.

Jin Yeong snarled at them and said to Ralph, very clearly, "I have *very many* teeth and I also can bite *very hard*."

He started up the stairs at a run, which startled the boy enough to make him take a couple steps backward, trip over one of the stairs, and sit down suddenly. The stairs bulged, ensnaring Jin Yeong's feet like massive bubbles of chewing gum, and the walls seemed to bend toward him, too. Undeterred, if a bit slower, Jin Yeong grimly waded through it, snarling at the encroaching wall.

"You're wooden," I told the stairs fiercely, and started after him without waiting to make sure that they obeyed. They must have listened, because they felt solid beneath my feet when I dashed up the stairs to Jin Yeong.

"Stop it!" shouted Ralph. "You can't tell my house what to do!"

"That's all you know, kid," I told him. To the stairs that ensnared Jin Yeong's feet, I said, "You're wooden. You can't do that."

"They're not wooden, they're tar!"

It was too late; Jin Yeong already had his feet free. I heard him mutter, "Ah, I will bite that child!"

I opened my mouth to tell him not to bite the kid, but he pushed me away before I could get the words out, and all that came out was a startled, "Oi!"

JinYeong snarled, his waist banded by blue paint with golden stripes that would have embraced me but now wrapped around him instead, and the stretchy edges that reached for me too writhed in what looked like annoyance.

"Flamin' heck!" I said, and grabbed for him. I missed by centimetres: the wall snapped back into itself, taking JinYeong with it before he had a chance to even bite it, and the entire thing immediately flattened and hardened as though it had always been flat and hard, and, above all, a wall.

I turned a very nasty look on the kid at the top of the stairs and said, "You'd better tell it to let him back out, or you and me are going to have a problem."

"Get out of my house!" yelled Ralph. "Or I'll tell it to eat you, too!"

I reckon he wasn't feeling too brave about it, though—maybe he hadn't seen anyone else copy what he'd done to the house before—because he turned and leaped through the wall behind him that had begun to swirl in a distinctly watery way.

"Come back here, you little brat!" I said wrathfully, taking the last of the stairs two at a time. "Give me my vampire back!"

I ran for the section of wall that was still swirling in a combination of Between and water or paint, and burst through it with the refreshing feeling of running through a waterfall and into the coolness of the cave behind it.

Someone's bedroom, I realised, forging forward as the wall tried to cling to me and draw me backward. Plain floorboards were beneath my feet, unpolished but clean, and an old metal frame bed with a mattress that had seen better days—or was it a carpeted bedroom with a set of bunk-beds?

I didn't bother to try and figure out which one it was, because the wall, wet and clammy, was still trying to drag me backwards, and it was beginning to feel more like a whirlpool than a wall, too. I had the distinct feeling that I might end up drowning if it managed to pull me back again.

"No, you don't!" I said sharply to it, with dread in my heart for Jin Yeong. Things that ate other things could always be forced to spit them out again—things that *drowned* other things weren't as easy to fix. "You're a wall, not water, and you're not going to drown me! *Down* boy!"

The wall released me and I couldn't help taking a couple of swift, instinctive steps away from it. I looked around the room a bit more carefully and found the interior of the room just as hard to comprehend now that I wasn't fighting to escape the embrace of a wall.

"Heck," I said irritably to myself. "What's it matter whether it's got bunkbeds or a single? Jin Yeong! Oi!"

There was no answer, but I hadn't expected there to be one. I threw another look around the room and caught a faint trail of reddish *something* that wasn't exactly red and wasn't exactly visible, wafting out the door.

I said savagely, "Gotcha!" and started off after it.

I stepped from bare boards—or maybe carpet—and into snow, a frigid breeze whipping colour into my cheeks and a teal-tinted snowflake wafting past my nose. At the end of the snowy hallway, a very surprised-looking Ralph said, "You can't do that!" and disappeared between tree trunks that began to look more and more tree trunky and less and less hallway-ish by the second.

Branches reached out to me, icy with snow and glittering teal paint, and I said to them firmly, "Get back into your lattice, you flamin' creepers!"

They didn't quite go back into the lattice work that ran along the hallway, but they didn't stretch out quite so much, either, which gave me just enough space to pass down the hallway, slipping my phone out of my pocket at the same time to call Zero.

He answered just after I followed the lingering trail of red into the lavish upstairs living room, giving my heart a jolt of relief.

"Yes."

"Zero?"

"What is it, Pet?"

"Reckon you'd better get here quick," I said, in a hushed voice that helped hide the way my voice shook. "'Cos the walls just ate Jin Yeong and I reckon they're about ready to try for dessert."

"Are you all right?"

"Yep, but this kid *really* knows how to use Between and it's taking all I've got to keep catching up with him. I need reinforcements to get Jin Yeong back."

"I'm coming. I'll put out a message to Athelas too. Is there anything I should know?"

"Yeah, come in via the flats and ask Vesper in unit nine if you can use her balcony to get over the wall. Heck! He's just changed the house again; I'd better go."

"Don't pull anything from Between that could get you noticed," Zero said, his voice distinctly warning, and then the line went dead.

I stopped and took a moment to settle myself in my surroundings again as I shoved my phone back in my pocket. Ralph had outdone himself this time: the floor was now the ceiling, and vice versa, and if I looked at the windows for too long, I could see a world outside that wasn't the human world.

"Come out here, you little sniveller!" I yelled, crossing the floor and avoiding a giant, blue-glassed chandelier that looked like a blooming tree from this perspective. It made my head feel weird, but it wasn't exactly dangerous: the thing I wanted to avoid was the distinctly Behind world outside the house.

I wondered briefly if this was something I'd be able to do with my own house, but there was no time to think about it, because the house had begun to tilt again, sending me sliding back across a suddenly sloped roof and toward the windows like a pinball in a pinball machine. I grabbed the chandelier on my way past and held on for dear life while the whole room did a loop-de-loop around me, and didn't let go until it was back up the way it should be. It was a bit of a drop down, but at least there was carpet, and not much of a chance to go flying out the windows.

Since the room seemed pretty stable for a little while, I took a closer look out the windows. There wasn't a courtyard in sight, just a sky that was too bright and something glassy and slowly moving below that couldn't possibly be the sea of slow-moving crystal that it looked like because crystal seas weren't something that existed.

Not in the human world, anyway.

I shivered a bit with the stray thought that as an heirling my position between worlds was very different these days— wondering suddenly if I would have to go Behind to submit my resignation to the crown. I didn't think I'd be able to rest comfortably in a world that had crystal seas. It was too alien; too dangerously other.

Even if I had a Zero to stand behind, it was too much.

When I cracked the window open just a bit, even the air smelt and felt different.

"Flamin' heck," I said, and shut it again firmly. No way I wanted to be going outside right now. Whatever else happened, I had to try and make sure the house didn't kick me out while Zero was still coming. Hopefully he wouldn't find it too hard to get in.

I'D MANAGED TO FIGHT MY WAY THROUGH A SANDSTORM ALONG the upstairs landing, nearly nabbed the kid by a coat-rack that turned into a far too affectionate octopus, and slid down the bannisters to avoid a suddenly-lava grand staircase before Zero got there.

Thankfully the outside I could see from the downstairs windows was still courtyard and apartment block out front; it was even more of a relief when I saw Zero drop down into the court-yard and cross it at a run.

The door opened almost before I touched the handle, which

made me grin sourly. Apparently the house knew how to behave when someone in authority was legging it across the yard to get in.

There was a deep frown between Zero's brows when he stepped through the door, but it vanished as soon as he saw me.

"Jin Yeong?"

"Somewhere in the walls. He doesn't have to breathe, right?"

He stared at me. "It's not necessary."

"That's good; he's probably fine, then." I caught the faint touch of amusement to his eyes and explained, "The walls can get a bit...watery every now and then."

"All right. Can you stop it if the boy tries to do it again?"

"Mostly, if I'm expecting it."

"Where is he?"

"In the sitting room," I said, tipping my head to the left. "He's been leaving little red trails around the house everywhere."

"Red?" Zero looked around, and nodded. "No sign of Athelas yet?"

"Not a thread of tweed," I replied. "You know how the kid's doing that red thing?"

He strode toward the sitting room. "I've got an idea. You did well, Pet. Come along."

That left me with a pleasantly warm feeling. It was nice to know that Zero wasn't too worried about Jin Yeong; I already had a good idea that he was going to be fine, but I didn't like not being able to *see* that he was fine.

I followed Zero into the sitting room and found him doing a swift once-over of the place. A few taps on the wall here, a bit of wriggly magic there.

"Can you see the boy?" he asked. "Or even the trail you mentioned? I'll need to talk to him."

"Don't worry about that," I said grimly. "Reckon I can bring him out here. The house is fighting me, but Between is willing to work with me as usual."

"Do it."

I reached out my hands to that trail of red and fairly *reefed* it toward us as if it was a bungee rope. Maybe thinking of it that way did some good, because the kid came flying through the wall and sailed over our heads, startled and struggling all the way. He caught himself lightly against the far windows and alighted on the window-seat that was striped with blue and gold, terrifyingly familiar with his lack of gravity.

"You'd better get out of my house right now," he said, his feet planted obstinately in a way that made me think of Peter Pan. "I've been nice until now, but when it gets dark, it'll be too late for you."

"Give us back our vampire," I told him.

"Leave my house!"

"Give him back," said Zero, his voice terribly cold. "Or I'll burn this entire place to the ground and salt the remains."

"Try it!" the pale boy said, his eyes flashing with red fury. "You'll burn your friend as well."

"I think not."

"Anyway," the boy said scornfully. "You can't burn this place down—people have tried before. It just eats the flames, or collapses the bulldozer, or eats the dynamite. Whatever you try to use, it won't work. There's nothing in this world that can destroy my house, and I *don't give you permission to be in here.*"

"I wasn't going to use anything from your world," Zero said, and with a smile even colder than his voice, he snapped a blue flame into being between his fingers.

"Look, kid," I said. "You don't know any better, and I know this is your house, but when he goes all quiet like that, it's a bad sign."

Maybe he'd already figured that out. At any rate, his eyes grew very large and fixed on the blue flame. At a whisper, he said, "What—what is that? You can't have that in here!"

"This," said Zero, prompting the flame into growth until it

licked all across his hand and leapt eagerly toward the ceiling, "is fae light. It is *very good* at eating away at the appearance of things."

"Put it away!" shouted the boy. "You can't have it in here!"

"We'll put it away when you give us back our vampire," I said.

He was definitely scared now, but his chin was still mulish when he said, "I w-won't!"

"Very well," said Zero, and flicked the blue fire at the closest wall.

I don't know what I expected, but whatever it was, it wasn't for the entire wall to fairly explode with flames that ate into bricks and plaster like acid through flesh, the entire lot going up with a roaring that sounded suspiciously like screaming.

The boy shrieked, half his face alight in blue flame that lit up a skull as pale and empty-eyed as any sugar skull instead of the flesh and blood that ought to have been there. Behind him, in the reflection of the window, I saw a skeleton burning, burning.

"Stop! Stop! My house! Don't touch my house!"

"Give us back our vampire, revenant," Zero said, through his teeth.

If the kid hadn't been screaming, I might have laughed aloud. *Give us back our vampire.* Not something I ever thought I'd hear Zero say. Not the us. Not the *our*. If I was to be really hopeful about it, I'd think we were actually a family. Nothing weird or uncomfortable—just family. The kind of love that would mean I could sit snuggled up with Zero again without worrying about what he'd think of it.

The revenant, its face and torso consumed with blue flame that showed the white bones beneath, howled, "Stop!" once more before that howl devolved into a many-layered screaming that merged with the screaming of the walls, the ceiling, the whole flamin' *house*.

And then one of the walls bulged and Jin Yeong came tumbling through, all cobwebs and slime and mould. I grabbed him by the mucky collar and heaved him away from the wall, and one of his hands closed around my wrist as he scrambled to get away, cursing in Korean.

Zero saw; I know he did. He didn't stop the flames, though, and the revenant's wailing grew wilder and higher, screaming without pause for breath.

"Zero!" I yelled. "Stop! Jin Yeong is out! You don't have to kill the kid!"

"It's already dead," Zero said grimly. "It's a revenant. The flames show it for what it is."

I grabbed his arm with my spare hand, Jin Yeong still staggering beside me, and said again, "*Stop*! I don't care if he's already dead; you're killing him *worse*!"

His eyes flickered with a wholly human amusement, and the flames sank, then died.

"Pet," he said, as the revenant leaped for cover behind one of the couches and began to weep noisily, "you can't kill something that's already dead. I was trying to separate it from this world."

"Yeah," I said, glaring at him. "That's killing him. He might not be alive in the same way that we are, but he's still interacting with the world. *And* we need to talk to him."

Zero looked as though he struggled with himself for a moment or two. Eventually, he said stiffly, "I may have overreacted."

I exchanged a startled look with Jin Yeong, who seemed even more disbelieving than me, and said, "Yeah, maybe. Thanks for coming and rescuing us, though."

Jin Yeong sniffed, but I was pretty sure he was grateful, too. "That pretend boy is hiding behind the couch," was all he said.

Have any of you blokes ever tried to coax a revenant out from behind a couch? It's not easy. Especially after you've set fire to his house and half of his face with fae light, showing the extent of his...deadness.

Zero sat down on the other couch to wait it out, and Jin Yeong vanished into the bathroom to clean himself up, but returned a few moments later because there was no running water. By that time, I was cross-legged beside the couch, peeking around the back of it to catch the red-glowing eyes of the revenant boy.

"You can come out," I said to him. "We won't hurt you; just don't try to get the house to eat us again, okay?"

The revenant, clinging to the fabric of the couch, only wept harder.

"I won't let Zero throw fire at you again. I won't let him set the house on fire, either. We didn't come here to hurt you, we just wanted to talk to you."

"We did not," said Jin Yeong loudly, "expect to be *eaten*. That was *rude*."

"You weren't invited!" yelled the revenant, making me jump.

"Okay, that's true," I agreed. "But feeding him to your house was a bit much, wasn't it?"

"An over-reaction," Zero said, in an aside. If I didn't know better, I'd think he was on his dignity about having to apologise earlier.

"Who are you, anyway?" demanded the revenant, wiping its nose on its sleeve.

Goodness knew why: it wasn't like it actually *had* bodily fluids to wipe away, if the fae light had actually exposed what it really looked like. I took it as a good sign that it wasn't actively sobbing anymore, though.

Encouragingly, I said, "We're just here to talk to you. We're... investigators. We want to know what happened to you."

There was the very slightest forward motion: the revenant crawled forward on its hands and knees and crouched just a foot away from the end of the couch, gazing at me. "Really?" it said. "Nobody ever cares about that. They just want the house, and it's *mine*."

"Come out and tell us about it," I said soothingly. "Start with your birthday first."

Of all the things that could have made him suspicious, that one didn't. He said, "April fourth, nineteen sixteen."

Marazul had already told us, so I knew what his date of birth was—or at least, I knew what the date of birth was for the boy who had supposedly been killed in this house in nineteen twenty-five. It was still weird for me to be looking at his face and having the thought that he had been here nearly a hundred years running around the back of my mind, screaming.

"Your name *is* Ralph, isn't it?"

He crawled out properly and crouched there to gaze up at me. "How do you know my real name? No one ever knows my name!"

To my right, I saw Jin Yeong and Zero become more still than they had been a moment ago—the stillness of predators, yeah, but at least they were trying. I threw a quick look at Zero, and he nodded: they didn't want to frighten Ralph back behind the couch, so they were willing to let me handle things for now.

"So, what," I said, turning back to him as he settled himself gingerly on the couch, facing us all, "you've been haunting this place for the last ninety-five years?"

"I don't *haunt*," said Ralph the revenant, with dignity. "That's for ghosts and shades. There's more of me than a bit of shadow and left-over personality. I have a skeleton."

"Yeah, sounds like the opposite of creepy," I said. "I heard that this place was supposed to be haunted, though."

"People keep trying to move in," said Ralph sulkily. "And they don't listen when I tell them that I was here first and that it's *my house*. They just keep coming in and making noise and trying to move things, and my house doesn't work like that. Things have to stay in the same places."

"Not haunted, then," I said, nodding. I thought about that for a bit, and grinned. "Bet you show them your skeleton, though, eh?"

"Sometimes," Ralph said, with a guilty sort of grin. "Mostly, I just let the house eat a few of them and spit them out. Sometimes

I keep them here for a while so they get the idea that it's stupid to hang around."

I glanced across at the still sodden and visibly irritated Jin Yeong, and grinned. "Yeah, I see that. What about the ones that don't come back out?"

"What, the three men and the one with glasses? They went somewhere else when the house swallowed them. I couldn't get them back out. The one with the glasses won't leave, either."

He sounded injured about that, which made it hard to stop grinning. Obviously the investigator that Vesper had told us about had found something to believe in.

I didn't like to think where the three young men with the cameras had got to, so I asked Ralph instead, "Oi. How come you don't have water here?"

"In my experience, empty human houses don't usually have water and power," Zero said, but he said it quietly so as not to startle the revenant.

"Yeah, but what if the realtors are showing it to people? He said there were people moving in and out: the real estate people must have kept on the lights and stuff so they could show it to people."

It was weird: even though I still had power and water at my house for those years that I was alone, it wasn't as though the house got shown to people often. Here, where the house had evidently been rented out and sold so many times, it would have made sense to keep them on. I remembered, suddenly, a water or power bill that I'd seen in amongst the paperwork I'd given to Five-Four-One, and wondered if I should have another look at it.

"The water and lights go when the people go," the revenant said sadly. "They don't care about me."

"Maybe they would if you weren't always flashing your skeleton at them," I pointed out. "Some people don't like that. And if you're going to be doing eyes-like-coal, they're going to run first and ask questions later."

"I like water, too," Ralph muttered. "They shouldn't just take it with them when they go. That's rude."

"What does a revenant need with water?" asked Zero in a voice that was closer to his normal rumble. The sound of it made Ralph jump a bit, but he didn't make a leap for it behind the couch again, which was a win.

"I like watching it flow," he said. "I can touch it, too. I can touch everything: I have a skeleton."

"How'd you know what you are?" I asked him curiously. If he was anything like Morgana, he wouldn't have got out much, and even with the way his house was all threaded through with Between—

Hang on.

"Flamin' heck!" I said, looking around at the squishiness and malleability of the entire house. It was Between, but Between in a way that wasn't quite the Between I was used to. "You've got access to Behind, haven't you? Not just the Between bit that's useful for getting the house to eat people."

"Monsters used to keep coming through," he said gloomily. "Different ones from me. But then I found that most of them couldn't hurt me, and I found out how to use the house to protect myself. Now they don't come in anymore. I think it was a fairy that told me what I am. He had fire that burned the house, too; we nearly died kicking him out."

Maybe I shouldn't have pushed it: he'd drawn up his legs and wrapped his arms around them again, just a little kid who had lived for over a hundred years, and ninety-odd of those years by himself. But we had to ask questions—we had a murderer to stop, and I had questions of my own that needed answering.

And yet suddenly I felt that I hadn't had too bad of a life, compared with him.

I sat next to him, close enough so that our arms were up against each others', just sorta nudging him. "Oi," I said, a bit more gently. "The night that you turned into a revenant—what happened?"

"There was a radio play," he said, his face lighting up. "It was new and exciting, but mama said I wasn't allowed to listen to it because I got jam on the knob that morning. I had to be locked in the coal cellar to remember not to touch things."

"She locked you in the *coal cellar* for getting a bit of jam on the radio knob?" I stared at Zero and then at Jin Yeong before remembering that to them, that probably wasn't so dreadful. Zero's dad had actively killed his pets to break him of the idea that he could have anything that couldn't be taken from him. I nudged Ralph a bit more and said to him, "I'm sorry, kid."

"If I touch things, I make them dirty," he explained. "Mama has to work very hard to fix them, so I can't touch things. But sometimes I get excited and forget. If I go in the cellar, it will help me to remember because it's dirty like me."

"You're not dirty, kid," I said, after I'd recovered from that. Flaming heck! At least I'd had good parents before they were murdered: I didn't have a messed up childhood and then get turned into a revenant. "What happened after that? After you got out of the cellar?"

"She came into my room later, after I'd had a bath," he said, wrapping his arms around his knees. He sank into a heavy kind of silence, his mouth becoming a tragic bow, and around us, the house began to whisper and move and bulge.

"Did she come in to kiss you goodnight?" I asked, keeping an eye on the movement. It wasn't like I thought we were in any danger now that Zero was here with his fae light, but if I had to coax the revenant out from behind the couch every time he got upset, we'd be here far longer than intended.

"Don't be silly," he said, his head jerking backward like I'd suggested she came in to throw a boot at him. "I'm little and dirty, and if I kiss her, she'll be smudged."

I managed to stop myself from retorting that kids were

supposed to smudge things, because it seemed as though that might offend him. Instead, I switched to the opposite seat and slung an arm around the dishevelled and sticky Jin Yeong's neck and said, "What's a bit of muck between friends?"

Jin Yeong's brows twitched up, but it was the revenant's face that caught my attention: there was a kind of starved look to it that he either didn't or couldn't hide. I switched couches again and put my arm around him instead.

"You are making me messy," he said, in a small voice.

"Feels good, doesn't it?" I said cheerfully. "Not worrying about mess."

"Feels good," he repeated, but I wasn't sure if he was just repeating what I'd said, or if he really meant it. He didn't move away, though, and his pinched little face seemed a bit warmer.

I patted his arm. "Ralph, if your mum didn't come in to kiss you goodnight, what did she come in for?"

"She brought in the fairy," he said solemnly. "The one that killed me."

There was that stillness from Zero and Jin Yeong again, but this time it was definitely a predatory stillness.

"The one that you nearly died trying to kick out?" I asked slowly. I'd thought this kid was more aware than Morgana, but it looked as though he was having trouble remembering he was dead. "Or the one who killed you?"

Ralph shivered, even with my arm around him. "It was him, the same one. He killed me but I'm still alive. We kicked him out."

"You're doing good, kid," I told him quietly, wishing I could be more gentle. "Don't suppose you remember his face, eh?"

"No," said the revenant hollowly. "I remember his face."

CHAPTER TEN

I don't think any of us actually expected him to say he remembered it, because there was a blank kind of silence from all of us as we stared at Ralph and then at each other.

"Hang on," I said at last. "You *do* remember it? You remember the bloke's face?"

Ralph nodded and pointed at a black-and-white photograph across the room. From a distance it looked like someone had scribbled across it: an autograph, probably.

"It was him," he said. "But he had a moustache."

I crossed the room to peer at the photograph and tried not to sigh. Strolling back to the couch, I showed it to Zero and Jin Yeong, then sat down again next to Ralph.

I pointed at the picture. "Leslie Howard is the one who killed you and your mum?"

"It was him," he said, shoulders hunching a bit. "He was even black-and-white like in the movies."

"Must have been scary for you," I said, still fighting back disappointment. As far as I knew, Leslie Howard hadn't been in the actual movies until after Ralph was dead: he must have seen the man on telly one time while his house was rented out.

Zero raised his brows at me just slightly, as if to ask why I wasn't more interested in the identification, and JinYeong murmured to him in Korean. Trust JinYeong to know about black-and-white stage and film stars.

"Never mind what he looked like for now," Zero said to Ralph. "Tell us about the year that you died. What else happened around then?"

"Lots happened," said the revenant in surprise, looking up at me and then at Zero. "All of my champions died, one by one, and then—"

He stopped, because Zero had said something I was pretty sure was a Behindkind swear, slow and vicious. To me, he said, "Try to get Athelas on the phone. Leave a message if you have to."

I took my phone out of my pocket, but asked, "What's he talking about, *champions*?"

Instead of answering, Zero said sharply to the revenant, "Your champions died? How many? How did they die? What clan and kind?"

Ralph shrank into me and I put my arm around him again, squeezing his shoulder comfortingly. "They didn't tell me any of that clan or kind stuff. They just said they were here to protect me and to support me. Mama said not to mind them: she said royalty doesn't need to mind the servants."

"*Hyeong*," said JinYeong in astonishment. "Did someone stand up for this one secretly? They were *all*—?"

"How many were there?" Zero repeated, more patiently this time. "How did they die?"

"There were three," said Ralph. He looked comfortable again, but still rather puzzled. "Mama said they were hanging in front of their houses so they could see their mistakes. She was very upset about it."

"Anyone gunna stop and tell me what champions are, or am I just supposed to guess?" I said to the room at large. It wasn't much good asking Ralph, mind you; he might know the right words to say, but it was obvious that he only knew one facet of the things he was talking about. Royalty, huh? Was that how someone had sold it to his Mama to get her on board for whatever it was they were trying to do?

"Champions are what we call any of the Behindkind houses who throw their weight behind a particular heirling," said Zero, his voice still stiff with shock. "Or, specifically, the fighters they choose to protect their heirling from the other heirlings. If each of the murder cycles was made up of champions…"

To Ralph, who was still looking confused, I said, "For a skeleton, you're doing a pretty good job of putting meat on the bones of our investigation."

Ralph giggled and said, "I don't know what that means."

"Don't worry, kid, I'm still trying to figure it out, too. I s'pose someone was trying to get a sneaky leg-up in the competition and didn't tell anyone they'd found an heirling?"

"It is worse than that," Jin Yeong said soberly. "If it was just one here, another there, it would seem natural, *an gurae*? But it is not just one team of champions here and another there. For this many champions to find this many heirlings—"

"They were all working together. One organisation," agreed Zero grimly. "Besides the Family, I don't know who has such a reach."

"What about a subsection of the same bunch who were running Upper Management?" I suggested. "You blokes didn't even know about them until they turned up and started making trouble for us with Athelas. If they kept themselves that well hidden, what makes you think they couldn't keep a whole network of heirlings and champions hidden for as long as it took the king or whoever to find out?"

I had another thought, too, but this one I kept to myself. What if…what if, just like Blackpoint with Abigail's group and the humans who had allowed themselves to be used by Upper Management, there were humans who had sold themselves to

Upper Management for the safety of being cared for and the promise of maybe a throne if they lived? Unlike the Family and the King, Upper Management were very good at working with humans—what if that connection had allowed them a closer look at the human world and other potential heirs?

What if they still had contacts with people like Abigail?

For a brief moment, I understood Abigail's utter abhorrence at the idea of working with any kind of fae. It was like a cancer: give one bit of leeway and it got into absolutely everything.

"Pet—"

"I don't know anything about champions," I said. "If my parents knew, they didn't tell me. What, you reckon I had some, too?"

"Almost certainly," he said. "Whether or not they approved, they would have had watchers at the very least. If they made a bargain, they would have had champions for you."

"Bit of a shame we can't question the king, eh?" I said shortly. "Reckon he could give us a few answers."

"It would be as useless as questioning my father," said Zero, and I shivered from pure reaction. Of Ralph, he asked, "Did your mother tell you who your father was?"

He wasn't quite young enough to say with confidence that he didn't have a father, but he was young enough to look confused by the question. "Mama didn't tell me," he said.

"Pet, call Athelas," Zero reminded me.

"Right."

I dialled and stepped away from the conversation for a bit of quiet, but there was no answer. I tried again, and this time I left a message when the beeps sounded.

"You better get over here quick, Athelas, or at least answer your phone. Come through unit number nine: Vesper. This kid says he remembers a face and this house likes eating people. Plus there's a um, *champion* new lead for us to follow. Also I reckon Zero is worried about you but he won't admit it, so—"

The phone chirped at me to tell me the message had ended, and I sniffed. Oh well, that would have to do.

I came back into the conversation to tell Zero, "He's not answering. You sent him a text earlier, too, didn't you?"

"Before I came. I've heard nothing back, either; we'll have to make a detour on our way home to see if we can meet with him."

"You're going," Ralph said sadly. Not a question; a statement of truth.

"Hang on," I said. "We've still got something else to look at here."

"*Eomma*," said JinYeong, without translating it for the revenant. "Where is its mother?"

I nodded. "Exactly. Oi, kid, is there a part of the house that's different from the rest?"

The revenant looked at me with big eyes. "Mama's resting room. I don't go there anymore."

"Yeah? What's different about it?"

"I don't know," he said. "I'm not allowed in there, but it feels different from the outside. A few people went in there and didn't come out again, but it wasn't me that did it."

Great. So there could be a few bodies in there, too.

"We'll come back and talk to you," said Zero, already moving toward the door.

"Don't worry," I said to Ralph, who was looking distinctly worried, "we won't do anything to hurt the house or you. We're just gunna take a look."

"Is it about the fairy who turned me into a revenant?"

"Yeah," I said. "Gotta check a few things. One day, I'll try to introduce you to a zombie I know. Don't think she'll be worried about a few bones, so you won't need to worry about keeping up appearances with her."

"I'll show you where it is, then," he said, and trotted out ahead of Zero.

He led us back into the hall and down the stairs, then in a u-turn that had us walking toward the back of the house along the hallway there. He stopped halfway down and said, "I'm not allowed to go in there, but you can go in. You won't touch anything, will you? She doesn't like it when you touch things."

"Don't worry, we won't mess the place up," I said, because I didn't think we could promise not to touch anything. "We'll be out in a bit."

He hung back there in the hall while Zero opened the door to the resting room, a sorry little spectre in the darkness that seemed to gather the walls around him in a riot of wall-paper patterns climbing over him like vines.

I was happy for Zero to go ahead; I was pretty sure I knew what we were going to see, and I wasn't anxious to get a look at it too quickly. JinYeong followed close behind me, still smelling of mould and something else that I assumed was the Between equivalent of house digestion juices, shifting his shoulders in irritation that he was still dirty.

"Don't worry," I said over my shoulder as we entered the room. "I'll hose you down in the garden when we get back."

He made a *psh* sort of a noise at me, his upper lip lifting in the tiniest of snarls, but that could have been because there was a distinctly musty smell to the room we'd just entered and I'm pretty sure JinYeong likes to be the most strongly smelling thing in any given room.

There was a body, of course, sitting in a chair toward the back corner of the room. She wasn't really easy to see, draped in shadows that had no real source and clung to everything in the room, but I could tell that she was female by the fringe of her skirt. I could also see that she'd been dead for a long time now, because her body was more skin-plastered skeleton than flesh.

"Flamin' heck," I said, rather thickly. "I'm getting pretty tired of finding people's parents mummified in their houses."

"She's not mummified," said Zero briefly, lifting one of the woman's dehydrated arms by the black fabric of her sleeve.

"How *dare* you!" said a female voice at the same time. A shadow detached itself from the wall, soft, sticky strands of something clinging between it and the wall, and wafted behind the body, spreading stickiness as she went.

"I do not like spiders," Jin Yeong said, his voice short with dislike. "What is she doing?"

"How dare you touch me!" said the spidery woman from behind the body. She passed along the wall as swiftly as she'd emerged, filaments streaming out from behind her, and circumnavigated us, dulling the sound around us.

"Should she be doing that?" I asked Zero, and my voice sounded a bit more muffled, too.

"She can do as she wishes," he said coldly. "There's nothing for us here: we should leave."

"Heck no!" I said savagely. "We are *not* going to leave her here to keep telling him what a grotty little thing he is and making him think he deserves to be locked in the coal cellar!"

"Her voice can't reach him," Zero said. "In fact, I'd be surprised if he's been able to hear her for the last fifty years at least."

I frowned, looking around the room, and said, "Do you mean the cobwebby feel to it? Is that why her body is still here instead of buried?"

"Yes," he said, on a sigh.

"Lemme guess: that's something I shouldn't be able to see?"

"It's magic; and yes, you shouldn't be able to see it if you're not...more than just human. The older the house grows, and the more she weaves herself into this place, the less she can touch the outside world. All she can do at this point is feed the house, which is—"

"—Feeding the kid," I finished. I jabbed Jin Yeong in the ribs and said, "Familiar, isn't it?"

"Everything is familiar," he said. "*Hyeong*, why have we not come here before?"

"We weren't focusing on peripheral cases," he said. "The method of murder was different and we had no reason to think that they were anything other than ripple effect murders."

"And they were only humans," I said. I didn't mean to say it, but it came out. "All of the peripheral murders—they were all humans, right?"

Zero took a very long time to answer. When he did, it was to ask, "Do you want me to apologise? I prioritised Behindkind deaths, yes, but I didn't ignore these deaths wholly because they were human. It was more that we didn't expect them to be so important because they *were* human."

"You lot really need to work on that thing you do where you think humans aren't important, considering every one of your heirlings needs to have at least a bit of human blood in them," I said.

"Leave this place!" whispered the spider ghost in dark tones. "You will never flourish here!"

"You don't look like you're doing a flamin' lot of flourishing, yourself!" I told it, as it swept around for another layer. "What a bunch of garbage!"

"I layer my nest," she said, drifting around behind her own body again. "Warm and cosy and perfect. You're not to touch anything!"

"What about your kid?" I asked her. "He's outside thinking he can't come in because it'll make his mum mad."

She faltered briefly, then continued on. "He can't come in. He'll only touch things and make them dirty. Such an awful little thing, ever since he was born."

I said bitterly, "Yeah, we heard you shut him in the coal cellar."

"You can't let him in here. I was made a promise that I'll never have to see him again if I stay in here."

"Funny," I said, and I think right then that my voice was about as cold as Zero's. "That's just what I was about to ask you. I heard that someone might have asked you whether you wanted to save your own life, or his."

There was a soft, dismissive sound from behind me, where she was still webbing her darkness. "He had no life that wasn't from me. He's mine, my flesh and blood; I can do with him what I want. Of course he should die for me."

"Yeah? And how did that work out for you?"

"It's not even a human anymore," Zero said. "There's no use trying to make it change its mind or understand what it did wrong. It's a memory with shadows."

"I *know*," I said, with angry tears at the back of my eyes. "But it's so horrible and that poor kid—!"

"It's not a kid anymore," he said.

Jin Yeong shrugged. "It is not dead, either."

"Like Morgana," I said. I didn't know exactly what a revenant was, apart from looking like a skeleton if you caught it in the wrong light, but there was another connection here. "Technically dead but still alive."

"I suppose you could say that," Zero said.

"Then your killer is definitely fae," I said gloomily. "Dodgy and manipulative about fulfilling bargains. Why am I alive, anyway? Messing with the pattern a bit, isn't it?"

"We'll talk later," he told me briefly. "This thing may not be alive, but it can still answer questions if someone comes to see it."

"Oh."

"All is death and decay," murmured the spider ghost, wafting around us again. "All will be what it once was. Life and death have no meaning."

I glared at it as it circled. I probably would have let it have a bit more of a mouthful, even though it wouldn't really do any good, but Zero had already turned around and was walking through the door. Jin Yeong grabbed me by the hoodie and tugged me back across the room, too, leaving the spider ghost to her endless circles and gloomy predicaments of decay that silenced as soon as we shut the door to her room.

Ralph stood just down the hall, his hands clasped together, and said when he saw us, "Did you find what you were looking for?"

"Yeah," I said slowly. "Oi, kid."

"What?"

"Don't go in there, all right?"

He nodded solemnly. "That's what he said, too."

"He?" I had a bad feeling about this.

"The fairy that took Mama away. He said that if I went in there, he'd come back and find me and burn my bones."

Sickness churned in my stomach. I didn't have memories like that—just nightmares. I wondered if I'd got those nightmares because the murderer had once said something like that to me, and I just didn't remember it. It was another sharp, jolting reminder that I needed to find some way of bringing those memories back out—some way of letting my mind know it was okay for things to bubble to the surface where I could see them. Simple questioning with Athelas hadn't got me too far, but maybe...maybe something a bit stronger would do the trick. Something like Zero's dad's little brain worms. Just preferably not from Zero's dad. Maybe that was how I could approach it with Athelas.

"He won't come back and burn your bones," I said to him. "Don't worry."

"But Mama said for me to stay out first, so I ought to listen to her, oughtn't I?"

I put my hand on his head and instead of hair beneath my hand, I felt smooth bone. I patted it anyway, just as if there really was hair to ruffle. "Don't worry about anything else she said: just that bit."

He smiled up at me in a trusting sort of a way, and I felt a pull at my heart.

Was that how Zero felt when he patted me on the head? Comforting and sort of protective—an older sibling who could see the unfortunate truth the kid couldn't be allowed to see yet? I found myself frowning and rubbed at the frown with the palm of my hand.

I didn't know exactly why it bothered me so much: I'd been protesting against the way that Zero took charge of me and kept me in the dark since nearly as long as I'd known him. Maybe it was how uncomfortable that thought was alongside the one Morgana had planted. *I think he likes you.*

He'd opened up a lot more recently—almost as if he was going to give me the full measure of what I was asking for, just to show me how uncomfortable it was—but that pat on the head that was becoming more and more regular still stuck in the back of my mind. Any sign of physical affection had almost always come from me before now, and I couldn't deny that there was a change.

Trying to push the discomfort away, I asked Ralph, "You got a computer in here somewhere? Or a TV, anything like that?"

"I put them in the coal cellar," he said. "So it doesn't mess up the house."

"That's something, anyway," I muttered. "Oi, kid: remind me to sort you out with an internet connection and power or something next time I come around."

His eyes lit up. "You're going to come back again?"

"Yeah, so long as you don't try and get the house to eat me again."

"Pet," Zero said in a low voice. "It's not wise for heirlings to spend too much time togeth—"

"What, like me and you?"

JinYeong chuckled, low and malicious. "Do not fight, *hyeong*," he said, and sauntered away to the front door despite his disreputable condition. "You will not win."

"I resent the implication that I'm hard to deal with!" I called after him, but he just laughed again and went down the staircase.

Zero, his eyes very light blue, said, "Very well, I yield."

"Heck, that was quick."

"We'd best go and see if we can find Athelas," he said. "You've still heard nothing from him?"

I shook my head. "Nothing. You reckon he's in trouble?"

"I think I sent him somewhere alone when I should have gone with him," Zero said below his breath. "We'll find him: he's unlikely to have run into something that could kill him, but if this house is any indicator, he might be finding it hard to leave."

I stared up at him. "He went to the other house? The one from his file?"

"I thought it wise to divide our assets," said Zero rather curtly. "Apparently, I was wrong. Out, Pet. We'd best go see if we can find him."

"What about the kid?" I asked, in a low voice. "What if someone gets in here?"

"No one knows he's here, apart from our murderer—and I very much doubt anyone's going to be able to get in if he doesn't want them to do so."

"That's not enough," I said stubbornly. "Your dad's out looking for people like this kid, I'll bet you—and at least seven humans have already disappeared here for good. What about that thing you did to Morgana's house? Can you do that?"

He didn't even hesitate. "Wait outside with Jin Yeong. I'll work something out."

WE WOULD HAVE GONE OUT BY THE LANE, BUT WHEN WE WERE nearly out in the street, Zero said softly, "Stop," and I saw what he'd already seen: out on the street were a couple of loiterers who definitely weren't human.

"Reckon they're looking for us?" I asked, gazing at shadows that didn't match their bodies. Their bodies said normal human male, but their shadows suggested something far squishier and prickly, with powerful shoulders.

"They're adjuncts of my father," Zero said shortly. "Whatever they're here for, they can't be allowed to see us coming out from this house. Not when we're so close to an heirling—he'd have the boy burned and salted before we could get back."

Jin Yeong shrugged. "It does not matter if they see us come out," he said softly. "It matters only if they see us come out and live to tell your father."

"No need to kill people if we don't have to," I said. I didn't think that adjuncts of Zero's dad deserved any particular consideration, but it certainly wasn't right to chase down and slaughter them just to make sure they didn't open their mouths. "We can go back through Vesper's flat and find a way out from there. She said it was okay."

"I suppose we should think ourselves fortunate that you endear yourself to other humans so easily," Zero said to me, interrupting Jin Yeong's muttering that it was *easier* to *kill*. "Jin Yeong, stop complaining. There's no need to expend the energy killing minions when we could just slip out where they can't see us. The less attention we draw to ourselves, the better."

"I'm just too adorable for my own good," I told him, dragging Jin Yeong along with us toward the wall. He leaped up ahead of me as though he hadn't had to be dragged across the yard, showing off his vampiric ability to defy gravity, then reached down and snatched me up before Zero could give me the boost he'd briefly knelt to offer.

"Heck," I said, grabbing Jin Yeong's arms to stop myself overbalancing into the uncomfortably tiny space pretending to be a backyard on the other side. Zero joined us in a powerful leap, and used the wall-top as a springboard to disappear over the top of Vesper's balcony.

His face appeared again for a moment: he said curtly, "Get in here, Jin Yeong."

It was only after I lowered my gaze to blink at Jin Yeong in confusion that I heard the noise—the unmistakeable noise—of battle.

"No!" I said, sharp and pleading. Not Vesper. They couldn't fight in that little old lady's flat—she was too weird and nice and alive.

"Up," said Jin Yeong, and threw me upward without any sign of effort. He was beside me in a second, the both of us swinging a leg over the balustrade and tumbling onto the balcony. He darted ahead of me into the unit, but dove straight across the living room, and I saw why a moment later.

It wasn't just one or two Behindkind, and they hadn't stayed in the street. Athelas, jacket-less and with his arms bloody in tatters from fingers to bicep, equipped with only a single, short sword, slashed and stabbed in Vesper's kitchen, whirling furiously amidst a group of five or six assorted Behindkind. Through the broken door, I heard the sound of shouting in the corridor, and saw Ezri and Cadence scuffle past, swinging hard and fast with cricket bats. Zero's voice shouted out there, too, so I abandoned the thought of helping the girls and concentrated on Vesper, instead.

She was crouched in her chair, even her feet off the floor as though it was contaminated, knitting furiously with her face turned away from the vicious snarl of teeth, vampire and Behindkind that roiled around her easy-chair and occasionally bumbled into it, shaking her nearly out of her refuge.

I darted across the room, without weapon and almost without thought, and wrenched Vesper's chair around to face the wall just in time to avoid the sword that plunged into the back of it and emerged inches from her cheek at the front instead.

"Got any more knitting needles?" I asked her, gasping. "Set, please."

"Anything for you, my dear," she said, and her voice was barely shaking, though her hands were when she reached into the knitting bag beside her and passed me two very sturdy 15mm needles.

"Keep knitting," I said before I left her. "Jin Yeong will make sure they don't touch you."

"If I don't see it, it can't hurt me," she said, eyes still on her knitting.

"That's the spirit," I said. A Behindkind head loomed behind the headrest of her chair and I sliced at it backhanded with the needle in my right hand: a needle which grew and lengthened and *sharpened* and took off the creature's head in a spurt of green blood that I sincerely hoped Vesper didn't see.

Jin Yeong, snarling, shoved the body out of the way and whirled to leap on the Behindkind with too many arms that was trying to grapple with him. It took him only a moment to rip out the thing's throat, so I left him to his gory mess and started toward the kitchen and Athelas. I didn't make it in time, for as the corridor grew silent outside, Zero plunged through the door and into the bunch around him.

"You girls all right?" I yelled through the door.

"Yeah," called Cadence, poking her head through the door. Behind her, Ezri raised a supercilious brow but grinned at me anyway. "Just a few scratches and some bruising; caught most of everything with our bats and the big bloke took care of the rest. You good, Pet?"

"Yep," I said shortly, with my eyes on the kitchen. Zero and Athelas were done with their opponents, but I didn't like how tattered and bloody Athelas was. A lot of it was blue blood, which meant that it was likely to be his own unless he'd been fighting fae before he got here.

The two girls shouldered their bats and ventured into the unit just as Jin Yeong started a careful prowl around to make sure all the Behindkind were really dead.

"Well, I s'pose none of them are gunna be reporting back," I said to Zero. "This is Ezri and Cadence, by the way."

Zero nodded at them briefly, then called to Jin Yeong, "All dead?"

"*Ne*," Jin Yeong said, stalking back to us. "The ones from the street are in the corridor, and the street is also clear. *Hyeong*, this little lady's house is a mess."

Zero stared at him. "Yes?"

"You need to fix it. She gave us cake and weapons."

"I would venture to suggest that we need to do more than fix the unit," suggested Athelas, and I didn't like the look in his eyes. Neither did Cadence, because she glared at him and let her cricket bat fall away from her shoulder as if ready to use it again if need be.

"It's only Vesper," I said. "She's been knitting since everything began and she's very determined not to see things she shouldn't see. Do anything to her and I'll finish what the Behindkind started."

The look I didn't like vanished and Athelas smiled in genuine amusement. "Will you so, Pet? Should I be fearful for my life?"

"Pet—" began Zero.

"Don't even bother," I said, starting back across the room to Vesper. "Figure it out. And fix this flamin' mess while you're at it!"

Rather to my surprise—and the open astonishment of the two human girls—they did clean it up. I'm pretty sure they did it with magic, but the important thing was that it got done. While they did it, I crouched by Vesper's chair as she knitted and gave her back her knitting needles, then chuntered about Jin Yeong's pretty face for a little while until her hands moved smoothly as she knitted once again.

Once the unit was clean again and I could turn her around safely, I did so, with Jin Yeong on the other side to make it a smoother transition than last time. Vesper didn't stop knitting, but she did slow a little, and she smiled warmly at the others.

"Would you like tea and cake, my dears?" she asked, utterly impervious to our bloody and battered appearance.

"Probably not just now," I said, with a worried eye on Athelas, who was swaying a little and still dripping blue blood. None of those drips reached the floor thanks to whatever magic Zero had done, but there was enough of it to worry me. "You all right, Athelas?"

"I am perfectly well, thank you, Pet."

"You don't look perfectly—" I began, but he was already turning to Zero.

"I'm very sorry, my lord," said Athelas, and he was as pale as I'd ever seen him. "I rather think they followed me. It was appallingly careless of me, but in my defence I had seen what was done to the house I visited and it occurred to me that something similar might be happening over here. I met with a few...hurdles... in my attempts to get here before the current ones you assisted me with."

"We're just glad you weren't trapped in the house somewhere," I said cheerfully. "We're all alive."

"We're alive, too," said Ezri, eyeing my psychos in distinct respect. "That was the quickest fight we've ever been in—never come out of one this clean, either. You guys actually do fight against fae."

"Told you," I said, grinning at her. "Don't forget to mention it to Abigail, yeah?"

Ezri snorted, but I was pretty sure that she'd mention it anyway. If she didn't, Cadence was sure to.

"Were you able to salvage anything?" Zero asked Athelas, ignoring our asides.

"The house," said Athelas wearily, "was set alight moments before I got there. I made an attempt to save what I could, but I was already too late."

"Flamin' heck," I said, staring at his arms in horror as the extent of his injuries sank in. "You're burned!"

I hadn't seen the damage because I thought it was Behindkind blood he was sporting, but now that I knew it for what it was, I felt more than slightly sick. That would be why he hadn't dropped the single sword he was still holding: it was literally stuck to his hand. I could see the damage to his other hand, too, strips of flesh that must have been pulled away when he lost grip of a second sword.

"You two," said Zero to Ezri and Cadence, "why were you following my steward?"

"We weren't following your steward," said Ezri. "We were following the bunch that attacked you here; we got a tipoff that they were on the move. They've been doing some stuff they shouldn't be doing and we heard they were going to be going after a kid somewhere in the neighbourhood if they could track down their lead."

"You must have been their lead," I said to Athelas.

"I do beg you not to belabour the matter, Pet," he murmured. "I feel sufficiently small about it already. I was…in something of a hurry to get here."

"Yeah, I can see that," I said. It was past time to get him back home and look after those burns. "Figured if you got my message you'd want to get over here as quick as you could."

"I wasn't in receipt of your no doubt delightful message," said Athelas. "I was otherwise occupied, but it occurred to me that if the place I visited was in such a mess at such an inconvenient time, yours was also likely to be so and that haste was no doubt necessary."

"Perhaps we could take this discussion outside," Zero suggested, with a meaningful look at Vesper, who had gone back to her knitting with all the cheerful self-absorption of someone who is very good at minding their own business.

He and Athelas started for the door without any more ado, followed by the two human girls, but Jin Yeong, who to my utter astonishment had been badly brewing tea in the kitchen, put that tea down in front of Vesper and carefully allowed her to kiss the un-bloodied skin of his forehead in a grandmotherly sort of way.

I stared at him but he just shoved his hands into his pockets and sauntered out of the door as well, leaving me trailing behind.

By way of comfort, I said to her, "It should keep pretty quiet over there from now on."

"So I gathered, my dear," she said, looking away from her knitting again at last. "Look after that pretty boy of yours."

"Don't worry, I won't let him get hurt," I said, grinning, and joined the others outside.

As I closed the door behind me, Athelas asked from further down the hall, "Why did you join in the fight if it was fae against fae? I didn't request your help, I believe."

"You're welcome," said Cadence, rolling her eyes.

That put a bit of a twinkle back in Athelas' eyes. He said, "I won't acknowledge that you helped if I didn't ask for it, you know."

"I know," she said. "That's the fae way. We helped because we recognised you. We figured if you were here, then Pet would be, and Abigail has told us to help where we can."

"You didn't help when we were fighting the petalmen in the court," I pointed out. I looked over at the sword still stuck to Athelas' hand and wondered if I turned it back into what it had begun as, would it drop away without damaging him?

"New orders," she said, grinning. "Abigail changed her mind for once: we're to offer help if you need it now."

"Yeah?" I stared at her. "What changed that?"

"Perhaps it would be better to take this conversation elsewhere," Zero said, looking around the corridor with a frown.

"Somewhere with tea, preferably," said Athelas, his face just a little whiter.

"Reckon we'd better go home instead," I said, a bit grimly. "You need to get this lot looked at, and we can talk once that's done."

"He'll be fine; he can heal," pointed out Ezri.

"I'm sure I will manage, my dear," said Athelas.

"*No*," I said, more loudly, gripping his elbow above the burn line. Athelas had a very bad habit of running around while he was injured nearly to death—he was probably even worse than Zero when it came to that. "We will go *home*, make sure you're *healed*, and *then* we'll talk about it."

Jin Yeong, chuckling maliciously, took hold of Athelas' other elbow. "Do as you're told, old man," he said.

"My lord, it would seem that I'm to be carried off; perhaps you could intervene?"

Zero stared at him, then laughed. "Go home, Athelas," he said. "In fact, we'll all go home. Anything that needs to be discussed between us can be done there; the humans may contact us if they wish to debrief."

"Hang on, we want to know what all this is about, too!" Ezri said to me, frowning. I didn't know if that was because they had been so casually dismissed, or because I was making a fuss over Athelas, but I didn't really care. "And—wait, is that *blood* around your boyfriend's mouth? I thought he was human? Do fae drink blood now?"

"What blood?" said Jin Yeong silkily, and the girl blinked a couple of times.

She swore. "I must be seeing things. I could have sworn there was blood all down your chin and throat."

"There is no blood," Jin Yeong said, a dark red trickle seeping into his collar from his neck and another dripping from his chin to his chest. "You must have imagined it."

"Guess so," she said, frowning.

"Abigail would have known if he was fae," Cadence told her. "So would I. He's already been vetted. Are you *really* going to go home without telling us anything?"

"Looks like it," I said. "What, do you lot leave your injured to fend for 'emselves? I'll talk with you later."

Ezri scowled. "Yeah, but they're *fae*."

"Absolutely appalling," Athelas said, *sotto voce*. "The kind of prejudice one encounters!"

Zero lifted his eyes skyward and said, "Enough. There has been enough excitement this morning."

It seemed like he said it to everyone, and even the humans stopped grumbling. It didn't stop them from scowling at us until we disappeared Between, though.

CHAPTER ELEVEN

It was *very hard* not to say *I told you so*. I made a heroic effort and didn't say it, but it was sweet to know that the information that was likely to have given the psychos the best lead they'd ever had in finding their murderer, had been gained directly from humans.

Not to mention that Athelas had been helped by two human girls to fight off Behindkind, and that had to stick in their gullets a bit.

I threw a sideways look at Athelas. Now that he was in his chair and had been imbibing tea and biscuits for the last couple of hours, he was actually healing up pretty well. That's one of the useful things about being fae: you heal up flamin' quick. The burns up and down his arms were now pink and smooth instead of bloody and fleshy in strips, and he had commandeered his own teacup instead of having to suffer me perched on the arm of his chair and tipping it up for him. I could even very soon ask him about getting my memories back, I thought. If I posed it as useful to the investigation, perhaps I might not even have to bargain for his help.

Jin Yeong had seen us home and then headed out again almost

immediately with Zero, who hadn't liked the thought of leaving Behindkind bodies around as a signal to his father, but they both turned up again at about four o'clock; JinYeong to retire to the shower without any sign of emerging soon, and Zero to gulp down coffee and check on Athelas' burns.

He must have been satisfied with what he saw, because he sank down into his chair with a fresh cup of coffee and said to Athelas, "Well?"

"Someone knew I was coming, and they wanted to make sure there was nothing for me to find—no one for me to question," said Athelas. "Whatever and whoever was in that house, it's all dust and salt now."

Zero heaved a sigh. "We're going to have to go back over all the deaths that didn't have peripherals attached, and find the peripheral."

"No champion without an heirling, you mean?"

"Exactly. Now that we know the peripheral will be someone with a significant amount of human blood, they might be easier to find. We'll also need to make sure that we have access to the humans group's records: we're likely to find a few matches there."

"They said they were doing a vote," I reminded him. "We have to wait and see."

"We'll see," he said, which was a bit worrisome. I didn't want him ruining the new relationship that seemed to be flourishing between us and Abigail's group by insisting on something they didn't freely give. Or by going and just taking it, for that matter.

"You lot notice anything weird about these kids?" I asked, by way of turning his mind to something else. "The peripheral kids, I mean?"

Athelas gazed at me with a slightly quizzical expression. "My frame of reference is quite wide, my dear," he said, "but I'm rather certain that everything about them was, as you have so quaintly put it, *weird*. Both revenants and zombies could be considered something out of the ordinary way, even in the world Behind. I would imagine that the boy I went in search of today was also...weird."

"I meant, how come they're all from the twenties except me, so far?"

"A very good question," Zero said briefly, "and one to which I would like to know the answer. You said the humans seem to think that there were other cycles after the twenties, but from our research, all of the human peripherals that we now know to be heirling deaths occurred in the twenties."

"What if it's not about the ones that are dead?" I asked. "What if it's about the ones that are still alive?"

"Are you suggesting ineptitude, or a smokescreen?"

"Not sure, yet," I said. "But—"

"The children we've found are all very good contenders as heirlings," Zero agreed. "Either skilled in using Between or significantly dangerous as Behindkind. Including yourself."

"Reckon Ralph could give me a run for my money," I said. My psychos were often surprised at what I could do when it came to Between, but I was pretty sure Ralph was better again. I couldn't see myself being able to weaponize my entire house. "But it doesn't make sense that the ones still around are the best contenders: why leave them around, alive or dead, if so?"

What if the ones remaining had been the ones no one considered worth much—the ones who weren't a danger? But then I thought of the nightmare again, and I remembered the bargain that the murderer had struck with each of the sets of parents that I knew of: Die for your child, or they will die for you.

"What if it's about the decisions their parents made, not their strength? Morgana and Ralph are both technically dead, and their parents decided to let them die. Mine didn't, and—"

"You think the murderer is helping to decide the fate of the Behind throne based on human decisions?"

I didn't need to look at Zero's face to get an idea of the incredulity it must be displaying. I could hear it in his voice.

"It's possible," said Athelas thoughtfully. "But we'll have to find another case more similar to yours to know for sure. That is where your friends will be able to help us."

"Perhaps," Zero said, but he didn't sound convinced. "I think it's far more likely that the murderer is playing games with no losing outcomes for him, and so he's allowing himself to have fun. No matter what he does—no matter whether the child dies or doesn't die—the result is the same. A child alone in a house, alive or dead, who will never emerge to fight in the heirling trials."

That was fine; he didn't have to agree with me. I would have to wait and see what Abigail came up with, but I was pretty sure I'd hit on where the difference lay—at least with the kids that were still around, alive or dead. It was something personal where there ought to be nothing but business—an aberration that had made it invisible to Zero, who tried so hard to ignore his human, personal side.

How did a person—human or Behindkind—get to be that way? I wondered. Someone who could kill innocents without regrets, but someone who also took revenge on parents who betrayed those innocents? It wasn't as though I wasn't very well aware of the duality of Behindkind—and particularly fae—but this was something different.

I remembered Vesper saying, "The world is full of oddness," in her warm, thoughtful voice, and then, suddenly, another memory flip-flopped in my head. Athelas, fighting desperately in the kitchen of Vesper's unit while she knitted defensively over in her corner and tried not to look too closely.

How had he known?

If he hadn't listened to my message, *how had he known to come up through Vesper's room to find us?*

Athelas, who had told me more than once that being badly injured was the best way to gain trust. How had he known?

My stomach sank like lead, and all desire to ask him to help me regain my memories utterly vanished. I looked up to find his eyes resting thoughtfully on me. He said, as though repeating for the third or fourth time, "Perhaps it is time to revisit our questions about your own experiences, Pet. For example: your champions—you ought to have had them, and yet, curiously, you do not remember them."

I couldn't. I couldn't sit here and answer questions with this sickening suspicion sitting in my head. I stood abruptly, said, "Reckon I need a bit of air first," and went straight out into the backyard, ignoring Zero's surprise.

They must have been worried about me—funny how the thought made my stomach twist right then—because Zero came out after I'd been sitting in the afternoon sun for less than five minutes, pulling up grass and wishing my fingers weren't so cold.

"You said you could do this," he said directly, without sitting down. "You need to either get back in there or stop pretending this is something you can do."

I just looked up at him, wondering rather numbly if he knew exactly how momentary weakness worked with humans. Even if it had been that, I'd still need time to gather myself before I could jump back in.

Instead of getting into that with him, I just asked, "What message did you send Athelas? Earlier, when JinYeong got eaten by the house and you sent him a message?"

"I told him to contact me as soon as possible, since I had to meet with you at the Standforth house and we might need his help."

"Did he get that message?"

Zero gazed down at me, and I thought he was exasperated. "What exactly are you trying to ask, Pet?"

"It's probably nothing," I said, but the idea was already well and truly festering away, dark and awful. "But earlier, Athelas came right to Vesper's apartment to find us."

The silence continued for a few moments, before Zero said, faintly perplexed, "Athelas was aware of the address, Pet. He fought through my father's men just to get to us because he knew we were likely to be in as much danger as himself."

"I get that," I said. I climbed rather wearily to my feet, because my neck had begun to hurt and it didn't look like he was planning on sitting down any time soon. "But what I *don't* understand is how he knew to come through Vesper's apartment? Unless he's lying about reading my message, how did he know to come that way?"

"Why would he lie about reading your message?"

I said, with acid in my stomach, "Exactly."

It was the thought that had made me feel so sick that I had to leave the house.

Properly exasperated now, Zero demanded, "What is it you suspect him of?"

"Dunno," I said, even though I did know. If Athelas knew more than what he should know when it came to getting into the houses of murdered heirlings, if he had purposely allowed himself to be injured to throw off suspicion, then...then...

"Let me set your mind at ease," said Zero coldly, and I knew that he had understood me perfectly. "If you really must have it, I have a story that is not so different from yours. I woke one night after sneaking into my brother's room to sleep and found my brother...very dead."

"You don't—you don't have to tell me this stuff if you don't want to," I said. "You can just tell me that you trust Athelas, and I'll try—"

Sharp with ice, he said, "Don't interrupt, Pet. You wanted to know the truth, and you'll have it now with no complaints! At that time I was ten, and I didn't know that my brother was using my fondness for him to keep me conveniently close for that time when he would make a push to...change the succession of the Family. So when I found him in pieces in his room in the dead quiet of the night, and heard a whisper of sound behind me, I seized the first sword that would come to me and gave chase to the murderer."

"That was when you were in the same room as the murderer," I said, in cold realisation. "The sword—"

"Yes. That was the first time the Heirling Sword came to me."

"Heck," I said, very quietly. At least I'd had my parents until I was thirteen, and they'd been good parents. I hadn't been half an orphan and lost a sibling as well. "You see him?"

"His shadow, nothing more. Not even a scent of him."

"When did you realise it was the same bloke that was murdering other people?"

"The weapon he used for the kill remains the same," Zero said quietly. "A bone knife, single-edged."

"Heck," I said once more, sucking in a breath. "That's what does that—takes a head right off? A bone knife?"

"That, along with strength, savagery, and a knowledge of where best to cut."

"Still sounds like Athelas," I muttered. I caught the anger in his eyes and said as bluntly as I could, "You thought it was him at first, didn't you? You had to have."

"He seemed a likely choice," Zero said, and it seemed as though he was less angry. "Under my father's order, he had already —that's not important. I was wrong."

"Yeah? How'd you find out?"

"My father had nearly killed him that night during a training session," said Zero. "I found him in my own suite when I returned, in a state not much better than my brother. I haven't doubted him since—not when it comes to this."

"Yeah, reckon that'd do it," I said. I'd heard enough about how Athelas was trained to make me pretty sure exactly how injured he'd been, and who had done that to him. I wondered if he had even fought back when Zero's dad did it. I drew in a breath that was shaky with burgeoning relief, and said, "I'm still surprised someone hasn't killed your dad yet."

"Believe me," said Zero, without the slightest edge of humour, "my father still has that particular reckoning to come."

"Okay, but then what about—"

"The second floor," Zero said, with finality, "is the only sensible entrance to that house: the actual entrance is bound up in both the human world and the world Between. I saw it as soon as I got there. If you hadn't told me which way to come, I would have gone that way regardless."

"Okay," I said. It wasn't like I didn't *want* to be convinced: the thought that Athelas could be more heftily involved in the murders than I'd ever suspected hadn't exactly been a pleasant one for me, either. But now that I knew my parents had died for me, it had become overwhelmingly necessary for me to do everything I could to find their killer. If I wasn't going to let the awful drag within me stop me, I certainly wasn't going to let anything else do it.

"Then once Athelas has recovered a little more, we'll begin again," he said. "And perhaps it would help to remember exactly how badly injured Athelas has been on your behalf—more than once."

"I remember it," I said. "But I also remember that he killed me six times, so don't pretend that I didn't have any reason to be suspicious."

Zero huffed out a breath that could have been exasperated, but could have been amused. "Very well," he said.

I mean, it wasn't as though I'd wanted to believe any such thing about Athelas, but it also wasn't as though he wasn't just twisty and deadly enough to be believable in the role. Still, when I returned to the living room fifteen minutes later with a tea-tray, he looked so fragile that the suspicion made me feel faintly guilty.

"I trust you're prepared to continue, Pet," he said.

Zero glanced up at me from across the room, but when I said, "Yeah," readily enough, he went back to whatever cobwebby bit of magic he was doing on a corner of the room.

"Yeah," I said again. "But I've been thinking about it, and I reckon I've got a better way of trying to get some real info. About champions and...other stuff, maybe."

"How very useful," Athelas said.

If I was going to trust him, I had better do it: no looking back, just cards on the table.

"My memories," I explained. "They don't want to come out: I thought it was just that I didn't remember stuff, but whenever I do remember something for a little while, the memories try to wriggle away and pretend they're not important, or real. I don't think it's magic, but it's like my own mind is fighting against me. And two days ago when Zero's dad had a go at me, there was a bit of memory in my head that I don't remember having before, but I can't get it to come back out."

Athelas' grey eyes dwelt on me meditatively. "I see. And you wish to know if there is a way to regain those memories."

"Be handy if Jin Yeong's mojo really did work on me," I muttered. "Then he could get the truth out of me. Figured you might have an idea for something that would work."

"I have an idea, but I very much fear you won't find it palatable," Athelas said. "You once described your encounter with my lord's father as having a *little worm in your brain*, I believe."

"Heck," I said, feeling ill again. "I was afraid you'd say that. You know how to do that, too?"

"Fortunately for you, my dear, I have experience on both sides of that particular magic," he said. "I can both perform the magic required and explain the process of resisting such attacks."

"'Zat the bit where I give it something to chew on that's the truth but don't give it the truth it's looking for?" I asked. "'Cos that's what I do when Zero's dad gets a bit nosy."

I looked up from my coffee to see that Athelas was gazing at me once again. "I begin to understand exactly why and how you haven't been able to get to all of your memories," he said, on a sigh. "My dear, that method is highly effective for discouraging others from poking around your mind, but if you should learn it too well, it is inclined to turn on you whenever you have something you don't particularly want to remember."

"You're saying I did this to myself?"

"I'm saying that perhaps you learnt how to do it at such a young age, and with such proficiency, that you've managed to draw the wool over your own eyes as well."

"That mean you can't do anything about it?"

"I can try," he said. "But as I mentioned earlier, you will very likely find it unpleasant."

"I know," I muttered. "But everything in my life is flamin' uncomfortable these days, so you might as well do it anyway."

I mean, I *said* that, but even if I'd acknowledged how unpleasant the process was going to be, I'm not sure I really understood how panic-inducing it would be, having that little worm in my head again. Not until Athelas said, "Shall we begin, my dear?" and a horribly familiar bit of magic wriggled its way into my head and looked around.

"I should like to know about your champions," said Athelas gently. I caught my breath as the worm began to dig, and he reminded me, "Breathe. You said you don't remember having champions: I want to know about them, so think carefully."

I breathed. Tried not to panic. It was Athelas. He wasn't going to actually hurt me, I knew that.

Didn't have champions; didn't know what champions were. Parents didn't say anything about champions.

A thought was below that, but it was dark and hard and couldn't be forced out: a stubborn root in frozen ground. The worm chewed thoughtfully on my certainty that I hadn't had champions, then went on to look for more. Almost without thinking about it, I let other truth bubble to the surface for it to find so that it wouldn't dig painfully into the frozen ground.

Learned about champions today. Never heard of them before.

"Stop trying to find little bits of truth to satisfy the worm," said Athelas, his voice oddly loud. "That's just another method of deception: a very truthful one, to be sure, but deception nevertheless. It's likely to deceive you as much as it is to deceive anyone else. Don't try to satisfy the worm today. Let it dig through whatever uncomfortable things it finds by itself and don't try to stop it."

I tried. I really did. I managed to stop throwing bits of truth at the worm and let it mumble around in my mind, but then I discovered that I was just feeding it with empty thoughts instead of bits of deceptive truth and gave vent to an annoyed growl.

The worm froze, scenting lies, and I batted it away out of my mind, shuddering.

I unscrunched my eyes to see that Athelas was looking rather startled. He said, "Might I remind you that I'm trying to help you, my dear? Surely that was a little much?"

"Sorry," I said, hunching my shoulders, and added, "Don't reckon this is working."

"Perhaps if you were to consider me more antagonistic, Pet?" he said mildly. "Or perhaps we have not asked the correct questions yet. I'm inclined to think that now that you know what your mind is doing, if you were truly distressed—"

"We are not going to throw Pet to my father to get memories," Zero said, in a deep rumble from his corner.

"Certainly not, my lord. Even should Pet regain those memories for herself, it would almost certainly lead to your father discovering them as well. I rather think we can get somewhere with patience and application."

"I vote for not throwing the pet to the fae lord as well," I agreed thankfully. "He'd have me killed if he thought I was an heirling anyway—no need to give him other reasons to want to kill me."

It was chilling enough to have been approached by him in the mall with Jin Yeong and offered something I still didn't understand. I had the uneasy feeling that he wasn't done with me yet, and as much as I wanted to be prepared should he approach again, I didn't want there to be a second time.

"That's enough for now," Zero said, rising. "Jin Yeong will be back soon and it's time to eat. There's no further purpose in continuing today."

"All right," I said feeling disloyal for being so thankful about that. There was still a very real drag on me that didn't want me to explore either hidden memories or my parents, and even if I was prepared to push past it, it didn't mean I couldn't rest every now and then, too.

"We are by no means finished, Pet," Athelas said admonishingly. "For today, this is enough. One way or another, we will teach you how to reverse what you learned so well how to do."

"That's a nice way to tell someone that something's their own fault," I said, trying to smile. "All right, we'll start again tomorrow. You lot want fish and chips or lasagne?"

Athelas was significantly less burned the next morning, but when I came down from my room he was seated in his chair and mantled in an air of gentle melancholy that didn't seem to lift even when I sat down and wished him a good morning.

He returned the greeting but sank back into silence again, eyes distant, unemployed with any of his usual occupations. His paper sat on the coffee table in front of him, untouched, and I didn't think he'd even made a delicately insulting remark at Jin Yeong, who sat on the couch reading another book.

I had a sudden, horrible thought that Zero might have told him what I suspected, so I asked with the breath held in my chest, "You still hurting?"

"Merely contemplating," he said, coming out of his silence with a faint sigh. "It occurs to me that the first of many dominos has fallen, and I can't yet see how they'll all fall out. Perhaps I have become accustomed to our life here, but I feel it a shame that things should change."

"Reckon you're just feeling a bit blue," I said, letting out my breath in relief. "Let me check your arms anyway. Maybe you're getting a bit more pain than you think."

"I'm really not as delicate as you seem to think, my dear," he said, but he did allow me to roll up his sleeves and make sure of that, although he suffered it with a rather amused light to his eyes. He was right: he was healing very well into a nice pinkish, bumpy sort of finish that looked like it might smooth out some time tomorrow.

"Yeah?" I left him to roll his own sleeves back down and said over my shoulder as I went to get breakfast, "That why Zero's out without you? You can't tell me he didn't refuse to let you join him."

"I will tell you nothing of the sort: I refuse to incriminate myself."

From the kitchen, I raised my voice to ask, "Where's he gone, anyway? The other house?"

"To what remains of it, at any rate," said Athelas. "It was fairly heftily salted, so I rather doubt anything of interest to us will be visible."

"You know who did it?"

"Not officially, but I suspect my lord's father had something to do with it. My lord does, too."

"What a surprise," I muttered to myself. I gathered together a tray to take out; nice and light, because Athelas recuperating tended to stick to tea and biscuits almost exclusively, and Jin Yeong was reading again, which meant he would probably be content with a liquid breakfast, so long as that liquid breakfast included blood.

Athelas waited for me to pour his tea and pass it to him, so he must have still been feeling a bit weak. Jin Yeong looked up from his book, blinked at me, and took his blood-laced coffee with a brilliant smile.

"Good morning to you, too," I said. "What are you so happy about?"

"This is a very useful book," he said. "I am prepared."

"Good grief!" I said, catching sight of a distinctly romance cover but not the title. He was still researching? "Anyone'd think you already have someone in mind!"

I said it partly as a joke, but partly to see if it might actually be true.

Jin Yeong put his nose in the air. "I may date a human woman if I choose."

I stared at him. "You really are going to try and date a human woman? A *specific* human woman? Oi, what about all that Behindkind garbage about the superiority of Behindkind and the inferiority of humans?"

"Even if she is below me in—"

A book sailed across the room and very nearly hit him in the face. Jin Yeong, quick to catch and scowl alike, saved his face from damage and sent a smouldering look across the room at Athelas.

"Do not throw things at me, old man," he said.

"I rather fancied you might want to read that one first," suggested Athelas. He looked a bit brighter, which was nice.

Jin Yeong narrowed his eyes, but seemed thoughtful. He flipped the book around, and I saw that despite the cheap paperback cover, it was a copy of *Pride and Prejudice*. I hadn't read it yet —had been stuck on *Sense and Sensibility* with mum for about a year without moving before everything happened—but I was willing to bet that Athelas had, and that there was a dig at Jin Yeong somewhere in the suggestion.

"What's Zero gunna say about it, that's what I want to know," I said beneath my breath. Of course, I knew that they'd both be able to hear it anyway, and while Athelas shot me an amused look, Jin Yeong narrowed his eyes at me.

"*Hyeong* will say a great deal," he said dismissively. "That is not my affair."

"What if he chucks you through another wall?"

"That is my affair."

"It's mine, too," I said obstinately. "This is *my* house, and the more walls you get chucked through, the lower the value of it drops. I don't want you—"

"I thought you planned on living here indefinitely," remarked Athelas, crossing one leg over the other again. "It would seem that I'm mistaken, if you're worried about the value of the place going down."

"I don't have to be planning on selling it to not like people being chucked through walls," I muttered. I found that Jin Yeong was gazing at me with his chin resting on his folded arms, and said defensively, "What?"

"Shall I not date someone, then?"

"Heck, why are you asking me?" I demanded. My phone buzzed in my pocket, and I fished it out as I said, "Shouldn't you ask her? The one you wanna date, I mean."

The text was from Marazul, and all it said was, *I've got something for you.* I caught my breath a little and then glanced up to find that Jin Yeong was looking expectantly at me.

"What did you say?"

"I said," he said, surprisingly patient, "that perhaps she does not know I like her. Perhaps she thinks I am a friend."

"You have friends? You have *female* friends?"

I looked at Athelas with wide eyes, expecting him to share my surprise, but he just sat there and watched with an air of quiet delight. It wasn't like I could say that Zero wouldn't approve of Jin Yeong having female friends, either, so that left me with nothing much else to say.

Jin Yeong, still contemplating me, asked, "Then how shall I tell her?"

"Told you before," I said, with a touch of irritation. "I've never been on a date. What would I know? Ask Athelas—wait, no, don't ask Athelas. Just…I dunno, make it clear to her that you're interested in her in *that way*, I suppose. Make sure she can't misunderstand."

"*Hae bolkka?*" he muttered to himself. "Shall I? *Ya!* Where are you going?"

"Got something to pick up," I said, abandoning my coffee and making a quick trot for the front door. I had somewhere to be, and giving Jin Yeong romantic advice wasn't something I felt like I wanted to do right now. "See you two later!"

The old mad bloke followed me from about halfway down the street, so I took a few minutes to buy him a coffee and left it on the top of someone's red-brick wall for him. Despite the fact that it was probably wise to avoid the Harbinger if I didn't want to take up my heirling status, it was nearly habit by now to look out for the old fella. I wasn't like he hadn't done the same for me.

I didn't see him again after that, so it must have appeased him. That left me to stroll alone in the pleasant morning sunshine, wondering if Zero was following me again or if he'd really let me out alone now that his dad was hanging around like a bad smell. These days Zero and Athelas were more inclined to be open with me, so I s'pose the universal balance was upset or something: there had to be something unpleasant to make up for the extra.

I should have been legging it to get to Marazul with how long I'd been waiting to get my hands on the info he had for me, but I didn't seem to be able to move at more than a sleepy stroll, despite that. Maybe it was just a reaction from the last couple of days being full on; the need to stroll in the sun without worrying that anyone was going to attack me, or pat me on the head, or ask me for advice on how to ask someone out on a date. What was I supposed to do about any of it? At any rate, it left me sluggish and disinclined to hurry, and I reckon Marazul had been expecting me to be a bit quicker, because he opened the door as soon as I got there, like he was waiting with his hand on the button.

It felt cool and refreshing to walk through that tunnel of water and glass after the sunshine, though. The blue-green light was somehow soothing, and with a quickening of anticipation in my heart, I came out in Marazul's living room, wondering why I'd loitered when it was so good to see his smiling face again.

"Ah," he said, "I thought you might have decided not to come, after all."

"Sorry I took a while," I said, smiling back at him. "I was working on my tan: I've been a bit busy the last few days, so it's nice to stretch out without having to fight something."

"Perhaps we can go out in the sunshine after you see what I've got for you," he said, wheeling himself out from behind the kitchen counter.

I wasn't prepared for the little thrill that ran through me, or for the question that so swiftly followed and crouched at the edges of my mind.

Was that how Jin Yeong would ask out his human friend? Nice and easy?

I frowned a little, then found that Marazul's eyes were resting on me curiously.

"We don't have to if you don't want to," he said. "No pressure."

"No—I mean yes! that'd be nice," I said hurriedly. "You just... reminded me of something."

"Something unpleasant, by the look of it," he observed.

"No, just a bit weird," I told him. "Stuff has been...weird at home for the last couple of days. I left home for a little while recently and now it feels like we're between states and trying to figure out how to work together again."

"You'll have to tell me how you came to be working with three Behindkind one day," he said. I heard a slight hesitation on the *with* and wondered if he'd substituted it for *for*.

There was no fae food on the coffee table, I noticed, with a little tickle of relief. That wasn't the sort of relationship I wanted to build with friends, regardless of what Athelas said. I didn't do it with Five, and I wasn't planning on doing it with 'Zul, either.

"Not trying to feed me up on fae goods, I see," I said to him. "Thanks for that."

He gave a spurt of surprised laughter, and said, "I wouldn't dare. I think you'd manage to find those swords of yours and teach me a lesson. The USB's on the coffee table, by the way."

I don't know if he meant me to sit down but I did so naturally after I'd taken the USB back, and he passed me a cup of coffee. I took it gratefully, and that seemed to please him.

"Didn't get a chance to finish my coffee this morning," I explained, as he wheeled himself in at right angles to me. "This hits the spot just right."

"Yes, I noticed that you're very fond of coffee. I've had to get my own plunger pot since—well..."

"Since we messed up the café?" This time I was the one who couldn't help laughing. "Yeah, that place did really good coffee. It's a shame it was run by goblins who were trying to syphon off energy from humans."

"Do you—you looked like you really know what you're doing. Is that the sort of thing you do often?"

"Zero wanted to make sure I could defend myself if I needed to," I said, shrugging. "It comes in handy when you walk into a place and find that Behindkind are messing with humans."

"I meant, is that the sort of thing you do often—find Behindkind who are mistreating humans and fix it?" he clarified, opening his laptop. Everything in the room pinched and then sharpened with an extra glitter of Behind as it connected to whatever Marazul was using for his not-quite-just-internet. "It seems dangerous for a human."

"It's dangerous for humans, all right," I said, a bit grimly. "That's why I do it."

"I'm surprised Lord Sero lets you do it, in that case."

"Yeah, well, he's still not too happy about it," I remarked, trying not to watch him too obviously as he unlocked the computer and went through a couple of password screens. "But that's my choice, not his."

"Yes," he said slowly, looking over at me. "That's what interested me. Lord Sero isn't the sort of person who allows others to do things that don't please him, anecdotally."

"At the moment I reckon he's just waiting for me to skin my knees too badly and come crying to him," I said, with more than usual honesty. "I reckon he thinks if he gives me my head for a while I'll change my mind."

"You don't agree?"

It was impossible to tell him all the things that meant I didn't have the luxury of backing off; all the reasons that meant I couldn't do anything but keep going on, protecting humans as best I could. So instead, I just shrugged and said, "Don't reckon so. He'll learn, sooner or later."

Marazul murmured, "I see. And when he does?"

"There will probably be another fight," I said, just as honestly as before. "He's getting better, but he still doesn't think much of humans."

"I find that hard to believe, when he's had you to look at," said Marazul, glancing at me briefly beneath his lashes before looking back at the computer. "Here's what I texted you about: I made a copy to work from, just in case, and you've got the original on the USB, but I've taken the password off it. I thought you might like to have a quick look at the copy to see it's what you expected before I delete it. You can delete it yourself if you're worried."

"I don't know exactly what to expect," I said, but I didn't stop him from turning the laptop toward me, and I reached out for it readily enough.

I was still a little bit pink from his compliment, but I still scanned the desktop quickly, more by habit more than any inbuilt suspicion. There was the file he was talking about: a yellow one named *Pet's USB*: but I could see a second file with the same name, which didn't make sense no matter which way I thought about it.

No, I realised a moment later, not exactly a second file with the same name. It was a second file with the same name, but in the fae script that Zero's books were written in. Reckon Marazul didn't know that I could read fae script, because he would have made sure I couldn't see it if he'd known.

I could have told him I could read it—could have asked him what the heck he was doing making a copy of the files I'd asked him to unlock, and leaving them around on his desktop in fae script while reassuring me he was going to let me delete the one in English—but there was a simpler way to check if my sudden suspicions were correct.

I reached for the touchpad and rolled the pointer over the second, fae-scripted folder.

"Not that one," Marazul said swiftly, laying his hand over mine to sweep the pointer away from the folder. He caught himself almost immediately, but it was far too late. "Ah," he said. "You read fae script. How do you read fae script? Humans aren't supposed to be able to do that."

I let my hand lie beneath his, feeling the warmth and excitement of it for a moment longer, before I pulled it away. "You told Zero, didn't you?" I asked, very quietly.

His eyes met mine and he smiled at me: apologetically, charmingly, warmly.

"Pet," he said, and there was regret in his voice, too, but it didn't matter. "How could I not? You're beautiful and shiny, but he could kill me if I step wrong."

"He wouldn't kill you for me," I said. "Not if you weren't harming me. Not even if I'd gotten you to do something he disapproved of."

"And then there's the vampire," he added. "I can't afford to make enemies, and if I have Lord Sero behind me, he won't let the vampire touch me."

I don't know if it was the sheer disappointment of the moment that made me frown: there was no reason to be annoyed at anyone for calling Jin Yeong exactly what he was. "What do you mean? What about Jin Yeong?"

The rueful smile he wore grew a touch warmer with real amusement. He looked as though he were debating within himself whether or not to answer, and as he hesitated, a heavy knock sounded on the door.

"That'll be Zero, then, won't it?"

It was funny how light and clear my voice sounded when I felt so heavy and grey with disappointment—as though a brief warmth of sunshine had vanished away into the cold morning. Had he been planning on walking in the sunshine with me before or after he gave Zero the contents of the USB and I remained in ignorance?

'Zul gave me another smile, and it came just as easily as it had always come: bright and warm, but with nothing to bear it up underneath. I knew then that although I might come back to ask for help with something here and there, I would never again make up an excuse to do so.

"See you next time, then," I said.

I reckon he knew it, too. There was real sadness in his face: I saw it reflected in the glass of the tank as I walked back up the watery hall and toward the door.

I opened the door, and Zero stared at me, taken aback. I didn't make him fumble for words—I'm not even sure he would have fumbled for words. I said, "He's got it ready for you. Catch you at home later. Got a contract for you to sign."

"Pet," he said. "The USB."

He left unsaid that if I didn't give it to him, he would simply take it, but I knew it. I fished it out of my pocket, the glassy squareness of it familiar but mysterious between my fingers.

Maybe I had been living with Behindkind for too long: it was physically painful to hold out my hand and allow him to take the

USB from me. That little bit of leverage I'd had, it was gone. I had spent it. Used it. And now I had nothing else to bargain with. I was going to have to trust again, and I already had a pretty good primer to judge by when it came to how wise it was to trust Behindkind.

Zero didn't snatch it away. Maybe he sympathised with me; maybe it was a moment of real kindness. He waited until I released it of my own accord before he took it away and put it somewhere in his leather jacket.

"Pet," he said again. I stopped and waited, but he seemed to be having more trouble than usual coming up with something to say. At last, he said, "Bring the contract to me when I get home. I'll sign it."

"Beauty," I said. "Got it ready for you."

I wasn't paying attention to where I was going when I left, so when I found myself walking toward Morgana's house, I sat on someone's wall to pull myself together for a few minutes.

I know it wasn't the end of the world, but it had been nice to have someone smile at me for a little while. Someone to make me feel bright and light and *different*, even if I knew they were Behindkind and I was human. Someone to take my mind off the turmoil and uncertainty of the past several days.

Now that spark was gone, and I felt as though I hadn't had enough time to enjoy it. More, I realised as I sat there, I'd told Zero I had a contract for him to sign. That wasn't entirely true: I had it drafted and mostly ready to go, but I had wanted to get North to look it over for me. Having the North Wind look over your contracts for you doesn't sound like it makes much sense, but she'd recently started up her own business in Sandy Bay, helping humans deal with contractual issues when it came to Behindkind, and she'd already offered to help me out if I needed it.

It was time to call in that favour.

CHAPTER TWELVE

By the time I got home it was late afternoon. From the slightly conscious look that Jin Yeong shot at me before looking away and the very casual manner in which Athelas enquired, "You had a pleasant day, Pet, I trust?" it was fairly obvious that Zero had both been home before me and that all of my psychos had a pretty good idea of what had happened.

"Zero headed out again?" I asked, dropping down on the couch beside Jin Yeong with my hands in my hoodie pocket, fiddling with the wad of paper I'd stuffed in there.

"I fancy he thought you were likely to run into trouble," suggested Athelas. "He came back briefly and went out again."

"Didn't see him following me," I said, but it wasn't like I would have seen him if he didn't want to be seen, after all. "S'pose he'll be home soon, too, then."

"I should imagine so." There was a brief moment of silence before Athelas added, "Might I venture to suggest that making contracts between…friends…leaves those friends unable to act on their worser impulses?"

"What, you mean you wanna say *I told you so?*" I asked him. For some reason, that struck me as funny even though it wasn't really. "Fair enough: you might as well."

"Contracts with friends are a matter of protecting both parties, my dear."

I shrugged. "If I have to have a contract with my friends, they're not really friends, are they?"

"A very poor reflection upon our situation, wouldn't you say?" gently suggested Athelas.

I took a moment longer to think about that, because although my first instinct had been a rather soul-crushing agreement, my second felt a bit more just. "If you're going to try and tell me that's not about ninety-five percent show for Behindkind who don't like you lot getting too close to humans, don't bother. I wouldn't believe you."

"He cannot fight," said JinYeong, speaking up for the first time since I'd gotten home that afternoon. "The merman cannot fight, and some enemies are too dangerous to make."

"I know," I said, but I remembered a nearly dead JinYeong who had dragged himself to find me after fighting for my right to keep the very same information. He had had enough experience to know that Zero was far more than a match for him, and he had still fought, tooth and nail, right to the death.

I poked him in the ribs and said, "Thanks," a bit absently, then sank back into my own thoughts. From there, I became aware that Athelas was still watching me. I met his grey eyes and it seemed to me that there was a faint question in them.

"I don't do that," I said to him. "That talking without talking thing that you and Zero do. You're gunna have to speak up."

"Might I suggest a cup of coffee, my dear? While refreshing to see that you're not hurling invective at the merman, I feel that something of a mood-lifter can only improve the situation."

"Not much use calling him names," I said, but I got up. A cup of coffee would hit just right.

"A delightful reflection of your character, I'm sure," said

Athelas blandly, and met Jin Yeong's cold, dark eyes just as blandly. "I must say, from past experience I was not expecting such a mild response."

"No need to be sarcastic," I said, but it made me smile anyway. "Maybe I won't make you a cup of tea while I'm making my coffee."

"I will have blood," said Jin Yeong, slipping around me and into the kitchen.

I stared at his back in surprise. "I can bring it back with me," I called after him, but by then he was already in the refrigerator.

Oh well. More coffee for me.

It wasn't much later that Zero came back. He stood in the hallway like a shadow until I said, "There's still coffee in the percolator if you want it."

He still hesitated for a moment there in the hall; said, "Pet—"

"Got something for you," I said, flourishing the thin sheaf of papers that had been in my hoodie pocket at him. "I just had to run it by a friend before I brought it to you."

"Yes, I heard that North had established her own legal firm," Athelas murmured, taking the sheaf from me. He flicked a look between me and Zero, then turned his attention on the papers. "One can't help feeling it's a step down in life for the North Wind, but no doubt she knows best what suits her."

"You mean you think she's wasting her time with human affairs when she's Behindkind?"

"I mean, Pet," said Athelas, his gaze rising to dwell on me coldly, "that she is a specific kind of Behindkind. And whether or not she will, that calling will hold her, no matter what else she chooses to do with her life."

"Fair enough," I said, as Zero sat down in his usual chair opposite me. "Reckon there's a pretty needy niche for a Behindkind lawyer helping humans, though."

"Apparently so," Athelas said, passing the printed contract to

Zero. "I see that you no longer consider Jin Yeong as an owner, my dear."

"*I* decided," Jin Yeong mumbled into his blood bag. I dug an elbow into his ribs, but that only made him grin.

"What about you?" I asked Athelas. "I put you in there, but if you want me to change it—"

"Oh no!" said Athelas easily. "No special treatment for me, I think! I prefer not to be in so much debt."

"It's not special treatment," I said, startled. I had originally refused to be considered as Jin Yeong's pet, on paper at least, because I had thought he was a lying vampire who pretended to be my friend. I'd kept it as it was because now that we actually were friends again, it was a weird thing to put to paper.

Athelas smiled a little. "Is it not? Pet—"

"All right, all right, don't have a stroke," I said. "I've already drawn you in as co-owner with Zero, so you don't have to worry about getting too attached on paper. It's only until my twentieth birthday, though, or until we figure out who this killer of yours is. And all the other terms are the same: you keeping me in the loop, the house being mine at the end of all this. You have a year and three quarters to think about how you're gunna deal with having to think of a human in a non-pet context."

"That's very kind of you," said Athelas, his eyes glowing with laughter. "I shall endeavour not to disappoint you."

I don't even think Zero read through it properly—or maybe he can read at super-speed, who knows? He signed the contract in a fizz of yellow *something* that was probably the magic North had told me about, then passed it back to Athelas, who took his time to read and sign.

Zero said briefly, "Practise, Jin Yeong."

"I have already practised," Jin Yeong said, one of his incisors showing.

"Then we will practise *again*," said Zero, his icy eyes fairly pinioning Jin Yeong.

I saw the struggle on Jin Yeong's face—the bloody desire to slap his blood bag onto the coffee table and spring for Zero's throat to start the fight on his own terms, wrestling against the part of him that realised he had *too many feelings* and would like to do something about that.

"Oi," I said to him, pinching a bit of his suitcoat sleeve between my fingers, "don't forget to take off your tie."

Jin Yeong looked down enquiringly at me, one eyebrow flying up, and I saw the amusement spring to his eyes. "I was not going to break a wall," he said, but he got up anyway and stripped off both coat and tie, leaving his blood bag on the table. As he sauntered out of the room, he said mockingly over his shoulder, "Come along, *hyeong*. If you wish to talk, we will talk."

"I used to fancy that there was nothing more irritating than a reactive and destructive Jin Yeong," said Athelas mildly as he left the room. "I perceive I was entirely mistaken."

"Almost as bad as a pet that won't do as it's told?" I suggested, grinning.

"Very nearly," said Zero, but there was amusement in his eyes despite the crease between his brows. "Pet—"

"I'm all right," I said, before he could keep going. Like Jin Yeong, I felt as though I needed to be given a minute to reconsider the things I might do or say, so that I didn't regret them. "There's a vampire waiting for you out there, and if you don't go out he'll probably come back in and make a mess here."

"We'll talk later," Zero said, and rested his hand briefly on my head.

It felt like approval, but what do I know anymore?

It was just on five that evening when I got to the yellow skeleton mural in the alley beside Centrepoint, and Abigail and Ezri were already there waiting for me. They had one of the blokes with them this time as well, but I couldn't remember his name.

I'd received the text inviting me to join them just half an hour earlier. Like all of Abigail's other texts, it had been brief and to-the-point. *Majority yes. Got something for you. Yellow skeleton 5pm.* I'd told my psychos that they would have to sort out their own dinner and made a dash out of the house, hoping to get there in time.

"Sorted out your pet fae?" asked Ezri, as soon as she saw me.

I stared at her until she looked away, huffing out a disparaging breath, then said to Abigail, "You said you have something for me?"

"You might find these useful," she said, shoving a fat, rubber-banded manila folder at me. "Look after this lot: they aren't something you can access at the local police station, and I'll want them back."

"Got it," I said. "I'll make sure the boys know to watch out. No blood on the papers, that sorta thing."

The bloke behind them grinned, but Abigail just rolled her eyes.

"Don't make me regret this, Pet."

"I'll try," I said. "Thanks for agreeing to meet with me again. I know this isn't ideal for you."

She shrugged. "Well, we'll get something out of it, too, if it makes you more inclined to take care of those things we mentioned last time. Thanks for helping out my girls yesterday, by the way."

"Helping us?" Ezri snorted. "We helped her fae!"

"They were pretty useful," I said, grinning. "Oi, Abigail—were there any of the earlier groups you talked about that shared info with fae?"

Abigail stiffened. "Why do you ask about that?"

"Well," I said, scenting blood, "informational sharing goes both ways, right? For instance, there was a group of fae in the twenties who knew a lot about a few humans they shouldn't know about. They were trying to protect them, but—"

She raised a brow at me. "Protect them? Why?"

"They were important humans. Protecting them would give the fae a leg up."

"There have been mentions in the records," Abigail said. "A stupid way to do things, if you ask me. It always ended up badly, as far as I could tell—especially for the humans."

"Not really a surprise," said the bloke. He paused, and said rather diffidently, "I heard you had something happen to you like Cadence."

"It started out like that," I said. "It's not really like that anymore, though."

Not exactly. I was a pet again in contract as well as in word, but at least I had been able to gain a little while losing a little. I might still feel slightly bitter about how it had happened, but I'd been able to have a say, at least.

"You didn't get taken back there? To their land?"

"I've been in and out, but that was by myself, mostly. Why?"

"We found something in our records about you, that's all," Abigail said abruptly. "We wanted to double check that you weren't—you know. One of the ones who wears a human face. That's why he's here."

"Rude," I said, looking at the bloke again. So he could tell fae from human, could he? I would like to know how. "Oi, what did you find?"

"The official police records note that you disappeared for a while when you were younger, not to mention that you died with your parents that night."

"Checking up on me?" I couldn't blame them. I was pretty sure Zero and Athelas had been doing the same with them: I had seen a few texts pop up on Zero's phone with Detective Tuatu's name on them over the last week.

Ezri looked at me challengingly. "Looks a bit weird, don't you think?"

I shrugged. "Dunno. I stayed with some friends from out of state when I was younger: maybe that's what they're talking about. I don't know why the police would think I'd disappeared, though."

"Did you say *out of state?*" Ezri said sharply.

"Yeah." I shot a bit of a worried look in her direction, because she sounded very urgent about it, and I didn't see that my friends from out of state were anything to worry about. "Stayed with 'em for a bit of a holiday, but I don't remember much."

"How come you don't remember much?"

"Dunno, I was still young."

"How young?"

"About twelve," I said, and as I said it, I realised how weird that sounded. How come that had never seemed weird inside my head? You say *I don't remember, I was young* about stuff that happened when you were two or three, not about stuff that happened when you were twelve.

Ezri said, "Yeah, weird, isn't it? When you find out you can't remember stuff from when you were twelve and your brain says it's cos you were too young. What were your friends' names?"

It took me a while to open my mouth again, and while I was still trying to find my way to answer that question, Ezri looked at me with cold triumph.

"Can't remember, can you?"

"I can," I protested, even though I wasn't so sure anymore. "Just hang on a minute! It was—there was a bloke—and a—flamin' heck."

"*Out of state* is code," Abigail said, while I was still staring at Ezri in shock at the further betrayal of my own memory. "That's what they call it when fae get hold of a human kid and take them off to their own land. When they get back—*if* they get back—we usually say they've been *out of state*. It's a coded reference."

"Who with? What are you talking about?" There was no way it was code, because that meant that enough people knew about the fae to have developed a code. It meant that my parents knew about that code. It meant that I had—it meant that I had—

I shook my head and said defensively, "How do you even know that?"

Abigail hesitated for a moment, then pulled out her phone. "Watch this," she said, and there was a grin on her face like she couldn't help it. She pulled up an app that turned her screen green, and used the search function on it to type in something like *early Hobart records.*

A 3-D book representation appeared, floating in the centre of the app, and Abigail casually flicked it right out and into the air in front of us. She caught it with the effortless ease of practise, and there it was in her hand: real and full-sized, taking up space in reality that it shouldn't have been able to take up considering it was a book from inside someone's phone.

"The heck!" I said, staring at Abigail.

She grinned. "It's something Blackpoint set us up with. It means we can carry a lot more around with us than people think."

"We're gunna have to have a talk about Blackpoint one of these days," I muttered.

"Look," she said, flipping through the book and holding it open for me. It was a soft-cover book that looked like it had been stitched together a couple hundred years ago; handwritten and squiggly, it was almost illegible. "This is the first record we have—it's when they started using this code. *Alas, we were informed that Anne travelled out of the state some three days later. No word has been had from her a year since, but we all know what out of state entails and expect to see no more of her. Arthur continues to take it badly.* There are references after that, but this is the first we found."

The empty patches in my memory sprouted a sudden, single remembrance. Great grandma Anne, who had disappeared—that copy of her license. And what had mum said?

She went out of state and was never seen again.

The thought left me feeling slightly bitter. Five was right: mum and dad had been hiding things from me. Did that mean my parents knew about a group like Abigail's? Had they been part of one? Why hadn't they ever told me about it, if so?

"I'll look up some more mentions of it," Abigail said. Maybe she mistook my silence for disbelief. "You should do some digging of your own, Pet."

"Thanks," I said. "I'll do that."

"Give us five minutes before you leave the alley," she said. "We don't want to be seen with you if we can help it."

"Rude," I said, more from habit than conviction. Ezri and the man grinned, but Abigail just sniffed.

Heck, I thought as I watched them walk away. This was something I was going to have to tell Zero, wasn't it?

I heaved a sigh to myself and headed up the street five minutes later to get myself a latte by way of relaxing. It was probably time I asked Zero to take a gander at my great grandma, too. It wasn't that I had been trying to keep it from them while they were asking questions, but it hadn't bobbed up in my mind like it should have. Now that I knew—now that I thought I knew—what had happened to her wasn't human-related, it seemed doubly important. I would just have to make sure they didn't know where I'd gotten the information.

When I came out of the café a little later, it felt like a storm was there to chase me home. Maybe it was just the weight of all the new knowledge I'd gained that afternoon mounting on the information from the day previous. It could have been a combination of sheer befuddlement and the extreme likelihood that I was being followed by the old mad bloke as usual, though.

As I came back past the delivery bay at Centrepoint, just before the alley where I'd talked with Abigail, I caught a flicker of yellow and black movement in my left peripheral. There was a mural on the roller door there: a Tasmanian tiger with the words

All I wanted was a sheepie. Just one sheepie below it. Sure enough, when I peered into the gloom, it wagged its tail at me and half howled, half whined, scratching at the black painted words, scoring them with its nails.

I grinned, partly in relief, partly in delight. "Hello, boy," I said, taking a few steps into the gloomy delivery bay. Heck, maybe it recognised me: I'd walked past and smiled at it for a few years now.

It pranced along the roller door, back and forward, forward and back, just like a dog when it wants you to play. I laughed and bounced on the balls of my feet in reply, which sent it into an ecstasy of bouncing and whining.

I knew it was Between acting up, but it didn't occur me until I was just a few metres away from the tiger that there was usually a reason for Between to start moving around and getting creative with the world.

And that reason was usually something big and probably bad passing by in the human world.

I turned to make a swift and comprehensive run for it before whatever it was that was stirring things up could see me here *seeing* it stirred up, but the entrance was already dark with something that turned the street outside into a silk-screened version of itself. Around the edges of that screen, shadows coiled and reached out, and I threw a look around for whatever weapon was closest to hand.

The only things I could see were remnants of foam packaging and an old umbrella. I tried a length of the foam first, in hopes that I could make it into a sword, but it turned into a whip edged with teeth that looked more likely to bite me than anyone I could possibly hope to hit by absolute accident if I was stupid enough to try and use the thing.

So I snatched up the umbrella instead, panting, "You flamin' better not be *that* sword!" at it in sheer desperation. It was solid and secure in my hand straight away; a blade long and true and chased with a glow of yellow that faded only slowly, the grip familiar beneath my fingers.

Ah heck. What was the use of telling me not to pull the Heirling Sword out of Between when it was the only sword that felt like coming out whenever there was an umbrella nearby?

I turned back to the screened-off entrance, the tiger at my back whining in fear, and drew back the sword in a two-handed guard stance from which I could slash as quickly and effectively as possible at my height.

Then flowers sprouted and burped up grass from the entrance of the delivery bay, freezing my lungs.

Heck. It was Zero's dad. *Why was it Zero's dad?*

Before he could step through and see what I held, I tossed the sword into the darkness behind me, where it landed without a sound. That was a relief, I thought; it meant it must have changed back into an umbrella, right? Less relieving was the fact that I now had no weapon to face Zero's dad—not to mention that it wouldn't have done me any good to have one anyway. The brief, mad thought that I could test Athelas' postulation on my missing memories popped up in my mind and terrified me just long enough to make me break into a sweat before I remembered that anything I learned would be given to Zero's father in the same moment that I learned it. I couldn't let that happen.

The flowers sprouted forward until there was a path for him all the way to my feet before he stepped through the screen and into the bay. He looked around him as he came, his mouth in a pained sort of grimace, but he mustn't have felt endangered by me, because he came without his guards this time.

How flamin' cosy.

He stopped a few feet short of me and took a moment to look around again, turning all the way around and unresponsive even when I shifted a little to put myself opposite him with the side wall at my back and the entrance at my left. It was a small comfort, but better than the idea of having to get past him to run for the entrance.

I think he wanted me to know how very little he thought of me as a threat, because when he was finally done making a show of looking around, he gave the smallest, most mocking of bows, and said, "The pet, I see."

"Off the leash and in person," I said, with a shiver sitting in my bones. "You come here often?"

"Humans say such a lot of useless things," he told me. "I saw a loose pet sniffing around and came to see if it was doing my son harm."

"I'm out on his orders," I said. It stuck in my gullet to have to talk about having permission to be outside and being on orders, but that was better than the flowers and grass I could see sticking in my gullet if Zero's dad decided to see where else those perennially springing flowers could grow. "Just running a delivery."

His eyes fell to the straps of my backpack. "I see. What are you delivering?"

"Info for a case he's working on," I said. He was going to want to see what I had and I wouldn't be able to say no, but I *had* to say no. There was no way he could be allowed to see the files I'd gotten from Abigail. Not only would that give him the information—if he didn't already have it—but it would give away the fact that there was a guerrilla sort of group out there. Abigail's group were already on a shortened life expectancy; I couldn't bring about their fall.

"That is very interesting to me," said the fae.

And now...and now he would tell me to show him what was in my backpack. I had the instinct to reach up and grip the straps of my backpack defensively, but managed not to follow it.

"Yeah?" I said instead. "Didn't think you cared much about humans and their affairs. Didn't expect you to want to look at a bit of paperwork."

He said, "I care very much about what interests my son these days. Open the bag, human."

"Don't think Zero would like that," I said, my left foot shifting back slightly.

"Lady, lady!" called someone, to my left.

I froze again. Oh heck.

The fae's head snapped toward the entrance, a crazily familiar cleft etched between his brows, and at that very moment, the Tasmanian tiger bounded past behind him with the sword in its mouth and streaked around the corner before he could turn his head back to catch a glimpse of what had moved to his left. I would have been worried about letting loose a Tasmanian tiger on Hobart if I'd had the brain space to be worried by it.

As it was, all I could do was say "What the heck?" in a shaken sort of voice that didn't have to be faked.

"Lady, lady!" burbled a voice from the screened-off street again, and a familiar figure tumbled right through into the delivery bay, supporting his drunken walk with the tip of the sword I'd last seen in the mouth of a Tasmanian tiger.

"Go back to the road!" I hissed at him frantically, but it was already too late.

Zero's father laughed, a mirthless, cold thing that sprinkled chips of ice amongst the flowers, and said, "Oh, this is very interesting!"

Was the old bloke grateful for the food and drink; the occasional blanket or t-shirt? I didn't know, but I wished that he would be grateful elsewhere. He could only get himself and me into trouble in this situation. We needed to be quiet and sit below the radar when it came to Zero's dad. More than ever, I realised that today.

"Get out of here!" I yelled at him, and Zero's dad laughed again.

"Stay. Where. You. Are," he said to me, with a force that ossified my bones, and strode back toward the entrance and the old mad bloke.

The old bloke capered for two seconds, though I could have sworn it was panic in his eyes, not madness, then threw the sword high over the fae's head, straight at me. If I'd been capable of laughing I would have laughed at the expression of sheer, offended incredulity on the fae's face as the sword sailed over his head.

I caught it by sheer habit, and it fit me like an extension of my arm, not light but exactly the right weight to level at Zero's dad without my arm shaking as he turned back to face me. And I did level it at him, because as soon as it touched my hand, my mind was clear and I could move properly again.

"Back off," I told him, my arm taking on a tinge of the glowing yellow that had swept up the blade as soon as I caught it. "Touch one hair of his scraggly little head and we'll have a problem."

Completely undermining that sentiment, the old mad bloke scarpered up and out of the delivery bay, giggling madly, and disappeared. Flaming heck. I was gunna kill him myself next time I saw him, the flea-ridden old troublemaker!

The fae let out a real laugh this time, his eyes glowing with fascination, and I could suddenly see why Zero's human mum might have found him attractive enough to follow him into Behind to her doom.

"There's no problem here," he said to me, his eyes still running over me. It felt as though he was looking at me from the inside out. "You're a good pet, aren't you? Very territorial, as I can see. I have no quarrel with that, so long as you're protecting the right people."

I couldn't help laughing. Maybe I was hysterical, maybe I just knew I'd already gone far too far to pull back now. "You're soliciting me to stand beside your son if he challenges?"

"*When* he challenges. Yes."

It made no sense. Here I was, holding the Heirling Sword, and he *knew* it: there was no way he didn't know I was an heirling, too. He also knew that heirlings were there to fight other heirlings until only one remained to take the crown. By rights, he should be trying to kill me, not seek collaboration.

"Right," I said. "Well, I'm his pet and I'll be by his side contractually, so you don't need to worry about that."

"I'm sure you'll excuse me for continuing to worry about such things," he said, his voice crawling into my mind. Crawling like a worm. "As soon as one of my men returned without his commander and the story of a certain pet wielding the Heirling Sword, I was delightfully curious. I came to you once before to see what you would do: today I have been more successful, it would seem. While my son has never had need of Champions, I do like to ensure that his allies are well vetted."

The worm, indiscriminate, already sought for truth though he hadn't given it exact directions; it burrowed, and everything for which it burrowed was connected to that word, *champions*. Part of my mind wobbled, terrified of being pulled up by the roots with its secrets, and threw up a similar flurry of small, incomplete truths as I had used earlier with Athelas to feed to the worm.

Never met a champion. Only heard the word the other day. Dunno what any of this means.

The worm chewed on that while I wavered, caught between opposing instincts to use this moment to find out everything I could, or to keep throwing up little bits of truth to feed the worm and escape Zero's father as soon as I could; caught between desire for knowledge and self-preservation. But I didn't have the luxury of choosing knowledge—not today—because everything I learned was something Zero's dad also learned.

Unaware of and unaffected by my struggle, the worm burrowed until a memory pierced through the surface of my mind, honed by fear. I knew then that regardless of what I wanted, the worm really was going to find something—both because there was something to be found, and because Athelas had been right: an antagonistic force was far more inclined to invoke memories than a friendly one. I found, with an icy suddenness, that I did indeed know about Champions, and the worm went after that certainty with sharp, sharp teeth.

I knew I couldn't let Zero's father see any of what was boiling up to the surface of my mind. "Get *out* of my head!" I snapped, and slapped that little worm out before it could chew on what it had dredged up. It was too late, *far* too late, to push back what it had pulled up. Too late to make Zero's dad think I couldn't protect myself against him. Too late to do anything but make sure he couldn't see anything that might help him: that vast wave of memories that pressed up against my mind and made it hard to breathe or think or talk.

"Very well," he said softly, his words fragmented and hard to understand between rushes of memory. "I would not worry too much about stray memories if I were you, little human. You'll find me very forgiving if you're willing to leave behind what is behind and serve only me. Run along: find your master and look after him well. We will continue our conversation another time. And tell that traitor steward that the next time I see him he will wish he had chosen otherwise than he has."

I didn't wait for him to tell me again: me and my backpack, we legged it up and out of the delivery bay, memories crowding thick and fast in my throat, in my head, before my eyes. The sword came with me, but it was an umbrella again before my feet touched the footpath, and I was running, running blindly.

I don't know where I went or how I got there, but it was small and wet and had some sort of greenery that took away the city smell and tried to push peaceful thoughts into my head. I unfurled the umbrella in front of me, bright yellow, and it whorled in my vision until it was a vast, gravity-pulling hole into which I tumbled.

I remembered.

I remembered my parents pushing me into my room with

shaking hands, and the threatening and furious speech from downstairs.

"You can't refuse the contract! Who will protect you if you refuse our help? Do you expect that little weak thing to succeed in the trials?"

"We don't want a throne, and we don't want protection. We won't sell our child to you."

"If you don't sell it to us, you'll find it as dead as the others one day."

"Better than losing her soul to a group like you. We'll protect her our own way: we don't need your money or your protection."

I remembered one day out on the street, on my way home from the supermarket, when a man with a face like a fly peered at me with his huge eyes and said, *"This is the child. Take it."*

Being bundled into a world that looked as though I saw it through the bottom of a jar, all weird, rounded edges and wrong coloured sky, wrong smelling grass, wrong shadows.

Being passed around between men and women with too many arms and sharp teeth, screaming; the cruel pinches to get me to stop, and when that failed, the outright beating.

I remembered...I remembered the room disintegrating into a chaos of screams and blood as my personal nightmare carved a deadly path from the door and right into the centre of the room, while I lay beaten and almost unconscious on the bed, coiling the melee around him as he came.

I remembered dragging my broken body up and out of the room on the outskirts of that terrifying whirlwind, stumbling out onto the street and nearly in front of a bus somewhere, crazily, in Kingston Beach.

I had tumbled onto that bus and somehow no-one had seen me—or maybe no-one cared about me—and I hadn't moved again, pain-wracked with the shuddering of the bus, until it stopped at its final destination and didn't move again.

I saw yellow somewhere in the morass of my memories and clutched at it: I wanted *out*. I didn't want to see this anymore. I hadn't had memories of Champions because I hadn't had Champions—I had had kidnappers. My parents had refused to sell me, refused to let me be used as a pawn in someone else's game, and the Behindkind had stolen me and taken me Behind rather than give up.

As the tears slowed and I stared blankly into yellow canvas again, real thoughts began to flow through my mind once again. My parents hadn't just chosen to die for me, they'd also refused to sell me. I had been so precious to them that they had sold themselves rather than sell me; died rather than have me die for them. Was I allowed to ruin that sacrifice by going my own way, whether or not I brought their killer to justice—or whatever passed for it Behind?

Just do it, part of me said. *Listen to Zero, listen to his dad. At least pretend to help Zero take the throne and forget about digging into your past. Let Zero do it. He* said *he'd do it, and then you don't have to worry about his dad.*

No more memories to harrow me. No more digging for said memories. Just trust Zero and rest in the safety that it promised. Honour my parents' sacrifice by staying alive long enough to enjoy life when everything Behindkind was stripped from my life at last.

It was so tempting. And there with my forehead resting on my knees and something soft supporting me from the left, I actually considered it. I could live my life, if not free from danger, at least protected from that danger again. I didn't have my parents, but I did have Zero.

There was a kind of dead, sickness in the pit of my stomach, because as much as I wanted to do it, I couldn't. If I did that, who would be there to help the humans? Abigail and her group? How long before they died, too? I would be running away from what I ought to be doing because I was too scared to do it. Worse than Zero, who had stopped doing what he thought was right because it hurt too much to lose people, I would be someone who had stopped doing what I thought was right because I was scared that

I was going to be hurt. Because I wanted to feel comfortable and protected.

I might even lose my soul in a way, as my parents had feared.

I wanted to feel safe. I wanted to be comfortable. But right now, I couldn't allow myself to be either, and that thought made me press my head back into my knees and sob again until everything felt hot and tight and feverish.

When that passed, I felt the soft peacefulness of a breeze slipping around me, and smelled the freshness of some kind of greenery—moss, or maybe clover—as well as the comforting tightness of some kind of an embrace curled around me.

Perfume tickled my nose as the world became real again, coiling in between the peaceful green that clung to me, and after a little longer, I began to be able to see the real, present world around me again.

As I came to the knowledge that part of the embrace around me was highly scented vampire, the rest of that reassuring embrace began to slither away in a furling up of greenery that I would have recognised at once if I had been in any condition to do so. The green man had found me again, and instead of advice, this time had given comfort.

"The heck," I said quietly to myself, and dashed the back of my hand across my eyes. My face was sticky with tears, and Jin Yeong's shirt front was a bit damp with them, too. He didn't seem to care too much, because he wasn't muttering about his best suit today, and it seemed like he was reluctant to let me go when I started to disentangle myself from him as well as the remaining vines.

"Why are you sitting in the street, crying?" he asked, straightening his tie over the patch of teary shirt as I pulled away.

I sniffed a bit. "How'd you find me sitting in the street crying?"

"*Hyeong* sent me to look for you: he said you had been too

long. I followed your not-scent. Why are you sitting in the street, crying?"

"Met Zero's dad: had a memory," I explained briefly, trying to unfold my legs to get up. They didn't want to work—probably a lack of circulation from crouching in street-corners having a mental breakdown while covered in vines—but that was okay, because Jin Yeong lifted me up by either arm instead.

"This," he said, indicating me with a tip of his head, up and down, "does not look like a memory."

"It was a pretty flamin' nasty one," I told him, rubbing my legs as much for comfort as the desire to have some feeling back in them. "A few pretty nasty ones, actually. We'd better get going. I don't want Zero's dad finding me if he's still around."

"We do not have to go home," he said, releasing my arms but taking one of my hands instead.

"No," I said dully, curling my fingers into his. "Better go home and get this over with. Reckon I've got a bit of info the other two might find useful."

"It would seem that we know why your champions were not slaughtered around you," said Athelas, when I was done talking. "Our murderer helpfully slaughtered them all for you somewhere between Behind and Kingston, and chose to display the bodies there."

"Yeah," I said thickly, wriggling a bit against Jin Yeong to sit up properly. He had sat behind me and slung an arm warmly but loosely around my neck as I told Zero and Athelas what had happened, and that had been oddly comforting—the feeling that my neck was guarded—so I hadn't tried to pull away. He waited until I was still again, then settled the arm back around my neck loosely. "I wanna know why he did that."

"Perhaps if you had waited around long enough to discuss the matter—"

"I was twelve and terrified," I said, feeling another shiver deep in my bones. "I was just lucky the bus I jumped on was direct to Hobart instead of going around Kingston Beach first. It didn't stop the murderer finding mum and dad at home later, anyway, so I don't think he wanted to talk."

"It must have been an annoying day for him," said Zero thoughtfully. "First, his quarry disappears with the Champions that he also needs to kill; then, he kills the Champions and his quarry has escaped yet again. I wonder if he had such trouble with any of the others?"

"I don't really care how annoying his day was, actually," I said. "And if he's working for your dad or the king, I hope one of them punished him for it when he got back, too."

Athelas smiled briefly. "I'm quite certain he was punished."

"You're pretty flamin' happy for a bloke Zero's dad is making threats about," I told him.

"I was quite well aware of what I was doing when I did it," he said easily. "It seemed to me that it was time to cut ties entirely, since my lord's father had unfortunately become aware that I was serving his son rather than himself."

"Is that why you're always sneaking out at night? You've been feeding Zero's dad bad information about him?"

That...was another relief that I hadn't known I'd needed.

"Say rather *limited* than bad," he temporised.

"I was well aware of it," said Zero, his blue eyes on me. As if I'd make accusations again, after what I'd heard from him and his dad! "Obviously he had to know something, but we preferred him not to learn about the heirlings being alive if we could avoid it."

"And that reminds me! You lot told me that only an Heirling can grab the sword like that!" I added accusingly. With Jin Yeong at my back and the other two facing me, I was beginning to feel safer and less wobbly, my face less stiff with the tears that had been there earlier. But I still felt hard done by, and I wanted someone to take responsibility for that.

Annoyingly cool, Zero said, "Next time you go out, take one of us with you."

"It's a bit late for that now," I said resentfully. "Your dad doesn't want to kill me—I just told you! The old mad bloke picked up the sword and threw it to me—he didn't throw an umbrella at me, he threw the *actual sword*. He's gotta be an Heirling, too, doesn't he?"

"The Harbinger can fight for a favoured Heirling," said Athelas. He was as cool as Zero, but there was a tightness to his cool. "They can pick up and retain the sword. Congratulations, Pet. It would seem that the Harbinger favours you."

"Oh yay. Lucky me."

Zero, his eyes the brightest blue I'd ever seen them, actually grinned. "Now you might have some appreciation for my state of mind over the last eighty years."

"First of all—*heck. How old are you?* Second of all, is that your way of saying *now you know how I feel?*"

"I very much doubt you'll ever have to feel the level of frustration I've felt in dealing with you," he said.

"Garbage," I said, jerking a thumb at Jin Yeong, who was an easy, comfortable target. "I've had to deal with him. It can't be worse than that."

Zero opened his mouth at the same time as Jin Yeong made a startled protest, but I didn't give either of them time to finish.

"You *can't* say I'm worse than him. You've dealt with both of us: be honest."

Jin Yeong openly grinned as I tilted my head back to look at him. Anyone'd think he was proud of being annoying—he probably was.

"Anyway," I said, ridiculously comforted as I lowered my chin to look at Zero again. "Abigail gave me that bunch of files and said the police probably don't have 'em, either, so at least we've got something new to look at now that we know we're looking for dead champions and murdered heirlings. Hopefully we don't have to fight your dad or the king to get to each heirling before they clean up what the murderer started."

"If the police don't have the records, I rather doubt anyone else has them," Athelas said. "I'm inclined to think that although Upper Management had firmly ensconced themselves in the local police, my lord's father has managed to get a toe-hold in Upper Management."

"Well," I said, drawing in a breath that caught very slightly, "s'pose all of this answers the question of exactly how much your dad knows about the cycle starting again, anyway. Good news is he doesn't want to kill me."

Zero, echoing my earlier thought, said, "The fact that he doesn't want to kill you is more worrying to me."

"Rude!" I said, but it came out on another caught breath, and although Jin Yeong's arm tightened around my neck, I still felt cold.

I, too, wanted to know why Zero's dad was happy to have me alive and near his son when I was also an heirling. I wanted to know what he'd managed to see of those new, horrible memories his worm had dredged up, and why he had urged me to abandon looking for others. I also wanted to know exactly what he wanted of me, because I was pretty flaming sure that it wasn't just to support his son in a claim for the throne.

And I was pretty sure that whatever it was, I didn't want any part of it.

CHAPTER THIRTEEN

Evening came softly and quietly; we each took a file to look at without really discussing it. No one asked me for anything, which was somewhere between a relief and an irritation, so I went upstairs with my file, still feeling raw and damaged. Jin Yeong even brought me up a mug of coffee later on while I sat in my beanbag chair and stared at the ceiling, unwilling to do anything and trying not to think too much. My brain was a mess of terrifyingly new memories that had taken hold in my mind, a gut-wrenching knowledge that my parents hadn't been what I thought they were, and lingering sadness from Marazul's betrayal that morning. The last of those particularly irked me. The rest made sense, but it was stupid to feel sad about a non-relationship with a merman, especially when there were so many other things to think about—so many other things that needed attention.

Turns out your heart doesn't shut up talking even when you don't have the time or brain space to listen to it.

Luckily for me, my phone buzzed in my pocket with a call when I was only halfway through my coffee and the thoughts I was trying not to think. I took it out of my pocket and looked down at it rather listlessly, but my heart jumped when I saw the caller id. Morgana. It was Morgana.

I stared at the phone for a couple of seconds longer, then stabbed at the green *answer call* button before it had a chance to stop ringing, and said stupidly, "What? I mean, hey. Hi. Are you all right?"

There was a very small sigh, short and exasperated. "You're the last person who should be worried about other people," said Morgana's voice.

"Yeah, I know," I said, trying not to smile too much. I knew exactly what she would look like right now: sitting upright in bed, her hair up high in some elaborate, black-decorated do, her black-lipsticked lips pursed in mock exasperation even though her eyes were laughing. "It's the company I'm keeping lately. I'm getting too protective for my own good. What's up?"

She didn't answer for a moment, and the answer followed another sigh, this one quicker and less comforting. "Look, Pet, I don't mind your big boy Zero in the house, but don't let the one that wears houndstooth come back again. He apparently went upstairs last night and scared the kids and bothered my parents, then went off without a word to anyone else. He left all my mirrors crooked, too—it took us all day to get them right again."

"Flamin' heck," I said softly. "Sorry. I didn't know. I'll have a word with him about that."

There was another slight pause before she said, "Thanks."

"You could have texted me," I told her. "Or gotten Daniel to tell me. You don't have to talk to me until you're comfortable."

"Your partner came to see me yesterday, too," Morgana said abruptly. "He said you were working really hard to keep me safe for a while there. Thought I should say thanks for that, too."

The startled thought that Detective Tuatu had gone to see Morgana crossed my mind. "My partner?"

"Jin Yeong. He climbed up the outside of the house and stared at me through the window until I opened it. He told me not to tell you but he's not the boss of me so—"

"Flamin' heck!" I said, even more startled. "I'm surprised he's not the one you're complaining about, then!"

"He didn't upset the kids, and he was trying to do me a favour —well, he was trying to do you a favour, but I think he figured it'd help me, too. I'm just surprised your Zero didn't try to do the same."

I would very much have liked to ask her about what she'd said about Zero a couple of weeks ago, that suggestion that had been sticking in my head and making life uncomfortable ever since it had wormed its way into my mind, but I didn't dare. It wasn't the right time, and I didn't want to break the tenuous connection that felt like it had formed again.

Instead, I asked, "You decided you're gunna start talking to me again, then?"

"Maybe a bit," she said.

"Okay," I said. Nice and light, as if I was trying not to startle a banshee caught between the jam and the golden syrup with an arm wrapped around each one and far too close to the edge of the shelf. "That'll be nice."

"I don't mean that I want to see you," she added, but the hardness wasn't there in her voice anymore. "But if you need someone to talk to every now and then, I'll pick up the phone when you call."

"Okay," I said again.

"I'm not going to help with your weird stuff; you'll have to keep that away from me. It's just if you want to talk about blokes or makeup or something."

I opened my mouth to say, "Actually, there *is* something—" but before I could say it, Morgana added, "I'd better go. Daniel will be getting home from work soon. Just...thanks for everything."

She hung up before I could answer her, and I sat there in silence again until I heard the clash as Zero and Jin Yeong began fighting in the backyard—steel to steel, by the sound of it, which was a relief, because that meant it was just practise and not a real fight. Athelas must have been out there, too, because the house was empty when I went downstairs to put together some afternoon tea for them, and that was just fine by me. I had a lot to think about again, but the most pressing of those things pushed itself to notice as I boiled the jug and prepared a coffee plunger and teapot. Namely, that Athelas had never been higher than the first floor in Morgana's house while I'd been there. Exactly how had he known where to go to find the kids? Daniel had been with me at the time, and I'd never told my psychos where we found them. I'd mostly avoided talking about the kids with them because I was half afraid they'd say something had to be done about them, and I didn't think the kids deserved to have something done about them.

Athelas, it would seem, had either been in the house when I wasn't aware, or had already been to the house before I was there. Whichever one it was, I wanted to know about it—and I wanted to know why he hadn't told me about it. Why he hadn't told any of us about it, if it came to that.

Things were still swirling around in my head when I brought the tray out to my psychos, because as suspicious as it was that Athelas knew where the kids were, I was still more concerned about knowing why he'd gone to see them. I wanted to know if it was on Zero's orders, too.

"You seem perturbed, my dear," said Athelas, as I set the tray down on the small, sun-faded table beside the seat in which he was elegantly sitting.

"Heirling stuff to think about," I told him, and it was technically true even if it was the sort of twisted thinking that I would have had to use against the brain worm that burrowed for truth. I shivered a bit, but it was true that Morgana could be considered as *heirling stuff*, since she was almost certainly one herself, little though she knew it. "Funny how I've got less of a life expectancy these days than I did when my parents were killed."

"Don't say that word," said Jin Yeong, suddenly close and reaching for a biscuit. "I already *told* you about that."

Zero reached for the closest mug of coffee—Jin Yeong's spice blend—but Jin Yeong snarled and unerringly snatched it away before he could touch it, so I shut my mouth.

Zero coolly took the other one and said, "You should save some of that energy for fighting. You haven't been paying attention."

"I did not bite you," Jin Yeong said curtly, and strode back across the yard with his coffee.

Athelas smiled and reached for his empty teacup, and after a moment or two Zero's brows went up and he followed Jin Yeong into the fight zone again.

I didn't say anything straight away. I just put Athelas' teapot in front of him, then sat down beside him with my feet up on the last bit of the patio railing that wasn't rotted all the way through.

"Jin Yeong's getting pretty touchy these days," I said, after a while.

I saw the faint smile in my peripheral once again: I'd been expecting that. It meant that Athelas was very well aware of exactly why Jin Yeong was behaving the way he was, and that he didn't want to ruin his amusement by telling me why.

That was all right.

That wasn't what I really wanted to ask him about.

"He's certainly less considered in his attacks," Athelas agreed. "But then, he restrained himself from biting Zero just now, so I'm cautiously optimistic for his chances. You both seem to be expanding in...unexpected ways these days. I rather fancy that you're getting much better at fighting these days yourself, Pet."

I couldn't help beaming. I'd thought I was getting better, but it was nice to hear that from someone who knew what they were talking about. Of course, I still *very much* remembered those occasions that I'd fought Athelas—the last one notwithstanding—and I was very well aware that I would have to fight significantly better if I was to train properly with Athelas.

Looking at it one way, I was lucky that Jin Yeong mostly chose to fight with swords when it came to me; he wasn't lying when he said his body was a weapon.

"Been practising," I said, blowing multicoloured steam from my coffee out into the back yard. "But the weird thing is, the better I get, the harder it is to beat you blokes. Comes from fighting against you when you've got a handicap, I s'pose."

"Yes, Jin Yeong is significantly better without a weapon," said Athelas. "But he is also significantly good when it comes to double blades, so holding your own against him is nothing to sniff at."

I nudged myself down in my seat, and a bit closer to him. It was starting to get cold out here. I said, "You didn't tell me you'd met Morgana before."

There was a breathless moment where even the air stood still —or maybe it was just because I was hoping I had managed the trick.

Then Athelas sipped his tea and said, "Did I not? It didn't seem important at the time, but no doubt you know better."

I drew in a breath, my lungs warming with motion again, but it didn't seem to provide me with any oxygen. Had he been taken by surprise and answered with the truth? Had he told me exactly what he wanted me to hear because he thought I knew something and needed to tell me something as little useful as possible? Impossible to tell, because it was Athelas.

But now I knew that he had known Morgana. Had met her, if he'd answered truthfully. I just didn't know what that meant.

"Your friend is entrenched far more deeply in our world than she would like to think," Athelas said, surprising me again. "She should do her best to adjust to it: it will serve her well in the future."

"Reckon she'll be all right after a while," I said, though there was a hurting part of my heart that suggested she might do so without my help, and might very well want to do so. "She was already—she already knew a lot. She just didn't want to admit it to herself. Some of it she didn't know wasn't normal."

"Odd, the things a person can accept as normal that are easily perceived as unusual from the outside," said Athelas. I wasn't sure if he was talking about Morgana, or something else. "Now that she knows they're not normal, her new normal should expand and become quite comfortable. She should at least be able to walk."

"*If* she eats brains," I said, aware that the conversation had gone in a direction I had not planned. It was probably a direction that was more comfortable for Athelas, the sneaky old fae.

"A small price to pay if one has a good cook," he said gently. His eyes flicked away from me and back to the backyard, where Zero was tipping back his head to finish the last of his coffee and JinYeong was looking very sharp and toothy. "Do you suppose JinYeong is going to remember that he has a weapon, or will he revert to teeth?"

"Dunno," I said. "Told you. He's been weird lately."

"Perhaps I should interfere, then," he said, leaning forward in order to rise.

"Athelas?"

"Yes?"

"How did you come to meet Morgana?" I wanted to ask why he'd gone back there and bothered the kids, too, but I wasn't quite sure I dared. Maybe I was too worried about what his answer might be.

He could have sighed faintly. "I had some business with her parents."

"Before or after they were dead?"

The words tumbled out of my mouth, but I wasn't sorry they came out. I wasn't sure exactly why I asked, or even why it was important—but I knew I wanted an answer.

"After," he said. "Quite some time ago. They were newly dead at that stage, and I had a question that needed an answer."

"You just—you went to talk to a couple of ghosts? Did Zero know?"

"Zero was, and remains, unaware. It was not something done at his behest."

"You know she was a zombie?"

"They didn't see fit to tell me what she was, and I certainly wasn't rude enough to ask," he said. "I was aware that she wasn't human when we spoke. I will not," he added, with a faint, understanding smile, "tell you what we spoke of. It was personal business and I doubt she remembers me."

"S'pose you mean you want me to keep quiet about it," I said, somewhat disgruntled. Whenever I got some answers, more questions seemed to pop up.

"That would be appreciated," he said, gazing at the wary circling of Zero and JinYeong. "But should you not do so, I won't stop you."

"You just don't wanna owe me anything," I said, and I couldn't help grinning up at him, despite the awfulness of the day.

"You know me too well, Pet," he said, smiling down into his teacup.

"Suspicious!" I said. "Now I don't know if I was right or not!"

Athelas rested his hand on my head briefly, a warm patch of houndstooth and corduroy beside me. "You pick up things very quickly, Pet," he said. "Do be careful, won't you? Try not to forget the old lessons with all the new ones you're learning. It would be dangerous for a pet to become too cheeky."

Then he put his teacup down and rose to stroll leisurely out into the backyard before I could remind him that we needed to do more work on further memories of mine that were missing— particularly the ones from the night my parents died. I could have chased him down, but I still felt a bit raw to do anything but accept the delay.

Instead, I sat where I was as Athelas said, "Jin Yeong, perhaps you would add to your goodness for the day by allowing me to spar with my lord. I feel as though I need to shake out the cobwebs."

"Fetch your boots, Pet," called Zero, as Jin Yeong, surprisingly amenable, left the field of battle to the other two men. "You're next."

"Great," I said sarcastically. "Looking forward to it."

I sat down next to Jin Yeong on the patio step to watch them fight for a while despite that, sipping my fourth or fifth coffee for the day. I probably need to work on drinking less, but who can deal with the stress of drinking less coffee? I wasn't buzzing yet, and even if my leg was bouncing a bit it was still easy to focus on watching Zero and Athelas fight. It's always an impressive sight: Zero has all the advantage of height and weight, and he should be an easy win, but when I see them at it, it's clear to see why Athelas was chosen to train him when he was a kid. There's a kind of deadly, barely-in-control savagery about Athelas as he fights, too quick to block, too sharp to avoid being cut, too slippery to be caught.

If every one of Zero's cuts had landed, it would probably have made very short work of the smaller fae; but not every cut did land, and that made all the difference. Athelas was good at taking the hits he needed to take in order to get in his own hits.

That left me thinking of Athelas again when I went in to grab my boots for training, and my thoughts were hard to categorise. Obviously, he was suspicious. But exactly what those suspicions led to—or even exactly what they were—eluded me. Whatever it was, it probably had something to do with Zero, and whatever it was, he had only been getting more and more suspicious lately. If I learnt that he had been out and about grifting to make sure that Zero didn't have to take the throne he so desperately didn't want to take, I wouldn't be surprised.

But then, that would leave the loose end of Heirlings not

generally making it through the cycle if they didn't become king, even if they resigned their right to take up the challenge—and Athelas was not the sort of person to leave loose ends lying around where they could cause damage.

And I wondered how much Zero knew of Athelas' machinations, too.

What I meant to do was grab my boots and go back outside to take my turn training. Instead, I found myself sitting down in my beanbag and staring up at the ceiling when I got to the room, my boots on but not zipped up and my thoughts pretty much in the same state of half-readiness. Where was I supposed to go from here? I was an heirling, and my parents had been—whatever the heck humans became when they fought back against Behindkind who terrorised humans. Someone had thought I was worth championing when I was a kid, and had kidnapped me to make sure they had me—an attempt that hadn't survived a visit from our murderer. I nearly hadn't survived it, either, but somehow I had.

The cycle for the throne had begun again in earnest, and one day soon Zero's dad would find us and force his son to be king. Or the king would show up for both of us. My champions—my kidnappers—were already dead, years ago: I'd never known them, though I suppose my parents must have.

There was *still* the problem of not knowing whether or not Zero was—in love with me? fond of me?

And now, I realised, sitting up to flip through the pile of papers that should have included the copy of my great grandmother's license, that paper had definitely disappeared.

Heck, I thought in annoyance. It wasn't like the psychos went poking through my room at random, but if it was gone, it was likely that one of them had taken it. Why? And which one?

I heaved a sigh and tossed the whole lot back onto the carpet, flopping into my beanbag again. There was too much going on in my life and I didn't know what to focus on first, let alone what was the most important. And there were still new and terrible memories waiting in the back of my mind—just waiting for me to close my eyes so that they could come out again.

I probably would have sat there for the rest of the evening if Jin Yeong hadn't come up to fetch me. Ignoring Zero's explicit orders, he kicked off his shoes and sauntered into my room without stopping, crouching beside the beanbag to say, "*Hyeong* wants us to fight."

"What a surprise," I said. "We've gotta have a word to him about mixed signals, because when we're inside it's all *don't fight on the furniture* and when we're outside it's all *have fun kids*."

Jin Yeong gave a small *thch* of a laugh, looking away, and said, "*Hyeong* is working us hard today…"

He let that trail away, and it wasn't until he glanced back at me, eyes liquid, that I realised what he meant.

"What, vampire spit? Reckon I'm still pretty hopped up from the other day," I said doubtfully. "Do I need it?"

Jin Yeong half-shrugged, but stayed where he was, watching me with his head on the side. What was he, playing Zero?

"Oh," I said, understanding suddenly. "You want to have a bit of fun with Zero."

"Fun?" He shrugged, eyes liquid and amused. "It could be fun."

"Okay," I said, butting my head back into the beanbag and taking one last look at the peaceful ceiling. I'd probably be on my back coughing up grass and looking at the sky by the time training was over. "Bite me or whatever, and we'll do some matched doubles with Athelas and Zero."

As if we'd ever come out the winners in that. As if there was ever a different outcome for either Jin Yeong or me when it came to fighting things that were too big and too bad, other than being sent flying through a wall and having to get up and do it again.

I gave a small sniff of laughter and turned my head to say to Jin Yeong, "Maybe we can chuck Zero through a wall if we team up," but I didn't get the chance to do more than form the *m* because he leaned forward and kissed me, nudging me back into the beanbag. It was just a quick one, not even long enough to feel the fizz of vampire saliva-induced energy, but instead of pulling away afterwards he pressed forward again to give me another soft, little kiss that was nowhere near long enough or deep enough to kick-start that otherworldly energy either.

"That's not—that didn't give me vampire spit," I said stupidly after that kiss.

"No," said Jin Yeong, moving forward once more. "That is the point."

This time, he came forward with the whole of him, arms slipping between me and the beanbag, his chest lightly touching me, and through the sudden quickening beat of my heart, I went into a flurry of memories.

Jin Yeong carrying me home on his back. Jin Yeong's arms around me as he murmured nonsense numbers in my ears to drive away the remembrance of dying in my dreams. Jin Yeong bloody and beaten and leaning against me because he wasn't strong enough to sit alone.

And out I came again, because he had certainly never kissed me like this before, and it was hard to concentrate on anything else. I had the stray, wild thought that Jin Yeong shoeless wasn't the non-threatening thing I had thought; shoeless Jin Yeong was a dangerously *comfortable* Jin Yeong.

An abundance of soft warmth was what it was, if you didn't count the sleek firmness of his chest; warmth and softness beneath me, curling around me, warmth and movement of lips against mine. Did I kiss him back? I think I must have, and that made another warmth in my stomach.

He left me enough space to move my arms—to embrace or to push away—and I think that's what woke me up. I pushed, experimentally, and he moved away from me and even the beanbag at once, settling his back against the wooden beam, his eyes on me. I don't know how, but he managed to look exactly as if he had just been pressing kisses into unsuspecting lips: eyes half-lidded, tie askew and slightly loose, hair rumpled out of its usual tidiness.

He had already said as much, but even if he hadn't, I would have known that what I had just—no, what Jin Yeong had just—oh heck—I would have known that the kiss that had just happened was *not* a kiss for the purposes of providing me with vampire spit.

"What the *flaming* heck was that?" I said at last, trying not to gasp. Between the beanbag and the rush of dizziness, I managed to sit up with some difficulty, but it was ridiculously hard to breathe, and a so very obviously just-kissed Jin Yeong was startlingly hard to face up to.

"Ah," he said, leaning his head against the beam behind him. "I have wanted to do that for a long time."

"Hang on!" I protested. "You can't—you can't go kissing me like that! You're sweet on a human! You said you're going to ask a human out on a date!"

"*Kurae*," he said. Smugly, he added, "That human is you."

"I meant *another* human! It can't be me!"

He narrowed his eyes at me, but ruined it by grinning. "I thought you didn't want to understand. Did you really not know that I love you? *Jeongmal?*"

"You can't!" I said, alarmed. Jin Yeong being in love with a human woman was annoying but understandable. Jin Yeong in love with *me* wasn't possible. Wasn't doable. Definitely wouldn't work. I didn't want it to work. "You're not allowed."

"No," said Jin Yeong, sitting forward and resting his arms on one knee. "You do not get to choose if I am in love with you. Perhaps you will look to me, perhaps you will look to someone else. But it is my choice to love you, and you can't tell me not to do it. Neither can *hyeong*."

"*How?*" I demanded. "And *why*? Why on earth would you fall in love with me?"

"I would like to know why, too," he said, moodily. "You are

uncomfortable and you make me think too much. And then sometimes you are *nice* and I can't think and that is worse."

"You want me to stop being nice to you?"

"*Ani*. Always be nice to me."

"I'm not going to be nice to you!" I said, a bit more wildly than I meant to. Jin Yeong was prickly, and crazy, and annoying; he wasn't supposed to be *in love* with me. He definitely wasn't allowed to.

He wasn't allowed to because that would make things uneasy when I had just started trusting him again. Just started feeling like we were on an even keel. Just started feeling like we'd be able to be good friends, even.

Jin Yeong sent a reproachful look in my direction, but I scowled at him.

"I'm not," I warned him. "I'm not going to be nice to you."

"You are already often not nice," he told me. "Then be beside me and fight with me, and poke me in the ribs instead. I will wait for you to think about it."

I nearly said straight away that I didn't need time to think about it, and that he'd better get over it *right now*, but I'd underestimated how hard it was to say something like that to a solemn-faced vampire who was just *looking* at me.

"I'm not gunna promise you anything," I told him instead. "We only just got to being friends again. You can't expect me to look—to look at you like that."

"I have no expectations," he said, one shoulder shrugging. Instead of the devil-may-care look it usually gave him, today it made him seem oddly self-deprecating.

It left me with the definite impression that he really didn't expect anything—except maybe a kick in the shins, if I was to judge by the wary light to his eyes. That wasn't fair, either. If he was in love with me, and I wasn't going to be in love with him— and I definitely wasn't going to be in love with him; it was insane to think that I was—he needed to be protecting himself. Not laying everything out in the open like this, as vulnerable as a human with their neck bared.

"How is that gunna work with me kissing you for vampire spit?" I asked him sharply. If he wasn't going to protect himself, someone had to. "Because I'm pretty sure that's going to be the opposite of helpful for you, and—"

"*Nan quenchana*," he said, with a slow, soft smile that made my cheeks grow warm, much to my shock. "For me, it is fun."

"Hang on," I said, unsteadily. "What do you mean, it's fun for you?"

"I told you. Kisses are not a transaction."

"Yes they *are*, you bloodthirsty little mosquito!"

"For *me*," he said softly, eyes dark and liquid, "it is not a transaction. For me, it is—"

I yelped and clapped my hands over my ears, shocked to find myself recalling in detail the kisses that had just occurred. "I don't want to know!"

He waited until I took my hands away from my ears before he said demurely, "You should remember that next time you kiss me."

I glared at him. "I'm not going to kiss you again!"

I sure as heck wasn't going to let him kiss me again, either. Good grief! That was the last thing I needed on my mind, taking up space that should be kept for other things.

"Pft," he said. "You will need vampire spit again."

"Then I'll get you to bite me!"

Jin Yeong, just the tips of his teeth showing in the most satisfied smirk I'd ever had the displeasure of seeing on him, said silkily, "I enjoy that *too*. Very. Much."

I stared at him with my mouth open for far too long before I choked out, "I really want to smack you in the face right now."

"My face is beautiful and should not be damaged."

"Everybody knows your face is beautiful! You don't have to keep reminding us!"

That earned me another reproachful look. He said, "You never say so."

"Only because you never stop telling me!" I thought about that for a moment and added, "Okay, I might not mention it even if you didn't, but I definitely don't want to when you're always so certain about how good looking you are."

"I have a mirror, and—"

"It would be better if the mirror thing was true," I muttered.

"*Amuten*," he said decidedly, as if to prevent me from diverging too far from the subject, "what will you do?"

I wasn't sure if he was talking about the next time I needed vampire spit, the fact that he was apparently in love with me, or me occasionally telling him that he was beautiful.

"About what?" I asked gloomily. "Vampire spit? You being in love with me?"

He grinned at me unexpectedly, eyes bright and dancing. "You are so straightforward," he said. "You can't do anything about me being in love with you."

"Vampire spit it is, then. It would be easier if I could bite you instead," I said broodingly. Jin Yeong's eyes lit up again, and his mouth opened, but I said hastily before he could reply, "If you say you'd like that as well, I really will hit you. I won't make you any more kimchi, either."

His mouth shut, very prim.

"If I *need* to have vampire spit, you can bite me."

Jin Yeong grew very slightly primmer. "I will bite very gently," he said.

"Don't say it like that!"

"It is annoying, *an gurae*?" he said, his eyes alight with malicious laughter. "When someone says something normal in a way that makes it not normal."

"Okay, fair enough," I said grudgingly. It wasn't like I hadn't done the same to him, times past counting. "No more kisses. Just the odd bite or two, and not in any weird places."

"*Koll!*" he said at once.

Deal. Great. That made things so much better.

"I'm not going to fall in love with you," I said, more grumpily. My heart still hadn't slowed down by much, and while that must have been the effects of the vampire spit, it made it annoyingly hard to speak without running out of breath. "So you might as well get used to that right now."

"*Kurae*, so you said," he answered, and although he didn't sound happy, he certainly didn't sound downbeat. He rose, swiftly and precisely, and turned to leave: said softly over his shoulder, "Try your best, my friend."

I was left staring at him as he exited the room, and I'm pretty sure he knew it, too, because he fairly *sauntered*. I flopped back into the beanbag, found it far too reminiscent of an embrace and so far from subtly Jin Yeong-scented to be at all restful, and got up at once.

Flaming heck.

What was I supposed to do *now*?